The Switch

Neil Bradshaw

Matador
Unit E2 Airfield Business Park,
Harrison Road, Market Harborough,
Leicestershire. LE16 7UL
Tel: 0116 2792299
Email: books@troubador.co.uk
Web: www.troubador.co.uk/matador
Twitter: @matadorbooks

ISBN 978 1803137 292

British Library Cataloguing in Publication Data.
A catalogue record for this book is available from the British Library.

Printed and bound in Great Britain by 4edge Limited
Typeset in 11pt Minion Pro by Troubador Publishing Ltd, Leicester, UK

Matador is an imprint of Troubador Publishing Ltd

The Switch

Dear Graham
I hope you have
time to read and
enjoy 'THE SWITCH'
many thanks

About the Author

Neil Bradshaw was born in South London. He attended Haberdashers Askes Boys school in New Cross where he developed a love for English Literature. He spent most of his working life in the film industry as a freelance camera technician. This is his debut. He now lives in Bucks.

For more information please go to
neilbradshawauthor.co.uk

Dedicated to Mike and Joy Bradshaw.
Thank you for your love, your encouragement
and your inspiration.

•

Also thanks to

Gabrielle Bradshaw
Yvonne Bradshaw
Rebecca Rouse
John Burke
Liza Bell

for all your help, advice and guidance.

•

And to A.J. "Tony" Harding
for planting the seed.

1

Who's been a naughty boy again?

Déjà vu. Literally translated, "Already seen". In George Miller's case, already seen, experienced and most important of all, survived. In the five years since joining his current club he had been summoned before the manager on no less than three other occasions. He had lost count of the times he had been reprimanded at his previous clubs. He was not a troublemaker and he certainly wasn't the wild, self-destructive maniac the journalists and editors of the press made him out to be. He just had the knack of being in the wrong place at the wrong time; most of the time.

George had been a professional footballer for twelve years. He had graced the back pages of all the national and many international newspapers during his career. His sporting achievements and heroic deeds on the pitch were described with almost biblical glorification. Sadly, the same couldn't be said of his frequent visits to the front pages. The domain of royalty, criminals, politicians and natural disasters; they were certainly no place for a sportsman. It was tantamount to trespassing if a hero from the sporting world strayed onto the front pages. George Miller had been trespassing again.

He had been asked to come in and give his version of events regarding a story featured in most of the papers. Another chapter in the colourful life of George Miller had been splashed all over the covers of the morning editions. A picture of him leaving a nightclub with what looked like a rowdy bunch of drunkards was somewhat misleading. The headline "Miller in bar room brawl", was both untrue and unfair.

The previous evening he had been having a few drinks with Lisa, a young lady he met at a photographic shoot for his boot sponsor. They had gone to a bar he knew well. There were intimate little alcoves scattered around the perimeter that provided a modicum of privacy. The two of them had been there for about an hour and were enjoying the champagne and each other's company, when a man popped his head around the corner and peered into the recess. He had obviously been drinking as it took most of his concentration to keep himself upright.

'Hello, mate. Are you George Miller?' he slurred holding onto the wall for added support. He ventured in a little further and as his eyes acclimatised to the dimly lit cavern, he recognised him for sure.

'Hope you don't mind. Me and the boys thought it was you. Any chance of a photo?' He thrust his hand towards George. George was happy to oblige, shaking the man's hand and posing with him for numerous selfies. He had always tried to be as accommodating as he could towards the fans and give them as much time as possible.

Interruptions to his personal life were part and parcel of the job and although sometimes he could do without them, he always tried to put a smile on his face and look enthusiastic and interested in what they had to say. After the handshakes, autographs and photos, George was ready to say goodbye and continue his conversation with the lovely Lisa. Unfortunately for him the man simply beckoned to his mates. Five more equally inebriated men staggered in and introduced themselves. The same scenarios were repeated several more times, with each of the men wanting his private slice of George. He had managed to keep the atmosphere light and cheerful, but when the men sat down at his table to join the party, he decided it was time to leave. It took only a few seconds for the star-struck fans to turn into a spiteful, hissing mob. They began hurling abuse at both him and Lisa.

'It's the likes of us that pay your bloody wages, mate,' one of them snarled.

'Can't be bothered to sit and have a drink with us, then,' growled another.

'Wanker.'

'Prima Donna.'

By this time the noise level had escalated and the atmosphere had become decidedly toxic. Lisa was looking scared and uneasy as the men jostled and gesticulated in an alarmingly aggressive manner. George calmly took her by the arm and began easing his way through the unpleasant melee towards the exit. At that moment a number of security staff arrived and informed the men that it was time for them to leave. This did nothing to improve their mood and scuffles began to break out. More burly doormen joined in as the punches started to fly. Some of the blows drew blood. The angry, drunken men were no match for the bouncers and were quickly subdued. But as George, Lisa and the dishevelled, battered mob stepped into the late afternoon gloom, a battery of flashlights lit up the street. George Miller, a pretty girl and a drunken posse of hostile yobs. Blood, booze, beauty and brutality. An editor's dream. It didn't look good. Even George could see that.

He had always taken the rough with the smooth. He knew he was lucky to be doing something he loved and being well paid for it. Incidents like these were no more than a mild irritant. Something he had learned to take in his stride. Unfortunately, they were becoming an irritant to other people as well. Important people who could decide George's future one way or another.

The manager had asked him to come in for a chat about his recent behaviour and more worryingly, "his future". George was confident he could explain the latest newspaper articles and pictures. He was just a little concerned about the inclusion of the word "future". He had been injured for a couple of weeks and wouldn't be able to start training again for at least two more after he had twisted his troublesome right knee falling down some steps coming out of a nightclub at three in the morning. He and a couple of teammates had been celebrating after a game. Once again, the incident had been captured on film and the evidence printed in most of the tabloids. All the players involved had been reprimanded, but George knew the management had taken a particularly dim view of him as he was now "out of action" yet again.

He was six-foot-two-inches tall, famous, wealthy and apparently, if you believed what most of the social commentators said, charming, charismatic and handsome. At thirty years old he was far from being "over the hill", but knew in his heart his best footballing days were behind him. He felt he had a few more years left at the highest level and wanted to make the most of them. He had always hoped to retire at the top and not sink slowly down the divisions into obscurity. He didn't want to end up as a novelty attraction in front of 1200 people on a wet and windy Wednesday night, somewhere in the back of beyond, like some of his schoolboy heroes. He had no desire to leave his present club as this would almost certainly mean a move to a lesser outfit and start the downward spiral he was so desperate to avoid. His one burning ambition was to win something in football; a trophy, a medal, a place in the history books. A memorable night he could look back on once he had retired and think *that was the high point, that was the pinnacle of my career.*

At the height of his powers George Miller was the name that kept being mentioned when it came to international squads. It was thought he would be the perfect replacement for the soon-to-be-retiring England captain. His future had looked very rosy indeed. It was at that crucial time George found himself back on the front pages, photographed in a rather uncompromising situation with an older woman. For the sake of decency, the published pictures had required substantial pixelization. The woman turned out to be married. A couple of days later George was photographed with her husband who *turned out to be very angry.* The husband was a well-respected member of the FA committee. The shot that made the front pages of most of the dailies showed the two men in an unflattering brawl, writhing around on the floor, fighting like schoolboys. George's name was mentioned in divorce papers and he was told there was a possibility of a court case against him for "causing an affray". It was a dark and worrying time and his career was temporarily put on hold. Things were settled "out of court", but the repercussions were rather unsavoury for both men. The husband would move on from the FA and fade into obscurity, but the effects on George's career were more damaging. Although the scandal eventually blew over, his name was mentioned less and less in international terms. It appeared the people running the international game were less tolerant than those running the domestic one. He would get no second chance. At the time, this was a mortal blow. It had been a lifelong ambition to pull on the shirt for England and represent his country. It still irked him. He sometimes wondered how different his career would have been if he hadn't become involved with *that older woman*. It was one of his few regrets.

George had become a wealthy man through football. With wages and sponsorship deals he had signed over the years and investments he had made, he was sitting very comfortably indeed. He wanted for nothing and made sure his family and his friends shared in his good fortune. He polarised opinion both in the boardroom and amongst the supporters. To some he was a lovable rogue, to others he was nothing more than a disruptive influence without whom they would be much better off. George knew he was walking a very fine line. He wondered whether this latest episode had finally tipped the balance. Would this latest transgression prove to be the final straw?

He sat amongst the tacky opulence of the huge lounge outside the manager's office. The room was bright and airy. The second-floor vista afforded views of the main concourse and car park through the floor-to-ceiling glass panels that ran along its entire thirty-five-metre length. The low, early-spring sunshine filled the space with an ethereal golden glow. A large smoked-glass table sat in the middle of the room surrounded on all sides by four black leather sofas. The table's thick and stumpy legs disappeared into the thick cream-coloured carpet, giving the impression it had taken permanant root. Two large televisions threw out ultra high-definition images. Both were tuned to the sports news channel; both had the sound turned down. The other walls were lined with silver-framed photographs boasting some of the club's past glories. Each one individually illuminated by its own spotlight had a plaque below describing the characters and events depicted. Action shots of past heroes, frozen in time forever. George chuckled to himself. He wondered how many of those sporting greats had ever had to sit outside the manager's office waiting for a dressing down. He suspected not many. They didn't do that sort of thing back in the monochrome era. Did they?

George was acutely aware he was conspicuous by his absence. Not one of the framed pictures gave any indication he had ever been at the club. In his five years there he had somehow managed to be either injured or suspended for all of the big occasions

He looked around the room again. The whole place was eerily quiet. The smell of the leather furniture mixed easily with the aroma of freshly ground coffee and the scent of the fresh flowers dotted around the room in numerous vases. The cocktail of perfumes wafted about on the air, taking turns to arouse the senses. He leant forward and picked up one of the newspapers arranged on the table. He didn't even bother to read the type. He just scowled at the pictorial evidence and wondered why fate had once again been so unkind to him. He tossed it back onto the table with disdain.

Brenda, the manager's secretary, emerged from her small office. She had started working at the club about the same time as George. As an eighteen-year-old office junior, she had impressed everyone with her vivacity and enthusiasm. Now as the manager's PA, she had attained her goal: A sweet girl with a bubbly personality that immediately charmed everyone who met her. She was twenty-three years old. Standing five-foot-three in her stockinged feet, she regularly wore outrageously high heels to make herself look taller. There was an elegance and an innocence about her. She was naturally very pretty but did insist on wearing a lot of makeup. George always felt she looked nicer with less paint on her face. She was well spoken, but it was clear her eloquence required a little effort. She did her best to sound educated and sophisticated, but occasionally when her guard was down, her vowels became a little less rounded. She was fond of most of the players, but thought George was special. He was the type of bloke she could imagine taking home and introducing to her mum and dad. She thought he was warm, charming and of course, devilishly handsome. The first day she met him she instantly fell in love with him and in the five years since, nothing had changed. She knew about his reputation with the ladies and it was a reoccurring thought in her mind that one day George would ask her out and she would be the girl on his arm. It was a dream she hoped would one day come true.

Brenda brought George a cup of tea. She bent down and placed the mug in front of him. As she did, the generous low-cut "V" neck of her loose-fitting pink sweater billowed out as if in full sail, displaying an impressive and unhindered view of her cleavage and beyond. She was hoping George would shoot a quick glance at her flirtatious offerings. He had taken many a quick glimpse on previous occasions but this time he kept his eyes fixed firmly on hers.

'Who's been a naughty boy again?' she said in her best scolding headmistress voice, shaking her head disapprovingly, just enough to cause a ripple of movement through her body; just enough to cajole her flaunted breasts to animate and demand his attention. George leant forward and picked up his tea without breaking eye contact. He smiled at her. He knew the delights to be had if he lowered his sights, but he kept his gaze fixed on hers. She remained in her rather awkward and uncomfortable jackknife position, exhibiting herself for as long as possible.

'So, what have you been up to this time?' she continued. George's eyes were not nibbling at the bait on offer. Her pose had become a bit of a strain and so reluctantly, she straightened herself up, pinching and picking at the shoulders of her sweater to help return it to its normal, less revealing position. After a quick inspection showed it to be hanging in a more respectable fashion, she stroked out a few creases in her leather skirt and returned her attention back to George.

'Wouldn't you like to know?' he said mysteriously, winking at her. Brenda giggled and turned to go back to her office. As she did, she looked back over her shoulder at him.

'I wouldn't mind being there when you get up to something next time.' She grinned and raised her eyebrows suggestively.

'It's a date,' shouted George as her swinging hips disappeared from view.

Brenda loved flirting with George and she loved it when he flirted back.

The flourish of activity and conversation was over and the room was once again silent. George sat in his glorious isolation; the pictures on the wall still echoing the historic, ghostly roars of the crowd. All his peers from the last hundred years or so bore witness to his solitude. How he would love to be up there with them. To have his own illuminated square space on that wall to announce that George Miller had contributed something towards the rich and wonderful history of the club. *Maybe one day* he thought, but then that would depend on the outcome of that morning's little chat.

2

Thirty years earlier.

John Miller paced up and down the hospital corridors. He started to wish he hadn't given up smoking. What he wouldn't give for a cigarette now. His wife, Paula, had been taken into theatre for a caesarean section. They were expecting their first children. Twins! They had been aware for some time that the bump on Paula's tummy contained two little Millers, ever since the nurse pointed out two hearts beating on the scan. The news had come as a bit of a shock. As first-time parents the thought of being responsible for a new life was daunting enough, but to be told they would have two little humans to care for had initially started alarm bells ringing. As they became accustomed to the idea, the fear and panic gradually turned to excitement. They had asked not to be told the sex of their babies. It would add to the surprise once they arrived.

As he waited nervously in the corridors outside the operating theatre, John considered all the possible combinations they might be faced with. They might have two girls. Daughters were supposed to pamper their fathers and look after them in their old age. His daughters would hopefully grow up to become as beautiful as their mother. But what about boyfriends? It wouldn't be long before he had spotty teenage youths knocking at his door trying to take his beautiful girls away. He remembered what he had been like at that age and shuddered. He tried to put those thoughts out of his mind.

What about two boys? His friend Gary who lived a few doors away had two sons. They weren't twins but there were only sixteen months between them. They were constantly in trouble at school and with the law. It wasn't unusual for John and Paula's front room or bedroom to be lit up by the blue flashing lights of police cars parked outside Gary's house, all hours of the day and night. Poor Gary and Julie; they were at their wits end. They just couldn't control them. It was a mystery to John how two such lovely and loving people could have had two such awful children. Surely he and Paula would do a better job of raising two boys.

Then there was the possibility of a boy and a girl. One of each. That seemed to conform to everyone's ideal. A full set. The best of both worlds. But what about the logistics involved? They might need to go to different schools. They would need their own bedrooms much sooner. Every combination seemed to throw up different challenges. As he paced methodically up and down, a couple of nurses crashed through the swing doors at the far end of the corridor, rushing towards some emergency. As they raced past him, the silence and stillness of John's private and thoughtful world was shattered. The noise from their shoes clattering on the hard vinyl floor reverberated and echoed off the walls and ceiling, sounding like a troupe of tap dancers. He stopped his marching and his musing and watched as they whooshed past, their faces etched with anxiety and apprehension. He suddenly felt guilty. There he was pondering the pros and cons of his twins' genders, while Paula was in theatre under the knife. Maybe it was her he should be thinking about.

John looked at his watch for the hundredth time. It felt like he had been pacing up and down for hours.

The doors at the end of the corridor swung open again. A doctor walked briskly towards him.

'Mr Miller?' the doctor enquired.

'Yes,' said John, his voice betraying equal amounts of expectation and trepidation.

'Your wife is doing fine. You have two healthy baby boys. You can go in and see them shortly. Congratulations.'

Without breaking stride or slowing down, the doctor carried on walking and disappeared through the doors at the other end of the corridor.

'Thank you, Doctor. Thank you,' John shouted after him.

John and Paula peered into the incubators. Side by side slept their two little miracles. Mops of raven black hair sitting on top of wrinkled faces. Four little arms and four little legs. Everything in its rightful place. They were perfect. The doctor who had spoken to John earlier joined them.

'They are beautiful' said Paula looking at the doctor.

'Yes, they are.' He cleared his throat. 'Mr and Mrs Miller, the obstetrician has examined the placentas and it is highly likely that these two lovely boys are not just twins but identical twins.'

There was a moment of silence. John and Paula looked at each other trying to work out if this was good news or bad news. It hadn't been something they had considered. There was a history of twins in Paula's family, but never identical twins as far as they knew. They looked back at the two sleeping beauties. They looked similar, but then all babies looked the same when they were born. Didn't they?

As the boys grew, it became evident they were truly identical. George and Graham were two peas from the same pod. Even John and Paula struggled to tell them apart. They were identical in their looks, mannerisms and personality. They wanted to wear the same clothes, eat the same food and watch the same TV. There was absolutely nothing to differentiate between them.

Both boys enjoyed sport and they both had a good eye for a ball. By the time they were eight years old, they were playing cricket for their local club and were members at their local golf course. But the sport they loved most was football. Football had always been one of John's great passions. He had played a bit when he was younger, but never really had the time to devote to it. He had been a season ticket holder at his local club for years and tried to get along to as many matches as possible. He loved taking Graham and George with him. Their faces lit up with excitement every time they went.

The three of them made regular trips to the local park and for hours George and Graham would imitate their footballing heroes. John would invariably find himself elected goalkeeper. Standing between the sticks, he would have balls constantly smashed at him. As each goal was celebrated by the young boys wheeling away with arms raised, being congratulated by the other, the poor old goalie would have to trudge back and retrieve the ball.

One of their favourite games was penalty shoot-outs. Each boy would take it in turn to spot the ball, then hammer it past their dad. John tried to keep the scores reasonably even, but eventually they became too good for him. His ability as a goalkeeper rarely had much say on the outcome.

Telling the boys apart was becoming increasingly difficult. Instead of developing differently they became more alike each year. John and Paula came up with the idea of making the boys wear name badges. They explained it was for the benefit of friends, family and the teachers at school. Although they would not admit it, both knew it was as much for their own benefit as anyone else's.

On more than one occasion Paula had asked one of the boys to do something, only to castigate the other, when it hadn't been done. An easy mistake to make as a friend or teacher, but an embarrassing one to make as a mother.

Wearing the badges would be part of the twins' lives until they were eighteen. It was something they would have to get used to, but also something they would learn to have fun with and turn to their own advantage.

John and Paula had asked for the boys to be split up during lessons. They hoped that by sitting apart they might make different and varied friends. George was asked to sit at the back of the classroom while Graham sat at the front. George sat next to Sara Parker. He spent most of the time teasing and annoying her, trying to impress her with stories and anecdotes he had either read or made up; showing off at every possible opportunity. George was good at "showing off", especially in front of girls! Graham sat next to Paul Davis. Paul was a quiet boy. They were similar in many ways and they quickly became good friends. However, when the bell sounded for break time or the end of school, the brothers would rush to each other and fall deep into private conversation, oblivious to all around them.

One morning as the boys were getting ready for school, they inadvertently picked up each other's sweaters. As George pulled on his jumper, he saw Graham had the name George on his chest. He glanced down at his badge and sure enough it said Graham. They laughed at their mistake and started to swap them back.

'Hang on a minute,' said Graham, 'let's see how long it takes Mum and Dad to realise we've got the wrong tops on.'

George grinned. A cheeky, mischievous grin. Over breakfast the boys tittered and giggled as they peeked up from their cereal at each other.

'What is the matter with you two this morning?' Paula said. 'Go on, off to school with you.'

As they stood to leave, Graham brushed his glass of milk with his school bag and knocked the remnants over the table. The fast-flowing white river spread quickly, engulfing cups, bowls and cutlery, before plunging over the edge of the table and splashing onto the floor.

'Oh, George, watch what you're doing, love.'

George was already standing by the back door. Graham apologised to his mum and with an excited expression ran towards his brother. Neither their mum nor dad had noticed. How far could they go with this? Would they get away with it at school? If their parents couldn't tell them apart, the teachers wouldn't stand a chance. They walked into school together, shooting looks at every classmate and friend to see if anyone was going to say anything. Nothing. They went into their classroom and sat in each other's seats. George found himself sitting next to Paul Davis. Paul noticed Graham was a little more jovial and amusing than usual. He was fidgety and talkative, but Paul thought no more of it. Graham sat next to Sara Parker. She was pleasantly surprised by George's behaviour. He didn't tease her or get on her nerves at all. In fact, he was nice and polite. She could get to like him if he stayed like that.

Mr Collett walked into the room and started to call the register. When he called,

"George Miller", Graham answered from the back of the class.

'Here, Mr Collett.'

'Graham Miller.'

George responded from right under Mr Collett's nose.

'Here, Mr Collett.'

Mr Collett continued reading out the names. George looked over his shoulder at Graham sitting at the back. So far, so good. As the day went on, they were both sure someone would notice, or they would somehow give themselves away. But no. Lunchtime came and went and no one said anything. By the end of school, nothing. They had done it. They had spent the entire day as each other. They had switched identities and fooled their friends, their teachers, even their parents. It gave them a terrific feeling of power. They could literally become one another at will, and no one would be any the wiser.

3

Fly in the ointment.

The boys had many fond memories of their primary school. They had played "The Switch" many times for their own amusement and no one had ever suspected a thing. At the age of eleven they had to change schools. They suddenly went from being big fish in a small pond to being small fish in what felt like a huge ocean.

On the first morning at their new school Graham and George stuck together like glue. Never had they been so grateful for each other's company.

Everything looked bigger. The buildings, the teachers, even the other pupils.

They were relieved to discover they had been put in the same class; 1B. Mr Baldwin was to be their form master. He was tall, slightly overweight, smelt of cigarettes and cheap aftershave lotion and wore a tweed jacket with leather patches on the elbows. He had white hair, which made him look older than he probably was. He appeared more of a daunting prospect than Mr Collett, but then everything about the place was more daunting.

They started sitting together in class, but it didn't take long for Mr Baldwin to become confused and irritated by the twins' anonymity. He split them up moving Graham to the back of the room and keeping George at the front. He also came up with the inspirational idea of giving the boys name tags. He was rather proud of himself for coming up with these solutions to distinguish between his pupils. His vision and foresight had made it easier for the whole class to tell George from Graham. For the boys it was back to the old routine. It would however be a little while before they plucked up the courage to try "The Switch" on Mr Baldwin, or anyone else for that matter.

Secondary school didn't turn out to be quite as scary as they thought. As the years passed, the twins' confidence and popularity increased. They both starred in the school's football team. George found himself surrounded by a number of admiring females and Graham began to show an appetite for academic studies.

The only real fly in the ointment was a boy called Frankie De Costa. He had arrived at the school with two of his old henchmen from his primary days, Baz and Robbo.

Frankie, Baz and Robbo were all tall for their age and had an intimidating and menacing swagger about them. Individually, they were scary. Together, they were a force no one wanted to mess with. They had ruled the roost at their previous school and they planned to do the same at this one. Over the first few years their ranks had been swollen by a number of other new boys. They had enlisted in "Frankie's army", as much for their own safety as anything else. Being part of the gang gave them an immunity from his persecution.

Frankie's hold over the pupils became greater every year. With each new autumn term, 150 more prospective victims would innocently walk into Frankie's kingdom. He liked to think of himself as the omnipotent "gangland boss". He had read books and watched movies about the Krays and the Richardsons from the sixties and seen how they had ruled the London underworld with an iron fist. He craved the "respect" these men supposedly commanded and the power they could exert over others. He ran his empire based on terror and intimidation. His soldiers would do anything he demanded, just to stay in his good books. Violence or the promise of physical retribution was never far away and anyone who crossed him was dealt with in a brutal and unpleasant manner. Even his victims were too scared to point the finger for fear of a repeat performance. No one ever grassed on Frankie or stood up to him and that was the way he liked it. No one that is, except the Miller twins.

There was an uneasy truce between Frankie, his gang and the Miller boys. Frankie despised their popularity and their talents. He hated the thought that they were not part of his empire. They weren't intimidated by him. Graham and George were nearly always together between lessons and as a pair, had an aura of their own. Frankie had assumed the twins would buckle under just like the rest of his disciples and bow down before him. But they hadn't. The first time Robbo had attempted to rile and bully Graham, he'd received a bloody nose for his trouble. Ever since, the twins had treated the gang with contempt and on each of the subsequent occasions, when they had come face to face, Frankie never got the better of them.

Graham and George had belittled Frankie to his face and in front of others. Frankie demanded respect from everyone but got none from the Millers. He spent most of his time planning how he could make them pay a public and humiliating price for their ridicule of him. He knew he would have to take them on separately. The two lions, side by side, were a force of which even Frankie's cackle of hyenas were wary.

One of the more explosive encounters between them came in the fourth year. They were fifteen years old. During a short morning break, Frankie and his gang found themselves in a small room off the main assembly hall. The room was more of a large store cupboard for the hundreds of fold-up wooden chairs that came out whenever there was a play, concert or show. The gang were kicking their heels, wondering what to do. It was pouring with rain, so outdoor thuggery wasn't that appealing. Boredom was setting in when the doors to the room swung open and in walked George Miller. George too was trying to escape the rain using the room as a cut-through. But he had stumbled into a hornet's nest. As soon as he entered, the mood in the room changed. There was no need to go outside now. Frankie's prime target had just presented himself to his executioners. Gift-wrapped. George had fallen straight into their laps and most important of all, from Frankie's point of view, he was alone. The room was quiet and secluded. It was perfect. George's momentum carried him into the centre of the small room. He heard the doors behind him swing shut. When he looked back over his shoulder, he saw Baz standing in front of them.

Frankie and Robbo both leapt to their feet. They couldn't believe their luck.

'Well, look who's just popped in for a chat,' Frankie smirked.

George said nothing, his eyes darting around the room, taking in every detail and every face, before settling on Frankie's wide and wild stare.

'To what do we owe this royal visit then?' Frankie took a step nearer to George, his smile becoming broader with every second. 'Got nothing to say for yourself Miller? Well, let me say something for you. This could be the worst day of your miserable fucking life so far. And when we have dealt with you, we might just go and find that brother of yours, then he will get his.'

Frankie was now only a few inches away from George's face, with Robbo just behind. George knew the only chance he had was to land the first blow. He was outnumbered ten to one but he certainly wasn't going to go down without a fight. Frankie would be the first casualty. He tensed his body and clenched his fists. He readied himself. In a matter of seconds he would deliver a crushing right uppercut into the base of Frankie's jawbone. If he had time, he would swivel around and catch Baz square in the face with a straight left. He would worry about the rest of them after that. Everything seemed to be happening in slow motion. The other hyenas began to circle, although they kept a little more distance between themselves and their prey, waiting for their leader's signal. The muscles in George's arm twitched as the power surged into them, his eyes locked together with Frankie's. You could hear a pin drop. Everyone was waiting with bated breath, for the sign that would start the action. The stillness and tension crackled in the air.

A tremendous explosion of noise suddenly shattered the uneasy calm. The doors behind Baz swung open with terrific force, smashing into the side of his head and knocking him clean off his feet. A sickening bone-crunching sound was immediately followed by a scream of pain and a thunderous clatter as Baz collapsed into the nearest stack of chairs. The noise of the falling chairs and the howls of agony from Baz, echoed around the small room. The sudden activity had taken them all by surprise. Everyone was looking at Baz. He stumbled to his feet clutching and groping at the debris strewn across the room. He wobbled then fell back to the floor in an undignified heap, dragging another stack of chairs on top of him. He looked like an old heavyweight boxer who didn't know when it was time to throw in the towel. Blood was pouring from a wound above his left eye and the swelling was already plain to see. He thrashed about on the floor like a dying fish, trying to regain some sort of composure. But he was spent. Baz was out of the equation. Standing at the door like an avenging angel was Graham. The circling hyenas let out a collective gasp and edged back a few feet. Both Frankie and Robbo instinctively took a step back too. All in the room, apart from the floundering Baz, stood frozen to the spot. They were like gunfighters waiting to see who would draw first. Graham was the first to move. He stepped forward and stood beside his brother. A muffled groan came from beneath the mass of scattered chairs; Baz was making another effort to raise himself. Graham glanced over at the battered gangster.

'You should get someone to look at that, Baz, before you bleed to death,' he said with a hint of sarcastic compassion in his voice.

All eyes were once again on Baz. The gash around his left eye was at least two inches long and looked deep. His eye had all but vanished from sight beneath the swelling. Blood spewed from the lacerated, pouting flesh and flowed down over his face. It quickly soaked into the collar of his white shirt and down onto his chest. He held a white handkerchief shakily over the wound, but that too became sodden in the relentless crimson tide. Looking at the shock and horror on the faces of the rest of the group, it was plain to see they had lost their stomach for the fight. Now it was Graham and George standing face to face with Frankie and Robbo, odds that Frankie didn't find quite so appealing.

'Let's sort this thing out right now; once and for all, Frankie. You think you're so fucking hard. Well, let's see what you've got when the odds are even,' growled Graham straight into Frankie's face.

Now it was Frankie's turn to consider his options. They stared into each other's eyes. Graham's were full of hate and vengeance. Frankie's were full of fear and panic, but neither moved, and neither blinked.

The shrill ringing of the bell sounded and announced the end of break, but the stare between the two remained locked. Baz finally steadied himself. The blood was still pouring from the side of his head and dripping relentlessly onto the wooden floorboards. He pushed his way blindly between Graham and Frankie in a drunken stagger towards the door.

'Maybe we'll save it for another time, eh Frankie?' George said in an almost compassionate tone. 'When you're back up to full strength.'

Frankie's demeanour had completely changed. The victory he was eagerly expecting had been snatched from him and now he faced the prospect of a humiliating retreat. Frankie, Robbo and the rest of the gang slunk away. Not through, but around Graham and George. The room fell silent.

Graham and George surveyed the battlefield. The chairs were scattered around the room, lying still and lifeless. There were smeared bloody handprints from Baz's numerous attempts to return to the conscious world, evident over the floor, the chairs, the walls and the swing doors. The room resembled an abattoir. The carnage that surrounded them told a story of violence and pain. But it wasn't their pain, and it wasn't their blood. The brothers looked at each other and smiled. Together they were a match for anyone. Together they were invincible.

4

Enrico Morotoni.

As the Friday morning flight from Naples to Heathrow came into land, Enrico Morotoni checked his diary. He had a busy and hectic schedule ahead of him. Enrico was a scout. A football scout. He had worked for several clubs during his career and been responsible for the discovery of a number of young and talented players. Enrico enjoyed his work. He had been unearthing young footballing talent for over thirty years and could count among his successes numerous high-profile and international players. He was going to be in London until his return flight on Sunday afternoon.

On this particular visit he was due to watch a couple of teenagers his club Napoli had been nurturing for some time. Since they were boys they had shown exceptional promise and Enrico had marked them down as likely superstars of the future. They had been loaned out to two of London's top clubs and the speculation was they both had bright and exciting careers in front of them. The young men were both of Italian parentage and Enrico was keen and eager to bring them home as soon as he thought the time was right. He would be attending the Friday night Premiership clash between Chelsea and Liverpool to watch the younger of the two boys play, then on the Saturday evening he would be heading over to Islington to see the older boy perform in the big north London derby.

He had also been told by a friend that a couple of sixteen-year-old brothers had started to catch the eye at county and district level. A number of local clubs in the south east had already started to take note and the name "Miller" was beginning to be whispered around the circuit. Enrico's friend had suggested he might want to take a look at them whilst he was over. They would be playing in a match, albeit only an inter-schools league, on the Saturday morning, but it might prove worthwhile if he had the time. Enrico had spoken to his bosses in Naples before he left and they had given him permission to take a look. Formal requests had been made to the boys' school to attend the game, just to keep everything above board. If Enrico wasn't too exhausted from his toils on Friday night and could muster the energy before his trip to north London, he would make his way south and take a quick glimpse at the two siblings.

The excitement and elation Enrico felt at every new discovery was only matched by his disappointment and frustration when he thought he had missed out on an opportunity. It was a matter of great personal pride that he scarcely ever let any worthy talent slip through his fingers.

He *would* make the effort to watch the Miller brothers. Just in case.

5

They both liked pizza.

Between September and May, Saturday mornings were all about football. For Graham and George their routine started early. They were both up and dressed by eight o'clock. Their dark blue kit bags, so carefully and meticulously packed by Paula the night before, were unceremoniously disgorged and rechecked. Beautifully ironed and folded shirts, shorts and tracksuits were emptied onto their beds, only to be stuffed back in once all of the items had been checked. Paula never once forgot to pack anything, but it was part of the boys routine and happened every week.

They had both played in the under 12s, under 14s and under 16s and were now an integral part of the 1st XI. In all that time they had played with, and against, boys that had been regular fixtures in their own school teams over the years, growing older together.

On this particular Saturday they were due to play the team that was not only top of the league but also their fiercest, local rival. There were always friendships to be renewed and some old scores to be settled.

The boys were ready to leave the house by 8.15 a.m. Unfortunately, John, who would be driving them, was still fast asleep. It was a journey of only ten minutes to the sports field. They didn't have to leave until 9.15 at the earliest for the ten o'clock kick-off, but the boys liked to get there with plenty of time in hand. They liked to warm up and feel the atmosphere grow as the ground slowly filled with people. To be the first there made them feel like they owned it. It was their domain. So, at 8.15 a.m. John's alarm went off. There were no buzzers or bells and no TV or radios clicking on. Just two sixteen-year-old boys jostling him from his slumber and making the comfortable warmth of his bed a distant memory.

John was ready in a flash. A quick splash in the bathroom, a squirt of this and a gargle of that and he was there at the front door with his boys. The three of them shouted up to say goodbye to Paula who was trying her hardest not to wake up. It was the one morning of the week she could relax and enjoy a bit of peace and quiet. She let out a grunt from beneath her duvet which the three men downstairs translated as, 'Goodbye. Hope you have a good game. See you later.'

John, Graham and George then crept out as quietly as they could, slamming the front door shut behind them and got into the car. As the car pulled out of their driveway, John cleared his throat.

'Listen, boys, there is something I think you should be aware of today. I have thought long and hard about whether to mention it to you but feel it would be better you know, than to be kept in the dark.'

He glanced into the rear-view mirror and saw the boys looking puzzled.

'What is it, Dad?' Graham asked.

'Well, if I tell you, you have to promise me faithfully that it won't affect your game in any way. You should concentrate fully on what Mr Ellis tells you and put everything else out of your mind.'

He gave the mirror another glance. Both Graham and George were now frowning and looking bemused.

'Of course we will, Dad. What is it?' George demanded.

'Well, I heard a rumour there is going to be a scout watching the game today. An Italian scout. I don't know who he is coming to watch, or if he is coming to watch anyone in particular. He may be here to look at someone in the opposition. I really don't know any more than that.'

There was a silent pause as the information was processed.

'Italian, you say,' asked Graham. 'What club is he from? Who told him about us? How long is he here for? Can we meet him?'

'Hey, hey, hey.' John blurted out to stop the incessant interrogation. 'No one said he was coming to look at you. He is just going to be there, that's all. The headmaster let it slip yesterday. He obviously hadn't meant to say anything and tried to backtrack as soon as he had mentioned it. All I know is he has asked for permission to attend the game, but it's not common knowledge, so don't say anything to anyone else about it, okay?'

'What does he look like?' asked Graham bursting with excitement.

'I've no idea, son. You now know all I know. Just put him out of your mind and concentrate on the game.'

Another glimpse in the mirror reflected both boys deep in thought. They had already started to plan their Italian adventure. Which club would they be playing for? Milan, Juventus, Roma? Where would they live? Maybe they should have a word with Mr Allen the head of languages at school and ask if they could start learning Italian. Mum and Dad couldn't grumble about that; that was educational. And they both liked pizzas. Italy would be great.

6

Ricochets and mishits. Bobbles and bad bounces.

John parked in his usual space. The sun was just breaking through the early morning mist. It was a cold, damp morning; the ground was soft under foot. The goal posts were already up and the netting in place. The boys jumped out of the car, their eyes immediately starting to flash around the ground in search of a swarthy-looking European stranger. Where was he?

'What about him?' George said pointing to a man in a black leather coat and wearing a flat cap.

'No,' said Graham, 'he's just walking his dog. Look.'

'Put that dog on a lead. This is a private sports ground,' bellowed the voice of the burly groundsman, as he marched towards the pitch with the corner flags tucked under his arm. The leather-coated man called after his dog and hastily put on his lead, waving apologetically. No, it wasn't him.

'What about him?' George said hopefully.

A man was sitting on one of the numerous benches placed around the pitch. He was reading a newspaper and smoking a cigarette. He didn't look Italian, thought Graham. Italians were dark-haired and well dressed. The man reading the newspaper had red hair and was wearing an orange high-viz jacket. Definitely not him.

John got out of the car and locked it.

'Don't be silly, boys. He won't be here yet, it's far too early. Now go and get changed and start warming up. Just do what you normally do. He won't be here until kick-off at the earliest.'

The boys walked towards the changing rooms with their kit bags, every now and again, glancing back to make sure no one had entered the arena without being scrutinised. The un-Italian man in the high-viz jacket had gone.

As the boys entered the changing rooms, they saw Mr Ellis, their sports' master and coach. Although he was in his early fifties, he was still as fit as most of the boys and was regularly the last man standing at the end of their training sessions. He was more like an older brother, or favourite uncle than a schoolmaster; a very popular man with both parents and pupils alike.

'Morning, sir.'

'Morning, boys. How are you feeling today? Ready for the big game?'

Without answering or even acknowledging his question, George jumped straight in.

'Is it true there is going to be a scout from Italy here today?'

As soon as he had said it he wished he hadn't. With all the excitement, he had completely forgotten what his dad had told them about keeping it to themselves. George glanced at Graham with a haunted look in his eyes. Graham just glared back at him, shaking his head with an expression of disbelief. They both turned to Mr Ellis whose look was more shock than anger.

'Who told you that? It's supposed to be hush-hush,' he said.

George was silent. He didn't know what to say. Graham came to his rescue.

'Well, we sort of heard Mr Kerridge talking to Dad about it,' Graham explained quickly, not wanting his father to be identified as the leak. George let out a sigh of relief but was still excited enough to plough on.

'So, is it true?' he asked eagerly.

'Well, yes, it is true. But I don't want you telling any of the others. This is a big game for us and I don't want any unnecessary distractions. I want you all to focus on the match a hundred per cent. Even you two.'

'Yes, sir,' shouted the boys in unison, like soldiers to a commanding officer. The same barrage of questions was then hurled at Mr Ellis. He raised his hands to stop the tsunami.

'Look, you know he is coming which is more than the rest of the lads. Let's leave it at that, shall we?'

They were privy to information none of their teammates were. They would be able to raise their game. They would shine like jewels. They would catch this Italian's eye and make him take note of the names George and Graham Miller.

This top-of-the-table clash had now become their FA Cup final and World Cup final all rolled into one. The beginning of the rest of their lives. The road to success, fame and fortune. Their futures could depend on their performances in this very match. If Graham was excited, George was almost delirious with expectation. His warm-up routine was done with so much vigour, he was in danger of burning himself out before the start.

With ten minutes to go before the kick-off, the ground was a buzz of activity. Mums, dads, brothers, sisters, uncles and grandparents were packed around the pitch behind the red and white plastic tape. Next to the changing rooms was a small hut that doubled as a cafe on match days. A line of people queued up for tea, coffee and maybe a bacon or sausage roll. Next to the tea hut was the main stand, a covered block of about 300 seats. That was also full. George kept scanning the sea of faces trying to find an Italian-looking one. There were far too many to take in and he had no idea what this man looked like anyway.

'What are you looking for?' asked Barry Nolan, the team's goalkeeper, as George's eyes squinted and searched for the mystery man.

'Just trying to spot my dad.'

Barry frowned and looked confused.

'He's over there where he always stands. Every week!' said Barry pointing in the opposite direction to George's stare.

'Oh yes,' said George. But his eyes kept searching.

Mr Ellis called the team together. They gathered around him waiting to hear his words of wisdom. They were always the same.

'Right lads. This is the big one. You know what you have to do and you know where you are supposed to be. Remember your responsibilities and do your best.'

'Yes sir!' retorted the chorus of enthusiastic voices.

As the huddle of boys broke away, Mr Ellis called to Graham and George.

'That means you two as well. Keep your minds on the game and don't think or worry about anything else. Okay?'

'Okay, Mr Ellis.' They ran off to take their positions.

As they lined up for the kick-off, George made one last inspection of the faces lining the pitch, but still the Italian was not making himself obvious. He must be lurking in the crowd somewhere. George's eyes found his father. John raised two thumbs then made two fists, shook them and smiled. The whistle blew and the game began.

Once the game had started, both boys were lost in it. The perimeter ring of spectators became nothing more than a blur.

The time seemed to fly by. In their eagerness to impress, the ball never quite went for them. Ricochets and mishits, bobbles and bad bounces. It was proving to be very frustrating for both the Miller boys. The game was scrappy and disjointed and gave no one any opportunity to shine. Half-time arrived and Mr Ellis called the boys together. Drinks were taken and orange segments sucked. Mr Ellis produced the Churchillian half-time speech they heard every week. The ruck of bodies looked like a human bonfire, with the steam and condensation coming off all the boys.

'More of the same and your luck will change,' were Mr Ellis' parting words as they started the second half.

The boys were exhausted at the final whistle. They had won the match one-nil, but it had been a particularly poor game. The only decent moment happened four minutes from the end. George received the ball just inside his own half, dribbled into the opposition penalty area and was brought crashing down by a badly-timed tackle from one of the opposition defenders. There was a moment of concern as George lay there clutching his right knee in pain, but after a few minutes and a dousing of cold water from what Mr Ellis liked to call "the magic sponge", he was up and limped off the pitch. Graham calmly stepped up and smashed the penalty past their goalkeeper.

The beaten team gave the victors three cheers and the victors replied in turn. After all the excitement at the start, the game had been a huge disappointment. There had been no real chance to show what they were capable of. The rest of their team was ecstatic with the win, as was Mr Ellis, heartily congratulating each of his players as they left the pitch. Graham and George trudged towards their father, heads hung low and shoulders slumped. They looked like members of the losing team. John embraced his sons.

'Well done, boys. You were great.'

'Come on, Dad, the match was awful,' moaned Graham dejectedly.

'Well, it was no classic, that's for sure, but you both acquitted yourselves very well. You should be proud of your performances.'

John's efforts to raise the boys' spirits hadn't had much effect. They dragged themselves towards the changing rooms for a shower, George with the last remnants of the limp he had sustained from the late tackle. Their legs and lungs were aching. They had given their all. They didn't even have the energy to restart the search for the Italian face in the crowd. They were none the wiser as to what he looked like, which club he was from and more importantly, what he had thought of the game. Graham put his arm around George's shoulders.

'Well at least we won. I guess that's the important thing.'

George nodded and did his best to raise a smile.

'I suppose so,' he replied grudgingly.

The mood in the dressing room was upbeat and celebratory. The lads were amusing themselves, removing mud from their boots and throwing it at each other. There was a party atmosphere and laughter in the air. Friendships had been renewed with some of the opposition and even more importantly, some old scores had been settled.

'Hey, boys,' said Kevin Sykes, the team's right back. 'Don't tell anyone I told you, but I heard a whisper there was some big-time scout watching the game this morning.'

'Yeah, I heard something about that too,' said Richard Baker.

Graham and George looked at each other in shock. They weren't the only two on the team to know. In fact, as the conversation went on, it appeared most of the other lads had heard something about it. Maybe that's why the game had been so scrappy thought Graham. Everyone had been trying too hard to impress. Their shocked expressions quickly transformed into broad smiles. They laughed. Thank goodness their father had told them. How would they have felt if they had been among the small minority unaware of the Italian's presence. They would have been really pissed off.

By the time the twins walked out from the changing rooms, most of the other players and spectators had gone. The ground was returning to the peaceful, calm setting they had witnessed when they had arrived. It was a bright morning. The sun had won its battle with the early morning dew and mist. The ground was basking in the warmth and preparing itself for a week's rest before the next invasion. They could see their father on the far side of the ground talking with Mr Ellis. They walked towards the two men. John and Cliff Ellis were in deep conversation. So much so they hadn't noticed the boys approaching. As soon as they became aware of their presence, the conversation came to a halt. Before anything else could be said, a loud roar pierced the air. The four heads snapped round to see where the noise had come from. It was an aggressive roar, like a pride of lions or an angry grizzly bear. The four of them watched as a sleek red sports car pulled away, the shingle of the car park surface hissing and spitting like a snake from under the excessively-wide back tyres. The car accelerated and with one more roar from the engine, disappeared from view, leaving only a slow-moving white blanket of exhaust smoke hanging in the air.

'Was that him?' George asked as the smoke drifted away.

'Yes,' said Mr Ellis.

'What did he say? What did he think?' George pleaded.

'Mr Morotoni said he was very impressed and wanted to see you two play again,' beamed Mr Ellis triumphantly.

'But the match was diabolical,' sighed Graham.

'I know,' agreed Mr Ellis, 'but he saw something he liked, enough to keep his interest alive.'

Once again, the questions poured forth.

'How long is he staying in England? Can we meet with him?'

Once again Mr Ellis raised his hands to fend off the verbal barrage.

'I'll let your father talk to you about it on the way home. If you want to talk to me, you will have to wait until Monday morning.'

He moved his gaze from the boys to John.

'Of course, John, if you want to talk to me about it further you've got my home and mobile number. Please don't hesitate to call me.'

The boys looked at the two men. Words had been said. Opinions swapped and decisions made between the two of them; and probably Mr Morotoni. What had they said? How had they left it with the Italian?

'Well played today, boys. See you Monday. Put some ice on that knee, George. I need you to be fit for next weekend. It's another big game. Good luck, John. I'll talk to you soon.'

He waved his hand and wandered over to his car.

The boys' attention snapped back to their father. What did he have to tell them? What information was he about to unveil?

'Come on, Dad, tell us what's happening. What's going on? What did Mr Morotoni actually say?'

'Calm down. Let's get to the car and I'll tell you all about it.'

The boys rushed over to their father's car, tossed their bags into the boot and jumped into the back seats.

'Belt up,' said John. The boys obediently clicked their seat belts into place and waited with great anticipation for their father's next utterance. John looked into the rear-view mirror and saw the two identical faces looking at him with identical expressions, both leaning forward in their seats eagerly awaiting his next words.

'Mr Morotoni was very impressed with you. He said he would like to see more of you and he thinks you both have a very bright future ahead. Unfortunately, he has to go back to Italy tomorrow afternoon.'

'Can we see him before he goes?' pleaded George.

'No, I'm sorry,' said John. 'Not on this visit. Mr Ellis was trying to get us together for an early breakfast to discuss a few things, but I told him we wouldn't be interested at this precise moment.'

The expectation in the boys' faces instantly disappeared. They turned to face each other with a look of horror and disbelief in their eyes.

'What? Why?' demanded George. 'You said no!' He sounded incredulous and angry. His voice was raised with a threatening hint of menace to it, a tone he had never used before when speaking to his father.

'Dad, tell us you are only joking,' begged Graham, more conciliatory than his brother.

'No joke, son.' From his tone and his demeanour, they could tell he certainly wasn't joking. His manner was sombre, almost apologetic.

'Your mother and I have always wanted you to finish your education before getting too involved in other activities. It's something we have talked about on many occasions, but even more so recently as it has become apparent you both have such a talent for the game.'

'But schoolwork won't suffer, Dad, I swear. In fact, if anything we will work harder,' pleaded George.

'No ifs or buts. I'm afraid my decision, … our decision is final. Once you have finished school in a couple of years you can do whatever you like, with our blessing, but until then, it's schoolwork and exams. I'm sorry, boys, that's the way it is. That's the way it's always been.'

George and Graham slumped back into their seats. The excited barrage of questions had ceased; the silence within the car was deafening. They felt empty. Emotionally drained. Abandoned. They couldn't believe what they were hearing. They loved and respected their parents very much, but they had turned the first major scout away, when he had expressed an interest. They had been watched by so many people in the past with connections to various football clubs, but this one was from *the big time.* The Golden Ticket. Mr Morotoni had flown in to see them and wanted to know more, only to have the door slammed in his face. Everything they had hoped and dreamed of since they were young had presented itself to them. A once-in-a-lifetime offer, rejected by the two people they trusted most. They felt betrayed.

John glanced in the mirror again and saw the two faces staring blankly into space, mouths open, disappointment and anger in their eyes. John swivelled in his seat to face them.

'George. Graham. I have been watching football for many years. Long before the two of you were even born. I've seen a lot of great players. I've also seen a lot of young boys no older than yourselves with so much God-given-talent, who still failed to make the grade. There are no guarantees in life or in sport. There is no certainty of success, whoever you are. Some lads get injured and some just find the going too tough. It's not all about talent. If you find yourself rejected by the game at such an early age and you have neglected your education, you have nothing to fall back on. Trust me, ninety-nine per cent of boys your age will not make it for one reason or another. Of course it was difficult for me to say "No" to Mr Morotoni. I know how much it means to you and I understand how disappointed you must feel. Please, please believe me boys, I hate being the reason you feel like you do now, but you also have to believe me when I tell you we have done this for your own good. When you leave school, with whatever qualifications you get, you can decide for yourselves what direction you would like to take. Whatever you decide, your mother and I will back you and support you with everything we have. Until then, please trust us. We love you very much and would never do anything to harm or upset you. I truly believe you both have the ability and the commitment to make it in professional football and the offers from the likes of Mr Morotoni will still be flooding in, two years from now. I'm not just saying that. I really do believe it. Just humour your old parents on this one. Finish school and you can do whatever your hearts desire.'

The car fell silent. John turned back to face the front and began the drive home. He kept glancing at the two blank faces in the back. There was very little movement and no sound. The boys were trying to absorb their father's reasoning, but it was tough. John swung the car into their driveway and the three of them got out. From the far side Graham looked across the roof towards John.

'Dad.'

John looked over at Graham, expecting more anger and bitterness.

'Yes, son?'

'Thank you,' he said, in a soft, apologetic voice.

Somewhere amongst the heartbreak there was sincere gratitude. Graham looked at George.

'Yeah. Thanks, Dad,' said George. John smiled. It was an emotional moment. He held his arms out wide and the boys embraced their father. Both boys were still a little disappointed, but that had faded beneath the guilt they were feeling. The guilt that came from believing their father would do anything to harm or jeopardise their future. This man was their hero. He was their god. How could they ever have thought that, even for one second? They smiled at each other. John ruffled both the boys' hair.

'Come on,' he said, 'let's go and tell your mother all about the game.'

7

Adolescent cat and mouse games.

At the end of that summer the boys would have to sit their first major exams. Exams their parents had put so much store by. John and Paula had done their best to instil in them just how important the results would be in moulding their future. Graham had no difficulty concentrating on his schoolwork. His grades and marks had steadily risen over the past few terms and John, Paula and his tutors were very pleased with the progress he had made. The same sadly could not be said of his brother. George would do just enough to get by. He would only put in the time and effort required to scrape a mark that wouldn't incur the wrath of either parents or teachers. He was marking time, going through the motions. He already knew where his future lay and he was convinced it wasn't reliant on maths, history or geography. Schoolwork was a necessary evil that had to be endured. He would stumble through the next couple of years and do what was needed, but he didn't see the point in letting work get in the way of more exciting pastimes.

One of the pastimes George found infinitely more exciting than schoolwork was his pursuit of a girl called Debbie Morris. She was gorgeous and George was infatuated with her. With shoulder-length blonde hair and big blue eyes, she had everything an adolescent sixteen-year-old boy could desire. She had developed into a proper woman and filled out her school uniform in a most impressive way. She was the perfect blend of "the girl next door" and "the glamourous super model". Some girls were pretty and some girls were sexy. Debbie was both. He had fancied her for some time and had the impression she rather liked him. There had been adolescent cat and mouse games between them for a while, Debbie playing hard to get, making George work for any reward or recognition. And when George's attention to her looked like it was fading, she would tease him with a wink or a suggestive smile and reignite his interest. The challenge for Debbie was to keep the embers glowing without fanning them into flames. She knew they would eventually go out together, but it would be when she decided, not him. She was the one pulling the strings, and George Miller would just have to wait until she was ready. George knew the game she was playing and was happy to go along with it, but not for much longer. He had decided to take a more forceful and direct approach as soon as an opportunity presented itself.

The school bell sounded to announce lunchtime. George strolled out into the playground and saw Debbie standing outside the library. She was on her own, leaning on her shoulder against the wall, looking at her mobile phone and scrolling through trash. George walked up behind her. She was completely oblivious to his presence. Like a big cat stalking its prey George crept ever closer. Slowly, quietly and menacingly. When he was only a few feet away, he pounced, grabbing her around the waist from behind and pulling her into his body. His head nuzzled into her neck. He had taken her completely by surprise. She jumped, let out a little shriek, and nearly dropped her phone. A second or two later, she had regained her composure and her grip on the mobile. She knew immediately who it was. It had only been a matter of time until George tired of their games and employed new tactics. All subtlety had disappeared. He had jumped straight in. She quite liked it. She too had become weary of the childish play-acting. It was time to take down the barriers and see what lay ahead. George tightened his grip around her waist until their bodies were firmly packed together. He could feel her hair on his face and smell her perfume. Her skin was soft on his cheek and lips. She glanced at him through the corner of her eye, almost having to look backwards, waiting for his next move. George whispered softly in her ear.

'Why don't we stop all this messing about? Think of all the time we are wasting. All the fun we could be having. Why don't you come out with me this afternoon and we can start to see what we've been missing?'

Debbie relaxed her body and felt comfortable in his arms. She smiled. What he said made sense and although it wasn't quite the way she planned to end his torment, she had strung him along long enough. George's grip loosened. Debbie turned around and looked at him face to face. She rested her arms on George's shoulders. He squeezed a little tighter and their faces inched towards each other. She looked into his eyes. They twinkled with excitement and expectation. He smiled at her in a way that made her feel he could read her thoughts. She hoped he couldn't. God, he was gorgeous!

'Alright. This afternoon, after school. I'll meet you by the gates, but don't be late. I'm not going to hang around for you.'

It was her final gesture of defiance. George leaned forward to kiss her. As he did so, her head jerked backwards. He was now the one with the surprised look on his face. 'Later, George. If you're lucky,' she said. She kissed her fingers and touched his already pursed lips. George released his hold on her and she walked away. She turned and looked back at him over her shoulder and smiled. A cheeky, suggestive smile that made George tingle with excitement. She had played him for as long as she had wanted. She had made him work hard, but ultimately he had won his prize. She had given in at last. He was sure she wouldn't regret it. She was sure as well.

For the remainder of the lunch hour George was in a world of his own. His mind could only think of one thing; one person. He had met up with a few friends and been involved in a number of conversations, but he couldn't remember with whom or what they had talked about. As the lunch break drew to a close, George began to make his way back to his locker to pick up the books he would need for the afternoon lessons. Those infernal lessons that stood between him and Debbie Morris. Once again, schoolwork was proving to be a major irritant and hinderance to his social life. Walking down the corridor between the dining block and the main assembly hall he saw Frankie De Costa and his cronies ahead of him, blocking the way to the door. George was on a real high and felt there was nothing even Frankie could do or say that would change his mood. The gang suddenly seemed juvenile and pathetic. Childish and immature. He felt ten feet tall and they just looked like silly little schoolboys. They wouldn't start any trouble now, just before the end of lunch break, right outside the dining rooms. George carried on walking.

8

The Switch.

George barged through the first line of minions as if they weren't there, pushing several of them out of his path. But they had seen him coming and they had seen the broad smile on his face. The sort of smile Frankie would love to wipe off. The group of teenage Mafiosi reformed, drew together and blocked his way to the door. They were even more stupid than George had given them credit for. Frankie stepped forward and pushed his hands into George's chest, jolting him backwards.

'Where do you think you're going, Miller?' snapped Frankie. 'There's no way through here. You'll have to walk round.'

'Get out of my way, *Francis,* and take your toy soldiers with you.'

Frankie's face contorted with rage. He hated being called Francis. It was a girl's name. No one was allowed to call him that, not even his parents, who had cursed him with the name in the first place. Most of the pupils and teachers were happy to forget the name even existed. The penalty for using it was too ghastly to imagine. Frankie growled and gritted his teeth. His hands were clenched into fists. The rest of the gang let out a collective gasp of horror as the "F" word came out of George's mouth. The atmosphere changed in a flash. Frankie and the gang may not have intended to make a big scene before, but now Frankie was on the verge of losing control and then anything could happen. To be called Francis, in what was a truly mocking way, in front of his mates, would have to be punished. He couldn't let it pass.

'I've heard a rumour that you have been sniffing around Debbie Morris,' Frankie said stepping forward and pushing his fists into George's chest again. This time there was no backward movement from George. He was braced for impact and ready for anything.

'She's mine. So, keep your grubby little hands off her. Do you hear?' Frankie growled. George smiled. He could see he had infuriated Frankie. The tips of his ears had turned bright red, his lip was curled and his nostrils flared. George had certainly touched a raw nerve. Calling him Francis always did the trick. Their faces were so close, their noses were touching. George could smell Frankie's stale, nicotine breath.

'It's not a rumour. It's true. And I'm not trying, I am succeeding. We're going out tonight, didn't she tell you?' George said sarcastically. As Frankie became even more furious, George's smile became broader.

'I hate to point this out to you, *Francis*, but if you were the only bloke on this planet, she wouldn't want anything to do with you. You must be out of your tiny fucking mind to think that a girl like Debbie Morris would have any interest in a foul-smelling rancid jerk like you.'

George then pushed back, his fingers probing into Frankie's chest.

'You're a coward.' Another push. 'A bully.' Another push. 'And a fool.' The third push knocked Frankie back into the door. The gang had moved aside and were watching the drama play out. Frankie exploded. This was the final straw. George Miller was going to be humbled in front of anyone who was passing or cared to watch. With a loud growl, Frankie hurled himself at George. They both crashed to the floor, a mass of arms and legs thrashing about. Grunting and swearing came from both brawlers. The mobile boxing ring, formed by the gang, was quickly swollen by passing students eager to see this clash of titans. It was a spectacle not to be missed. Shouts of encouragement were coming from the spectators, although no one wanted to be seen cheering on George. Baz and Robbo might have been watching and could report back to Frankie after it was all over. But Frankie De Costa getting a beating would have been extremely popular throughout the school. Punches were flying everywhere. Most were ineffectual and missed their targets. Both Baz and Robbo connected with a couple of kicks to George's ribs when he came close enough to them, but apart from that, there were few scoring shots. George and Frankie rolled around like a rabid, convulsing animal.

George suddenly connected with two well-aimed blows. One flush on Frankie's nose, the other to his bottom lip. Both drew blood. The blood, mixed with his sweat and saliva, quickly spread across Frankie's face giving him the look of a beaten man. Frankie's strength and stamina seemed to drain away. Whether it was the physical blows or the taste and sight of his own blood that had weakened him, his ability to fight was waning. His crown was beginning to slip. George had his left hand tightly gripped around Frankie's throat. He could feel his fingernails burrowing into the soft, moist flesh of Frankie's neck, his left knee buried in Frankie's chest. Frankie's arms and legs were still valiantly thrashing around in an attempt to knock George off balance, but to no avail. The blood from his nose and lip had stained his yellow teeth making him look grotesque. Was this really the fearsome Frankie De Costa? George's grip tightened around Frankie's throat. Frankie's face was bright red and getting redder by the second. George's right hand clenched into a fist so tight his fingernails began to cut into his own flesh. The muscles in his arms were as hard as concrete and burning with the power coursing through them. The hairs on the back of his neck were standing to attention like a warring tomcat's tail. Breathing in so deeply, the air rushing up his nostrils felt like iced water. He felt no mercy or compassion towards Frankie. He would deliver the *coup de grâce*. A pile driver of a punch straight into Frankie's ugly, bloody, weasel-like face. Frankie was about to become Francis to anyone who wanted to call him that. He pulled back his right arm ready to plunge his fist into Frankie's gaping, crimson mouth. He felt his own lip curl, and his teeth grind together. He had never before felt so much strength in his own body. Just as he was about to "pull the trigger", a hand grabbed his wrist from behind. Had the gang finally decided to intervene? Were Baz and Robbo going to continue the fight? George didn't care. He would take them on. He would take them all on; he would leave them all bloody and beaten. He turned and scowled, like a lion interrupted from his meal. Whoever it was, they were going down straight away. He wasn't going to be kept from his kill for a moment longer. He released his grip on Frankie's throat and readied his left fist for action on the intruder's face. He began to swing around. Then he heard a voice.

'What's the meaning of this? Don't you gentlemen know how to conduct yourselves in public? You're sixteen years old, for God's sake.'

It was Mr Coulson, the history master. He still had hold of George's right wrist. The hate and violence were still in George's eyes as he got to his feet and turned towards the teacher. It was as much as George could manage to halt the progress of his left fist from smashing into the elderly man's chin. Coulson was frozen to the spot. He suddenly realised the danger he was in. George's eyes were wild and cold and had no reason. After a couple of seconds, Coulson released George's hand. George was breathing heavily and was trying to calm himself down. He glared into the old man's eyes with a look so passionate and hateful, Coulson's knees momentarily buckled. George turned his head and looked down at the carcass he had been about to devour. The lion had been denied his kill. Coulson regained his composure as best he could and tried to stamp his authority back on the situation.

'Get up boy,' Coulson shouted at Frankie, in a voice that betrayed some of the fear that was still pumping through his veins. Frankie dragged himself to his feet, rearranging his uniform and inspecting the damage done to his face. He fumbled about in his pocket and pulled out a handkerchief, mopping as much of the blood from his nose and mouth as he could.

Coulson questioned them about how the fight had started, but he got no answer. Amazingly, none of the spectators had witnessed the fights beginning. He berated both George and Frankie, telling them how unacceptable their behaviour was. George and Frankie heard none of it. They looked at each other with all the hostility that had been building up over the years.

'Okay, if that's your attitude, you can both report to the headmaster at the end of school. Now move along. All of you.'

He ushered the remaining onlookers away, the huge majority of them disappointed at his intervention. He sent Frankie and George off in different directions. As they walked away Mr Coulson shouted at both of them.

'The headmaster will expect to see you outside his office at four o'clock sharp.'

It was then that the reality of the situation hit George. The severest of all punishments. Not the dressing down from the headmaster. He had suffered that before and probably would again. It was the realisation he would not be able to meet Debbie at the school gates. Frankie, Mr Coulson and the headmaster were all just sideshows. The problem was Debbie. How would he be able to get a message to her to let her know what had happened? Neither he nor Graham took their mobile phones to school. He didn't even know Debbie's number. He knew he would be some time with Mr Kerridge. There were two of them to reprimand and even if he were to be seen first, he would still be at least fifteen minutes late. Would she wait for him? Would she give him another chance? She didn't seem like the sort of girl who would take too kindly to being stood up on a first date. The concern and panic spread across George's face as he tried to think of a solution. Then he heard Frankie's voice. He turned to see his blood-stained face sneering at him, his teeth still luminous with the vermillion varnish.

'Looks like you won't be able to make the date with your tart after all, Georgie boy. Looks like you'll be having a threesome with me and "Old Man Kerridge" instead.'

There was a smugness about Frankie's voice. A smugness that hinted at him having planned the entire episode. George shook his head and let out an audible laugh. Frankie was mean, nasty, violent and vicious, but he was no planner. He didn't have the brains to concoct a scheme like that. The events had however played into Frankie's hands, and the thought of George's irritation at the inconvenience of a trip to the headmaster's office would have cheered Frankie up no end, maybe even bringing a smile to his battered lip.

George had to think of a way to get a message to Debbie. None of their afternoon lessons coincided and he wouldn't be seeing Graham either. He wracked his brain to try and think of a solution but kept coming up blank.

The bell sounded for the end of school. Four o'clock. George rushed out of his classroom as quickly as he could and made a dash for the playground. Maybe he would catch a glimpse of Debbie or one of her friends. Maybe he would bump into Graham. If only he could find someone to pass on his message. Let her know he would be twenty minutes late and to wait for him. He burst through the swinging doors that led out into the open air. Before he had a chance to raise his eyes and start searching, he crashed straight into Mr Coulson. The books and papers the master was carrying were sent flying and the elderly gentleman was nearly knocked off his feet. He staggered backwards but regained his balance and shot George a furious look.

'Look where you're going boy!' he shouted angrily and bent down to pick up his spilt load. Coulson then stopped and looked up at George, suddenly realising who he was.

'You,' he shouted sternly. 'The headmasters office is that way,' he said pointing in the exact opposite direction. 'Mr Kerridge is expecting you now. Not next week.'

George slowly turned around, shooting one last forlorn look into the swarm of pupils making their way to the school's main gate. His chance had gone. He wasn't going to see anyone who would be able to help him. His shoulders sagged. He gave Coulson one more menacing glare, but knew he had no other option than to make his way over to the headmaster's block.

George entered the room outside the headmaster's office. Frankie was already there. He had cleaned himself up since lunchtime. The pathetic, vulnerable, bloody mess that had been lying on the floor only a couple of hours earlier was now sneering back at him from across the table. A comb had been pulled through his hair. The blood trails from his nose and the crimson stains on his teeth had gone. The smattering of blood flecks on his shirt had also faded. A small bruise was forming under his left eye and his lip was swollen. George could see the red broken skin on Frankie's neck where his fingernails had sliced into him. George smiled to himself. Frankie had escaped a real beating, but he still bore the marks and scars of his ignominious defeat.

The room was musty and cold. Disinfectant had been used liberally somewhere very close by. George sat down opposite Frankie. They stared across the oak table at each other with loathing in their eyes. There was no need for verbal abuse. Their looks said it all. George despised Frankie for making him miss his date with Debbie. Frankie knew it and was basking in the knowledge that through no real effort of his own, he had screwed with George's plans far more than he could have ever hoped. Frankie made an exaggerated effort to look at his watch, extending his left arm fully and pushing back his shirt sleeve. He moved his wrist slowly and deliberately towards his face.

'I'd stop worrying if I was you Miller. Your tart's probably walking home by now, probably with someone else. How do you feel about that, lover boy?'

George looked at Frankie's bruised and cut face. He tried to imagine what it would have looked like if Mr Coulson hadn't intervened. Just another couple of seconds and he would have delivered the blow that would have finally ended Frankie's reign of terror.

The un-oiled squeak and creak of the imposing oak door to the headmaster's study trumpeted judgement day. The door stopped tantalisingly ajar. The muffled conversation between two men seeped out from the privacy of the room. The boys swapped glances. Their firing squad was about to take aim. The creaking groaned back into life and the door opened fully. The suited visitor shook hands with Mr Kerridge and with a cheery smile and wave, left the building. He didn't seem to notice or acknowledge the condemned, waiting for their punishment. In an instant, the smiling face of the headmaster vanished. Frank Kerridge was a large and imposing figure. Well over six feet tall, he was an ex-regimental sergeant major from the Scots Guards. He always carried his swagger stick with its polished ornamental silver head; always tucked under his left arm. He never walked, he marched. To all the other pupils in the school he was a fearsome and frightening prospect, putting the fear of God into all under his "command". But not even Frank Kerridge, with all of his military bluster, could ruffle the feathers of the two protagonists sitting outside his office that afternoon. And he knew it.

He looked down at George and Frankie. He had seen both of these boys before, on numerous occasions. His happy, friendly demeanour had gone. He was now their executioner, dressed in his long, black gown like the "Grim Reaper". He was a busy man and didn't have time to be reprimanding pupils. He would normally now be enjoying a glass of finest malt whisky as the school day came to a close, but instead he had to deal with the two boys in front of him. It was as much a punishment for him as it was for them.

'Right, you boy, inside,' he ordered, gesturing at Frankie to enter his office. Frankie stood up, sneered at George and made his way into the study.

'You, wait here. I'll deal with you shortly,' he snapped at George. Mr Kerridge followed Frankie in and slammed the door. There was no time or opportunity for the squeaking hinges to break out into song this time. Just a mighty swoosh of air and a deafening thunderclap as the door crashed shut, sealing Frankie in. George was left alone with only his thoughts and his despair. He sighed and slumped back into the hard wooden chair, forcing a number of worrying creaks from its joints. Even the headmaster was against him, asking Frankie to go in first. George would be there even longer than he thought. Debbie would surely have gone home by the time he was let out. But what if she had waited? What if she had decided to hang on for him? Frankie would be first out. He might make his way over to the gates to see if she was still there. If she was, what would he say or do? What if Frankie made up some cock and bull story about him that would make things even worse? He looked at his watch. It was 4.15. He wasn't sure if he would have waited for her if she'd been that late. There was little point in worrying anymore. There was nothing he could do. As his desperation slowly morphed into resignation, the chimes from the large clock on the wall sang out in celebration of the quarter hour. George leant forward, forcing another series of creaks from the wooden chair and with his elbows on his knees and his head in his hands, stared at the threadbare carpet under his feet.

'Is the coast clear, George?' a voice whispered from around the corner. The whisper broke the silence of the room like the crash of a cymbal.

'It's me. Is it clear?' the whisper continued.

George spun around to see Graham's head peeping out from behind the door.

'Yes, it's clear. Frankie went in first,' replied George. 'What the hell are you doing here?'

'Roy told me Coulson caught you beating the crap out of Frankie and sent you here. He told me what it was about too. He said Frankie looked a total mess. Wish I'd been there to see it,' Graham chirped with a big smile on his face.

'He wouldn't have started anything if you'd been there,' laughed George. 'They shit themselves when we're together.'

'Sounds like he pretty much shit himself this afternoon, until Coulson saved him.'

The brothers chuckled. George started to recount the details of the fight, but Graham stopped him.

'Tell me later,' Graham said, cutting across his brother. 'I've just come past the school gates. She is still there.'

George's eyes popped wide and bright.

'Why don't you give me your badge and see if you can catch her before she leaves? I'll take the lecture from Kerridge.'

George suddenly came to life. He jumped up from the rickety old chair. There was a chance after all. They would pull "The Switch", fool Kerridge and George would get to keep his date with Debbie. There was always an adrenaline rush when they changed identities. It was so easy and yet so exciting.

'Thanks mate. I owe you one,' said George, hastily pinning his name badge onto Graham's sweater.

'Yes, I think you do, Brother, but my reward will be seeing Frankie come out of Kerridge's office and thinking I am you. I fuckin' love this.'

He patted his George badge and sat down, looking sombre and ready for a telling off. George scampered out of the door as fast as he could and headed towards the main gates.

Please be there. Please be there, he pleaded to himself.

Graham took in his surroundings. It was a forbidding place with nothing friendly or warm to commend it. He had never been there for a reprimand before, unlike his brother. A few minutes after George had sprinted off, the large oak door groaned open. Frankie emerged looking cocky and unrepentant.

'You, boy. In here.' He waved Graham into his room. 'And you, De Costa. Don't forget what I said.'

'No sir,' Frankie replied in a mock timid voice. As they passed each other in the doorway, Frankie sneered. He silently growled at Graham and mouthed,

'Fuck you Miller.' Graham just smiled. *If only you knew*, he thought.

Frankie made his way to the school gates. If he was lucky, Debbie Morris would still be there waiting for George. He would tell her he had seen him leaving through the back entrance with some other girl, laughing, joking and bragging about how he had stood "Debbie Morris" up. He would tell her she was far too good for a mongrel like Miller. Maybe even offer to walk her down the hill himself. It wasn't really his style, but anything he could do to upset George Miller was a bonus. Even if she said no, he hadn't lost anything. She was a tart, anyway. His mind was a conniving sewer of ideas. He would really show that fucking George Miller this time.

When he reached the main gates, he searched for Debbie, but there was no one there. He was disappointed she had gone and frustrated he wouldn't be able to spin his little web. That would have been the perfect end to his day. But his disappointment was tempered by the knowledge that she obviously hadn't waited. George Miller thought he was such a stud, but this time the girl had walked out on him and Frankie wasn't about to let that opportunity go. He would be able to remind George about it whenever he liked. Preferably when Debbie Morris was in earshot. He paused and leant up against the high perimeter brick wall. He felt a warm glow of satisfaction engulf him. He pulled another of his smug grins and lit a cigarette. As he started to walk down the hill, he thought about the events of the day. He hadn't planned any of it, but today he had scored his greatest victory so far against his biggest and most bitter rival. With almost a skip in his step, he made his way towards his bus stop. He noticed a couple of figures in what looked like school uniform at the bottom of the hill. His eyes squinted with concentration as he strained to see who it was. It looked very much like the blonde locks of Debbie Morris. She was with someone, but he couldn't make out who. Whoever it was, they were engaged in a passionate embrace. They were kissing. Frankie stood there transfixed, trying to work out what was happening. Surely Debbie wasn't that fickle to have gone off with someone else so quickly just because George hadn't shown up on time. For a split-second Frankie felt a twinge of sympathy for George. Debbie Morris was a slut after all. As the kissing couple stopped briefly for air, Frankie couldn't believe his eyes. It was Graham she was kissing. He watched the couple as they resumed their petting. He was totally confused. Had Debbie decided to teach one Miller brother a lesson by going out with the other one? But then Graham wouldn't have done that to George and besides, Debbie wasn't really Graham's type. As the endless stream of contradictions passed through his brain, the penny slowly started to drop. Even for Frankie the realisation of what had happened didn't take too much working out. His feeling of victory turned to fury and rage. He had been tricked. So had the headmaster. Frankie realised he had one last chance to nail George Miller and this time with the added bonus of dragging Graham Miller into the mire as well. He flicked his cigarette into the road and raced back up the hill, through the school gates towards the headmaster's office, eager to relate the hoax that had been perpetrated on both of them. He ran as fast as he could across the playground and into the doors of the headmaster's block. He slammed into them but they refused to open. He battered and punched them in an attempt to alert someone, anyone, but the lock had been turned and there was no one there. The headmaster had finished his lecture to Miller and they had all left the building. Frankie's master plan was in tatters. Glory had been snatched from his grasp not once, but twice in a matter of minutes. He pushed and rattled the doors again, more in frustration and anger than any hope that someone would come. If he could have exposed Graham Miller to Kerridge he would have inflicted a mortal blow to the Miller boys. But there was no one there to expose anyone to. Frankie's wretched day was now complete. He had been humbled and bloodied at the hands of George Miller, scolded by the headmaster, and then fooled by Graham Miller. With his blood boiling and with fury in his eyes, he swung a final and defiant punch at the locked door. With adrenaline pumping through him Frankie didn't feel the pain from his hand. He did feel the blood run down from his knuckles. He watched as it dripped off the end of his nicotine-stained fingers. As each drop of blood splashed on the clean floor, he swore to himself that the next bloodshed in this feud would not be his. It would be Miller blood.

9

Behind enemy lines.

A shrill and chirpy voice jolted George out of his daydream.

'You were miles away. Just staring into space,' said Brenda.

George blinked and quickly refocused his eyes and his mind back to the present. She had popped her head out to tell George that Mr Roswell wouldn't be long and that he was sorry to keep him waiting.

'Is there anything I can do for you while you're waiting?' she asked cheekily.

'No thank you,' George answered with a smile. And with that she disappeared back into her office.

George was very fond of Brenda. She reminded him of Debbie Morris. They had the same magnetic appeal and the same cheeky smile. They were both flirtatious and both had a twinkle in their eye. Their personalities were pretty similar too. Always upbeat and happy.

George found himself wondering if Brenda was as adventurous in the bedroom as Debbie had been. He wondered if he would ever find out. She was not married he knew that, but he had never seen her with anyone or heard her talk about a boyfriend, or for that matter a girlfriend. Like Debbie, George suspected Brenda would have been the prize catch at her school. Had she been hunted and hounded by a "George Miller" type when she was sixteen, and if so, did she play as hard to get as Debbie had with him? He hoped so.

Debbie had been on his mind. He had been thinking of her more and more. The wonderful memories he had of their time together replayed over and over in his head. He could see her face smiling at him. He could remember the touch of her lips on his. He remembered the scent he inhaled the first time his head nuzzled into her neck and the little noises she used to make when they made love. Those memories were all so precious. He often wondered what she had ended up doing and where she was living. Did she get married and have children? He found himself envying the unknown man who had taken her down the aisle and felt a wave of jealously wash over him. He smiled and secretly laughed at himself. He was covetous of a man he not only didn't know, but who may not have even existed!

Debbie had always wanted to see the world. She had always spoken about India, Australia, South Africa and Japan with so much enthusiasm. She had a list of places she was keen to visit and the list was a long one. She hadn't been the most gifted of academic students at school and had to work very hard to achieve even moderate success. So, it was something of a surprise to George when he found out she had been accepted into Durham University. He couldn't work out where she had found the time to study. In their two years together, they were constantly at each other's side. The only thing he remembered her studying was him and vice versa. Maybe she was smarter than he had given her credit for. They had never discussed history, literature, politics or the meaning of life. Their time together was more dedicated to exploring the animalistic side of life rather than the philosophical. They were totally consumed with each other and took every opportunity to indulge themselves in the lust and passion they felt.

There was one occasion in particular that George drifted back to in his mind on many occasions. It was a memory that always excited him.

They were seventeen and had been seeing each other for just over a year. They were kissing and cuddling during their lunch break at school. After a few minutes, the petting became quite intense. George was kissing and nibbling the bottom of Debbie's neck. She was purring with delight.

'Get a room,' George heard one girl say as she passed by. They were both revelling in each other's pleasure and paying no attention to the world around them. Without warning, Debbie pulled her neck away from George's kisses, held his head and pulled it close to hers. She whispered in his ear.

'I want you to fuck me right now.'

George yanked his head back in surprise, a look of incredulity on his face.

'What? Here? At school?' he exclaimed, his "amazed" expression slowly dissolving into a furtive smile.

'Yes. Here and now. If you don't, I think I will explode. I want to feel you inside me.' She pulled his face even closer to hers and whispered in his ear. 'All of you.'

She glared into his eyes with a look of desperation that he was not going to argue with.

George loved flaunting the rules, but they had never done it at school before. He smiled and tried desperately to think of somewhere they could go. He remembered the shortcut he had taken to the headmaster's study the year before after fighting with Frankie. It was out of bounds for all pupils, but was also quite overgrown and untended, so the teachers rarely used it. It was muddy, untidy, cold, dark and uninviting. It was perfect.

'Come on,' he said grabbing her hand and pulling her with him. She gripped his hand enthusiastically and gladly followed. They walked across the tarmac playground as naturally as they could, hoping their excited faces weren't giving anything away. Almost running, they turned the corner next to the geography rooms. They were about to go behind enemy lines. Leaving the colourful, bustling, vibrant, noisy world of school life, they slipped into forbidden territory. The contrast between the two worlds was stark. They had turned the corner into a dark, cold and soulless place. There was no sunlight or warmth. There was no colour. The noise and excitement of the other students playing and enjoying themselves had gone. The silence was only broken by the sound of the cold wind whistling through the empty branches of the trees and their footsteps on the crisp orange autumn leaves. They were alone. George walked a few more steps, pulling Debbie behind him, then ducked into one of the building's recesses. It was even colder and darker. They both shivered, but it was as much with excitement as it was the chill.

The recess was full of litter and leaves, blown in over weeks and months. Empty crisp bags and plastic bottles made up their carpet, with cigarette packets and sheets of old yellowing newspaper. To add to the excitement, they were just beneath the window of the teachers' common room. No one would be able to see them, but they would have to keep as quiet as possible if they were to avoid being heard. The surroundings were far from romantic, but this was not about romance, it was about lust in its most basic form. They looked into each other's eyes and smiled. Their mouths locked together again. Their tongues darted in and out of each other's mouths with even more vigour than usual. They groped at each other's clothing with a piranha-like frenzy. Debbie's hands were fumbling with the clasps on George's trousers. In seconds they were open. She found the zip, lowered it, reached inside and eased her hand behind the elastic of his boxer shorts, down onto his hot pulsing flesh. Her fingers wrapped themselves around his erection. George clumsily unbuttoned Debbie's blouse trying his best not to tear all the buttons off in his haste. He moved his hands inside the gaping blouse and unclipped her bra. He eased the lacy underwear up, exposing her beautiful breasts, then cupped them with his hands, kissing and sucking on each of her nipples in turn, nipping them with his teeth just enough to make her flinch. As he did so, Debbie eased her prize out of his trousers. She ran her grip along the shaft, back and forth. With her other hand she hitched up her skirt and pulled her thong to one side. She lifted herself onto her tiptoes. George bent his knees slightly, lowering himself into position. She spread her legs as wide as she could and manoeuvred him towards her moist portal. As the most sensitive parts of their bodies brushed together, she released her grip allowing him to slowly slide inside her. They both let out a muffled moan as they felt their union. He was hard and she was very wet. They looked lovingly into each other's eyes as he eased himself in deeper and deeper. George started to pump and push. She opened her legs a little more to try and accommodate his insurgence. They kept eye contact until George had pushed the last tantalising inch of himself into her. Debbie's head tilted back and her eyes closed. There was a look of sheer ecstasy on both their faces. As the momentum and rhythm increased, so did the power of the thrusts. George's pelvic punches were causing Debbie's entire body to judder. He was lifting her off the floor with the force of his penetration. Her arms were wrapped tightly around his neck, holding on for dear life. Her breasts were bouncing beautifully in time to their pleasure. Faster and faster. Harder and harder. There was no stopping now. George gripped her buttocks, supporting her weight and levering her back and forward, up and down, regulating the movement of her body in time with his. A stifled cry came from both of them as George emptied himself inside her. Their glorious rhythm reached its crescendo as George's orgasm shot repeatedly into Debbie's body. They continued for a few moments longer, making sure they had squeezed every last drop of pleasure out of the moment. The momentum slowed and they came to a halt. He kissed her deeply and passionately. He removed his tongue from her mouth and slowly withdrew himself from between her legs. Another contented squeal came from Debbie's mouth as George slipped out of her. They had done it. It had been quick and it had been intense. It had been passionate and exciting. It had been thrilling and magnificent. They started to re-dress themselves with as much urgency as they had undressed each other. They brushed themselves down, cleaned themselves up and tried to make themselves look respectable. They took each other by the hand and slowly crept back towards the geography rooms. After checking that no one was watching, they calmly stepped back into the world of colour, of noise and of sunlight. That world had carried on without even noticing they had gone. A stolen moment, from right under the teachers' noses. It was an exhilarating feeling. The buzz would stay with them for the rest of that day. The journey back into that dark, cold and erotic world would be repeated many times during the following months.

They had given each other so much joy during their two years together. Their lovemaking had known no bounds. They experimented and explored all the pleasures available. Debbie was as willing and creative as George. The more dangerous or bizarre, the more exciting; the more clandestine the geography the bigger the thrill.

There was nothing they didn't try. Debbie learnt as much from George as he did from her. It was heaven. It was magical. But after two years, it was over. It was inevitable. They had promised to keep in touch and try to get together whenever possible, but somehow it never happened. George did meet up with Debbie on one occasion. It was about five years later, by chance, when he was up in Newcastle. But apart from that, she had all but vanished from his life. Debbie was now just a horny, sexy, tingling memory.

He had been with many glamourous and sexy women since, but never for very long. He had experienced all the passion and excitement, even the lust, but he had yet to feel that special spark that ignited in his body when he was with Debbie.

Although they had only been together for two years, Debbie was still a massive part of George's life. Apart from his brother and parents, she was still the most important and treasured person in his heart. As fond as he was of Brenda, he found himself wishing it had been Debbie typing away in the small office. That would have cheered him up and taken his mind off the trouble he was in.

10

The last chance.

George started to go over his story and his defence regarding the incident with the drunks at the bar. As much as he tried, he couldn't think of anything better to tell them other than the truth. Brenda appeared from her office again. She knocked on Bernie's door and opened it.

'Mr Roswell will see you now Mr Miller.' She was no longer the flirty secretary, but the dedicated professional PA. George stood up and straightened his trousers and jacket.

'Thank you, Miss Cousins,' he replied in the same businesslike tone. He sucked in a deep breath and walked through the door into Bernie's office.

'Can I get you gentlemen anything else?' Brenda inquired.

'No thank you, Brenda, that will be all.' She shut the door behind her. George could sense an atmosphere and it wasn't a good one.

'Come on in, George. Sorry to have kept you waiting so long. Sit down,' said Bernie. There were three other men in the room with George. Bernie the manager, David Blackstone the club's secretary and CEO, and Doug Fenner the first team coach and Bernie's right-hand man. They had obviously been discussing his future while he had been waiting outside. Had they already decided his fate? Maybe his defence wasn't even going to be heard. Bernie and David took their seats facing George. Doug remained standing, gazing out of the window. When George had been in these situations before, they normally gave him a rap on the knuckles and fined him a week's wages, but the mood in the room was awkward. He could sense the tension. The body language between the three other men was prickly to say the least. George felt uncomfortable and slightly nervous, which he rarely did in Bernie's and Doug's company. He prepared himself for the onslaught.

David Blackstone was a strait-laced, God-fearing man. He was always impeccably dressed in a suit and tie, always well groomed and clean shaven. He was in his late fifties and spoke with a soft Scottish accent. From what George could surmise, his footballing heart lay with East Fife, but his footballing brain, focus and business acumen were committed to this club. Business was business and in the cut-throat world of professional football there was no room for sentiment. He said what he thought and you were never in any doubt what he was thinking. He would never say anything behind your back that he wouldn't say to your face and he was never afraid or intimidated to give his honest and sometimes brutal opinion. George and David had never really been friendly, but George had a grudging respect for the man and his honesty. David felt that everyone who was on the company's payroll should promote a good image of the club at all times. Womanising, drinking, gambling and brawling were definitely not part of his utopian vision. Although David had no outright control over decisions about who should stay or who should go, his opinions were always asked. He had been at the club longer than anyone apart from Mr Morton, the chairman. The chairman trusted him and valued his judgment.

Morally, David Blackstone despised George, but he was a businessman first and foremost and knew he had to put the financial facts ahead of his own personal feelings. Had David finally persuaded the powers that be to cash in on their wayward asset, before the self-destruct button made George's value plummet?

Doug Fenner smiled at George. He had turned his attention from the horizon outside to the drama inside. He was the only man in the room who didn't look under pressure. George managed a hint of a grin, but he looked nervous and hunted. Doug winked and nodded almost secretively as he walked over to join Bernie and David. Was that a sign everything was going to be alright? Doug should know; he had been part of the conversation. George felt a little easier and made himself comfortable.

Doug was there primarily as moral support for Bernie. They were cut from the same cloth and treated people like human beings, not just assets or liabilities. They were a dying breed in the world of football, but weren't going to change their ethos or principles for anyone. For that reason, they were both well respected and loved by most of the people in the game.

Doug had been the manager who first signed George as a professional. He had taken a gamble on an eighteen-year-old just out of school. He had had a number of chats and meetings with his father, but been told in no uncertain terms, nothing would be signed until George finished his education. Doug respected that and was prepared to wait until the time was right. It was only then that they sat down together and agreed terms. Doug had told George on many occasions that he was the best gamble he had ever taken. He treated him more like a son than a player and because of that, he had become, and remained, great friends with John and Paula. John trusted Doug to look after his young son and treat him right and he wasn't disappointed.

After a couple of seasons, John was invited up to Lancashire to talk about George's future. Doug had received an offer from a Premiership side that was more than he could afford to turn down. He didn't want to sell George, but the chance for his club to make a financial killing and more importantly to Doug, help George's career blossom in the big league, was too hard to refuse. It meant a move back down south, which pleased both John and Paula. Over the following few years, George's and Doug's paths crossed a few times before they both ended up where they were now.

The three judges were in place facing George. Bernie took a deep breath.

'George, you have been with us now for five years. Your playing record is good and your injury rate has been low, except recently of course. You are a valuable and treasured member of this club.'

'Thank you, Mr Roswell,' George interjected.

'We are all aware of the pressures a modern-day sportsman has to endure and we appreciate it's not easy.' He paused and glanced over at David Blackstone. David sat deadly still, staring directly and unblinkingly at George. Bernie took another deep breath. 'However, there are limits to how far our tolerance and understanding will stretch. The chairman is very unhappy about the current situation we find ourselves in. He doesn't want to be reading about his club and his players on the front pages of his morning newspapers.'

George hadn't seen Bernie look so serious before. He could see the stress etched into every nook and cranny of Bernie's weathered features. He shuffled awkwardly in his seat as he spoke. George felt the uncomfortable nervousness come back into his body. He gazed over at Doug, hoping to see another reassuring gesture, but Doug's head was bowed. He was staring at the space between his feet, with a blank and empty expression on his face. George's eyes returned to Bernie who was looking straight at him.

'The chairman has asked me to say this to you. He does not want to see any more of his players, especially you George, in the headlines for the wrong reasons again.'

The sternness fell out of Bernie's face and a look of resignation came into his eyes. 'George, its out of my hands now, this is your last chance.'

His voice had lost its authority. He spoke in a softer, kinder tone.

'I have done as much as I can. Don't throw it away son.'

David then informed George he had been fined a week's wages for bringing the club into disrepute. He said it in a very matter-of-fact way. He showed no pleasure or smugness in the announcement and wished George well at the end of the meeting. George felt only guilt as he shook the three men's hands, thanked them, apologised and left the office. The fine was incidental. He wouldn't even notice it, but he felt an emptiness inside him that really hurt. Bernie had stuck his neck out for him, only for George to carry on in his own selfish way. It was Bernie's reputation as well as his own he was damaging and it was Bernie's and Doug's trust he had been forsaking. He owed a lot to both men. Maybe, he also owed it to himself to keep his nose clean and prove all of the doubters wrong.

As George made his way to the stairs he saw Brenda. She was on the phone, but still managed a little wave goodbye. He waved back and slowly walked down the stairs, out of the doors through to the main reception, then into the car park and the open air.

'Wait a minute, George. Hang on.' George turned around to see Doug, slightly breathless, running across the tarmac towards him.

'Are you okay George?' he asked, panting, and looking a little red in the face.

'Yes, of course I am. A week's wages won't hurt much.'

As soon as he said it, he wished he hadn't. It wasn't the time or the place for humour or flippancy. Doug also failed to see the funny side. Doug placed his right hand on George's shoulder, as much for support as anything else. He caught his breath and looked George squarely in the eye.

'George. You and I go back a long way. I feel I almost discovered you. You had real talent and still do, but you've got to realise talent sometimes isn't enough.'

Where had George heard that before?

'It's a team game. It's a squad game. You've got to fit in or all the talent in the world isn't going to get you anywhere. You're great with the players and the supporters love you, but you've got to toe the line when it comes to the management and the owners. To them you are just a number on a spreadsheet. A value. A commodity. Something to be bargained with. It's shit, I know, but that's the way this business is nowadays. Before you came in, David was telling Bernie that the board would be happy if he decided to move you on. He had Bernie by the balls. After all of your previous…,' he paused and considered his next word… 'problems, he was more or less telling him to get rid of you as soon as possible. Bernie has bought you this last chance. If you screw it up this time it won't just be you facing the firing squad. George, you know there is only one way to fall once you've passed thirty. You've still got a couple more years at this level. Keep your head down, play the game by their rules and see it through. You're a long time out of the game and there will be plenty of opportunity to regret missed chances once you've retired.'

'I know,' George sighed ruefully. 'I really do appreciate what the two of you have done for me. Not just today but over the years. Don't worry, I won't let either of you down again. I promise.'

'Good. And don't let yourself down either,' said Doug, throwing a fake punch at George's chin. Doug's hand cradled the back of George's neck, then patted his cheek.

'See you tomorrow, son. Say hello to your folks for me when you speak to them.'

George climbed into his car. It had been an emotionally draining day and he could do with a good stiff drink. He sat in his car for a moment wondering what to do. He could hear Doug's words echoing in his head. Maybe a cup of tea would be a better idea. If he was going to turnover a new leaf, now was probably the best time to start. He drove himself home.

11

Newcastle. (Seven years earlier).

Debbie Morris was enjoying her year off. She had decided to take a break after her course at university had finished. She felt she had earned one. She needed some time to recharge and re-evaluate her life. It was the first time she could remember, when there was nothing to do, no one to see and no deadlines to meet. Each new day was a blank canvas. She was twenty-three years old. The previous seven years had been jam-packed with work, learning, loving, pressure, decisions and emotions. Her life had been hurtling along at a hundred miles an hour. After all that rushing around, her year off would be dedicated to taking it easy.

For her last two years at school, she had been involved in a passionate love affair with a boy called George Miller. They had spent every possible moment with each other. They were together at weekends, during school holidays, to and from school and as much of the school day as lessons allowed. Both sets of parents had started to show signs of concern at the intensity of their relationship, but they didn't know the half of it. Once Debbie knew she would be travelling up to Durham, it became clear that their relationship would have to end. They wouldn't be able to see each other for long periods of time. They would be embarking on new adventures, far away from each other. It was heartbreaking for them both. Debbie knew it wouldn't be easy moving away. She would see her family at Christmas and occasionally during the holidays and she could keep in touch with her friends via the many social media sites to which they all belonged. But it was the separation from George that would be the hardest pill to swallow. They had meant so much to each other. She knew she would miss him terribly.

During her years at Durham, Debbie had a number of lovers, none of them lasting, or serious. Everyone was experimenting with their sexuality, finding out, exploring and discovering new pleasures and experiencing new fantasies. She was years ahead of them. She had done it all with George at school from the age of sixteen.

Of the men Debbie had relationships with, none of them really matched up to George. Was he really that good? Or had his prowess been enhanced by the years and her frequent visits to him in her imagination and memory? Had she set the bar too high, or rather, had George? Would anyone ever live up to her expectations? Every time with George was a thrill. There was always something new, something different and always with incredible passion and energy.

The only occasion she had entered uncharted sexual territory was during her final year at Durham. She had been smoking a few joints and drinking wine with a couple of girlfriends. They were all a little drunk and a little high. One thing led to another, and the three of them ended up in bed together. She had never experienced love-making with other girls before. It was so natural, so nice, softer, less brutal. There was more kissing and stroking. More touching, licking and fondling. They all knew what they liked and were happy and eager to practise it on each other, performing treats they enjoyed so much, on someone else. Knowing the intimate places that could generate so much ecstasy. She had given oral pleasure to George and other men before, but never to another woman. It was somehow easier, maybe even more enjoyable. To make another girl moan with delight using her tongue, in the way she knew would bring her maximum rapture, gave her as much pleasure as if it was being done to her. There was no competition, no selfishness. It was slow and gentle, beautiful and erotic. It was one of the most sensual nights Debbie could remember. When she woke up, they were all entwined in each other's nakedness like three little puppies in their basket. She felt no embarrassment and no shame. If it hadn't been for the fact she had an appointment early that morning she would have loved to stay and start all over again. She remembered feeling a little jealous of the two girls left in the bed that morning, knowing that when they woke, they would probably start their day with more of the same, but sadly, without her. The memory of that night made her body tingle. She had never imagined herself receiving or giving sexual pleasure to another girl. She had never even given it a thought before. It had certainly never occurred to her that there could be that kind of intimacy outside a regular heterosexual relationship. That first experience of another girl's touch and tongue had, up until then, been a one-off delight. She wouldn't go out searching for another opportunity, but she knew if one presented itself, she would gladly and excitedly embrace it.

She remembered thinking at the time how George would have loved to have been there. Like a child in a sweet shop. But his presence would have changed the whole dynamic and atmosphere. It wouldn't have been the same. It was the only time Debbie had had sex and was glad George was not there.

Debbie's years at Durham had been fun and fruitful. She had worked as hard as she had played and gained a first-class honours degree in sociology. She was proud of herself as were her parents. The degree had opened a lot of doors for her. She just had to decide which one of them to step through. She still had a burning desire to travel and now had a number of opportunities as to how she could fulfil it. But after the helter-skelter of the past seven years, she had decided to take a holiday from responsibility and decision-making, to relax and recuperate, to collect her thoughts and plan her future. In the back of her mind she thought she would spend her year's vacation travelling through Europe. See some of the sights. Paris, Rome, Madrid. So many on her list. But she never quite got around to it.

She had rented a flat in the centre of Newcastle with a friend from university. Carrie was tall and angular with long, dark, curly hair and big brown eyes. She had a beguiling smile, was very attractive and had a figure that turned most men's (and some women's) heads. On more than one occasion Debbie had wondered if Carrie had ever had sex with another girl. Had she known the softness and intimacy of another girl's touch? It had remained only a thought. Carrie's boyfriend Daniel had moved in, "unofficially", soon after they got the flat. Debbie didn't mind. He helped pay the rent and was a good laugh. He had a job at Newcastle United Football Club. She wasn't really sure what he did there, although she knew he wasn't a player. He was the only one of the three of them who was earning a regular wage, so he was always handy to have about.

Debbie was living off a monthly allowance from her parents. They had been so pleased with her results that when she announced she would be taking a year off, they offered to help finance it with a decent sum of money each month. She felt a little guilty when she explained to them she would be staying up north instead of returning home, but they seemed to come to terms with it and were very understanding. She could be her own boss and let off as much steam as she liked before enrolling in the rat race. The following summer she would start to look for a job and the next big chapter in her life would begin to unfold. Until then, she would stay up in Newcastle and live a carefree existence.

Because George was a professional footballer and quite famous, Debbie was able to keep tabs on his whereabouts and see how his career was progressing. She wasn't particularly interested in football, but always made a special effort to read about George's team in the papers. She was pleased and proud when he made the right sort of headlines; lauded and congratulated for some exceptional performance on the football pitch. And she was mildly amused when he made the wrong sort. The number of times she had seen George's face beaming out at her from the front pages of various newspapers under some derogatory headline were too many to count. There had been scandals involving married women, irate husbands, irate fathers, drunken brawls and gambling. George was the one they loved to hang it on. Even a generic article about the drinking culture in football would have a picture of George alongside it to draw the readers in, even if the piece didn't mention him. There were numerous photos of him with his arm around various glamorous women. They made her smile. She looked at the women and thought how lucky they were. Had they experienced the George Miller that she had? All that intensity and passion. She hoped not. Debbie realised that every time she looked at these women, there was an element of jealousy and envy in her heart.

George had suffered terribly at the hands of the tabloids with their "kiss and tell" revelations over the years. She wondered how much of a stir some of her stories would have made. With her wealth of knowledge she would have the hacks queuing around the block for her story, probably offering her huge sums of money. But her memories were special and private. George was special. Even though she hadn't seen him in person for five years, the mention of his name, or sight of his picture in the papers made her pulse rate rise.

Over the last few months, she had thought of phoning him and having a chat. He would be easy to get in touch with. She knew what club he played for and even if they wouldn't give her his number, she still had John and Paula's old landline number. Assuming they were still at their old address.

She would normally get the urge to talk to George whilst sitting in the flat on her own. Three quarters of the way into a bottle of red wine and surfing through her memories.

The wine always helped with her bravery and confidence. Sometimes she would lie on her bed alone listening to Carrie and Daniel hammering away in the next room. Moaning and grunting through the paper-thin walls, their increasing and uncontrollable cries of joy and exhilaration blending with the ever-accelerating and frantic orchestral accompaniment of the squeaking bedsprings. She would wait with an almost voyeuristic anticipation to hear the triumphant, if stifled, announcement that they had both finished their journey. At those moments in particular she wished it had been George's fingers gently probing inside her and not her own.

Her urges to talk to him invariably floated off into thin air. The more thought she gave it, the less the idea appealed. Deep down she was scared he wouldn't be the same George. He might not even want to talk to her. He might have turned into one of those superstar brats with an enormous ego and sense of self-importance. He might be aloof and dismissive, superior and cold. All of her wonderful memories would be tarnished forever. It always came down to that. A sense of panic that things would simply just not be the same. Maybe ignorance was the only way to keep her memories alive and in pristine condition. Life had moved on anyway. She was sure she had changed as well. Maybe the chemistry they had enjoyed in those wonderful days at school had evaporated over the years. Was she still the same horny little teenager that fucked him under the teachers' common room window? Even she couldn't answer that question. There was no doubt a lot had happened to them both in the past five years. Had he thought about her as much as she thought about him? The chance the answer to that question might be "no" was always enough to dissuade her from pursuing the idea. Her memories would stay unmolested and unchallenged. They would keep her warm through the cold winter nights.

Debbie awoke on Friday morning with a splitting headache. She had been in the pub the night before and had drunk far too much. This was not unusual. Her head was thumping and her mouth reminded her of the shots she had been knocking back in the various drinking games they had been playing. She reached out into the semidarkness for the glass of water by her bed. She tried hard to focus on her watch. 9.45. The morning was doing its best to invade the room, but the curtains were just about holding it at bay. She didn't have to get up. She had nothing planned. She sipped the water and slumped back into her pillow. She let out a loud yawn and stretched her arms above her head. The sun had started to win its battle with the curtains and light was slowly seeping into the room. She gradually extracted herself from beneath the duvet, shuffled into the kitchen and made herself a cup of tea. The flat was empty and still. Carrie and Daniel had already gone out. Half-eaten bowls of cornflakes and two half-drunk cups of coffee had been abandoned on the table, evidence of the rush and activity that had taken place earlier that morning, to which Debbie had been oblivious. The local newspaper was open and half hidden under the breakfast paraphernalia. The prime minister looked up at her with a coffee stain around his face. Debbie folded the paper shut and was immediately greeted by a smiling picture of George Miller beaming up at her. She wouldn't mind waking up to that face every morning. She sipped her tea and read the article. The piece wasn't about George personally. In fact, he didn't even get a mention. It was about his team. They were one of two London-based clubs taking part in a charity event for a children's hospice on Sunday. They were due to play Newcastle on Saturday, then stay overnight and perform whatever charitable duties they needed to on the Sunday. When she had read the article, she propped the paper up against the Cornflake packet, with George's face looking straight at her. His eyes twinkled even in newsprint and his smile was just as entrancing, warm, loving and inviting as she remembered. She kissed the tips of her first two fingers and planted them on his lips. She stared at him for a moment in silence and once again began the process of convincing herself to get in touch with him. She would allow herself to go through the motions. It wouldn't be long before she decided it was a bad idea. But was it? This was obviously the best opportunity she had had for a long while and she was unlikely to get a better one in the future. He would be arriving on Tyneside that afternoon to prepare for the game. Then, Saturday night after the match, he would be on his own. He would have no game to worry about the following day. Daniel would be able to get her a ticket for the match. He had boasted as much not so long ago.

She started to convince herself that it was now or never. Time to grasp the nettle and take the plunge. To gamble her memories and dreams. She knew what she stood to lose, but the tantalising thought of actually seeing George in the flesh again was proving too strong. She failed to talk herself out of the idea. This time she was going to do it. As she got dressed, a shiver of excitement ran through her body. All the possibilities began to rush through her mind. The meeting, the passion, their undiminished love. As she put on her underwear her fingers slid between her legs. Her eyes were shut and dreaming of his touch. She let out a small whimper and whispered, 'Oh George.'

Daniel's mobile rang only once before he answered.

'Daniel. Hi, it's Debbie.'

'Hi, Debbie,' he replied slightly surprised. 'Is everything okay?'

'Yes, everything's fine, I want to ask you a massive favour.'

His voice became more suggestive.

'And what "massive" favour can I do for you, my dear?'

'Well, do you remember saying you could get me tickets for any Newcastle game, not so long ago?'

'Mmm. Yes.' He didn't sound convincing.

'Well, I wonder if you could get me a ticket for tomorrow's game.'

Debbie's voice was becoming increasingly excitable.

'Tomorrow!' exclaimed Daniel. 'That's a little short notice, isn't it?'

'I know. I'm sorry but I really need to go to the match. Is there any chance at all?'

She had sounded as helpless and as desperate as she could. A real damsel in distress. There was a short pause, before Daniel spoke.

'Well, this just happens to be your lucky day. I can't go tomorrow so you can have my season ticket. Of course, you will have to sit next to Carrie for the whole game and I warn you she can be quite opinionated and aggressive.'

'Brilliant. Thank you so much, Daniel. I owe you one,' said Debbie in an equally suggestive tone. She knew he fancied her, but he was harmless and at that precise moment he was also very useful.

12

Room 407.

On Saturday Debbie had arranged to meet Carrie in a pub about half a mile from the ground. It was a huge relief to her that she would be with Carrie. She hadn't thought about the stress and traumas involved in getting into the ground, finding her seat and watching the game on her own. Carrie was a regular and would be able to show her where to go and what to do. It couldn't have turned out any better.

'I didn't think you were interested in football,' Carrie said as they sipped their pre-match drinks.

'I'm not,' replied Debbie. 'This will be the first game I have seen since watching the school team play about five years ago.' Carrie looked puzzled.

'So why all the panic about getting a ticket for this game? Daniel said you were desperate and begged him to get you one for today.'

Debbie smiled. She *had* been desperate, but Daniel had a talent for the dramatic and had obviously dressed the story up a little for Carrie's benefit. Debbie then recounted in glorious technicolour some of the experiences she had shared with George whilst they were at school. As the stories continued Carrie's expressions went from surprise to amazement, horror, shock, even envy. By the time Debbie had finished, Carrie looked quite worn out.

'Well, aren't you the dark horse! Why didn't you say anything before?' she asked. Debbie explained she didn't want to become part of the George Miller circus. She didn't want the press hounding her or offering her money for any juicy titbits of information. She also didn't want her name linked with any of the stories they might want to concoct themselves. She wasn't going to be just another skeleton in George Miller's closet. She turned and stared straight into Carrie's eyes and raised her index finger, wagging it close to her face.

'And I'm trusting you not to say anything about this to anyone. Not even Daniel. Okay?'

There was a hint of threat about the way she said it, but both girls knew she was only teasing. Carrie looked at her, wide-eyed as if nothing had been further from her mind.

'I mean it,' she said. Carrie smiled.

'My lips are sealed as far as George Miller is concerned. Which is more than you can say.'

Carrie roared out laughing at her own joke. Debbie looked at her with as stern a face as she could manage, but Carrie's laughter was infectious and dragged her into the humour of the smutty innuendo. Carrie was helpless with laughter and Debbie unwittingly joined in.

'Mind you,' Carrie stuttered through her giggles, 'I wouldn't mind a little romp around the penalty area with him. He's not bad, not bad at all.'

Carrie was still wrapped up in her own comedy as they left the pub and made their way to the ground.

Debbie was awestruck by the size of the stadium and the amount of people there. The noise and atmosphere were like nothing she had ever experienced before and she wasn't even inside the arena. She knew it would be different from when she turned up at the sports field to watch George play for the school, but she hadn't expected it to be quite so intimidating or exhilarating. Carrie seemed to take it all in her stride, but then she did this most weeks. As they walked up the steps to the upper tier, all Debbie could see was the sky. Then in to view came the stand at the opposite side of the ground. It suddenly gave everything scale. The place was enormous. And then the noise. A wall of sound suddenly hit her. Thousands of voices singing in an almost tribal way. She was looking down on a whole new world. A massive structure with about 60,000 men, women, boys and girls, all chanting and gesticulating in unison. She felt the adrenaline rush through her. It was a truly spectacular scene. And the game hadn't even started.

Carrie supplied a running commentary throughout the match, never missing an opportunity to make some kind of suggestive remark about George. Had he ever scored a hat-trick with her? Was he as penetrating off the pitch as he was on it? Did he burst into her box? And what was his conversion rate between attempts and success? Debbie smiled at them all, but left Carrie to do most of the laughing.

When the game was over, they both stood to leave.

'I'm sorry your first match was such a damp squib,' Carrie said as if it were her fault.

'Was it?' Debbie asked. 'I thought it was quite exciting.'

Carrie looked at her with a quizzical frown on her face.

'I do hope you're not that easily pleased between the sheets,' she said. 'My estimations of you and Mr Miller would go down rapidly if that was the case.'

'Don't worry about that,' said Debbie 'your estimations are safe just where they are.'

As they emerged from the ground and into the street, Carrie asked, 'What do you want to do now. Pub? Club? Wine bar?'

'I'm actually going to George's hotel to meet him,' said Debbie, as if that was the obvious answer. Carrie's eyes widened with surprise.

'Oh great. I'll come along with you. Just to keep you company.'

'Oh no. Oh no, no, no. After all you said about hat-tricks and penalty boxes I don't think either of us would be able to keep a straight face. Anyway, I'm only going along for a look. I might not even be able to talk to him. It's just to satisfy my own curiosity,' she said unconvincingly. 'Besides, Daniel will be home soon. Why don't you go back and prepare yourself for a siege of your own penalty box?'

They both laughed. The two girls hugged.

'Thank Daniel for the ticket and thank you for all your wisdom and knowledge during the game. Especially about George. I will see you later.' Debbie paused and with a glint in her eye said, 'Maybe.'

Debbie managed to hail a cab and got in with a feeling of excitement and mild panic. The traffic was appalling. So many cars, all moving at a snail's pace. She had plenty of time to think about the next phase of her plan, but that was not a good thing. With self-doubts continually knocking at the door, she remembered all the reasons why she had never done anything like this before, every second telling herself there was still time to turn back. The hotel where George was staying was about six miles away from the stadium. She had managed to find out which hotel from Daniel. The journey had taken nearly three quarters of an hour by the time the driver pulled into the car park. She sat there for a few seconds breathing deeply. She paid her fare, picked up the small bag she had prepared earlier that morning, shut the door and walked purposefully into the hotel. She went straight past reception and into the spacious bar. All seemed normal and quiet. She chose a table that was tucked away, but also had a good view of the reception desk and main entrance. She removed her long black woollen coat and laid it carefully over her bag. She called the waiter and asked him for a large Jack Daniels with ice, then slowly scanned the panorama. The bar and lounge were relatively empty. There were only a few drinkers, most of them alone, all of them men. Her searching stare darted between her fellow imbibers trying not to catch anyone's eyes. Some were plugged into their headphones and some were reading newspapers or books. She wished she had bought a newspaper with her as much for camouflage as anything else.

She had been waiting for about half an hour and was into her second Jack Daniels, when a huge yellow and blue double-decker coach pulled up outside the hotel. A number of photographers had appeared from nowhere and were jostling for position as the coach doors opened. About a dozen large, thickset, suited doormen did their best to hold them at bay and formed a protective tunnel from the coach to the main entrance. *This must be them*, she thought. She drew in a deep breath and took a large gulp of her drink. Peering around one of the pillars that formed part of her defensive wall she watched as a steady stream of smartly dressed young men marched into the foyer. She didn't recognise any of them, until she saw George appear. He looked great. She suddenly felt a little breathless. They were all dressed in blazers, shirts and ties. She had never seen him look so sharp. He scrubbed up rather well, she thought. No sooner had the men entered the hotel, they were ushered through a large pair of wooden doors by an elderly and official-looking gentleman. George had disappeared as quickly as he had appeared. She had waited five years to lay her eyes on him again and he had gone within thirty seconds.

The excitement of their arrival had died down and the hotel had returned to normality. Debbie sat there with a great sense of anti-climax. She finished her drink. Should she have another? They had arrived, she had seen him and now he was gone. She had no idea how long they were going to be behind those imposing wooden doors, or even if they would be coming out at all. How long should she wait? She wasn't going to sit there all night. She ordered another drink. She had eyed the prize and he was certainly worth the effort. She would wait for another half an hour, no more and then leave.

An hour later the large wooden doors swung open. A wall of sound burst forth. Multiple conversations, all rolled together, poured out and filled the reception area with noise. The men slowly emerged, looking slightly less dapper than they had when they went in. Most of them had removed their blazers and loosened their ties. The atmosphere was less formal. They had been meeting the people involved in the charity event. The press were there and official duties had been performed. Photographs taken, items autographed and interviews given. Now their time was their own.

The men dispersed in every direction. Some of them wandered off, presumably to their rooms, some looked to be heading towards the bar. George was one of the last to appear. He was with two other men and two young and very attractive girls. Debbie suddenly felt sick. The worst thing that could possibly have happened was playing out in front of her. She saw George look over in her direction. She raised her hand and shielded her eyes, hiding her face with her arm. What would she do? What would she say if he recognised her and came over with his girlfriend? She would feel so stupid, and *so* jealous. To her immense relief, she saw George kiss both girls and shake both of the men's hands. The four of them headed for the exit leaving George standing alone. A number of people had formed an unofficial queue waiting for his attention. He started to chat with them and oblige their requests. She watched as he put his arms around the shoulders of men, women and children, all keen to have a record on their phones or tablets of them with "their friend", George Miller. She watched as he signed programmes, footballs, even a couple of shirts. She grinned as he was presented with a pen to autograph the chests of two very buxom young ladies.

Debbie called the waiter over.

'Would you give that gentleman over there this note for me, please?'

She handed the waiter a small piece of folded paper and watched as he walked over towards George. As soon as the last father and son combo had been dealt with, the waiter gave George the note. George opened it.

If you've got nothing else to do tonight, why don't you meet me by the school gates? If you can stay out of trouble and not get into any fights, that is!

He read the note. Debbie could just make out the confusion spreading across George's increasingly furrowing brow. He lifted his head from the note and spoke to the waiter. The waiter replied and pointed his finger in Debbie's direction. She was concealed well enough behind the various plants, people and pillars. George screwed his eyes in the direction of the waiter's finger, but could see nothing. He thanked the waiter, patted him on the shoulder and started to walk-over towards Debbie. He had a puzzled and inquisitive look on his face as he got closer and closer to her table, but as soon as he saw her, that look dissolved into a smile and his face lit up like a beacon.

'Debbie. Is it really you? Wow. How are you?'

George kissed her on the cheek. It was a kiss you gave to friends or family, not the sort of kiss she had been accustomed to from George Miller. He sat down.

'What are you doing here?' he asked.

'I was in a meeting and fancied a drink before I went home. I couldn't believe it when I saw you over there. What an incredible coincidence,' she said with all the sincerity she could fake.

They fired the same questions at each other. Fast and furious. Once the initial excitement had calmed down, they ordered some drinks. They chatted for over an hour, although it seemed more like five minutes. They discovered that they were both single, unattached, happy and both still treasured all of their fabulous memories from their school days. Without even noticing it, they were holding each other's hands across the table. The chemistry was still there. The sparkle was still there. They were still both fluent in each other's body language. The passion was rising in both of them.

'I feel like I'm sixteen again,' said George.

'So do I,' agreed Debbie, fairly sure where all of this was leading.

'What did we use to do to pass the time in those days, can you remember?' she asked with a cheeky smile. George could remember very clearly.

'Unfortunately, we have to share rooms. I've got someone else in with me tonight.' He paused. 'Why don't you see if you can book a room and I will be up in a minute?' he suggested.

Debbie nodded enthusiastically. She picked up her coat and bag and walked over to the reception desk, trying to look calm. She asked the girl if there were any rooms available. George watched excitedly from the bar. Debbie picked up a pen and signed a piece of paper. She handed over her credit card and took the plastic key card. Without looking back, she walked to the lift and was gone. George finished his drink and walked towards the girl on the desk.

'Excuse me, I wonder if I could leave a message for Mr Gilchrist in room 209. He is out at the moment, but will definitely be back by eleven o'clock.'

'Certainly, Mr Miller,' said the girl. George wrote the note and sealed it in an envelope.

Keith, I have just met an old friend from school. Will be back later. Cover for me if you can. Cheers. George.

As the girl took the note, a gentleman standing behind her spoke.

'Excuse me, sir, are you Mr George Miller?'

'Yes,' said George.

'There is a phone call for you, sir. Please pick up any one of those in front of you.' George picked up one of the receivers on the desk and put it to his ear. Before he could say anything, he heard a voice on the other end.

'Room 407. Hurry up. I've waited five years for this. I don't think I can wait much longer.' Then the phone went dead.

George pushed the button in the lift for the fourth floor. He hadn't been this excited for a very long time. He felt the same thrill as he had the first time they had crept behind the geography rooms at school. He knocked on the door three times.

'I'm still waiting,' called Debbie. George smiled and pushed the door open. There she was. Just as he remembered her, only better. She was a vision. She was wearing her long black coat with the collar turned up. She looked fabulous. George turned to shut the door. As his eyes returned to the beauty that stood before him, he saw the full-length coat slowly slide off her shoulders and fall to the floor, revealing Debbie Morris like he had never seen her before. She looked like something out of a lingerie catalogue. The girl of his dreams, in the sexiest, laciest, most erotic underwear he had ever seen. As he stared at her, Debbie spread her arms wide, as if displaying her wares. Showing him what was on offer. That morning's shopping trip to *Victoria Secrets* had been worthwhile after all, Debbie thought. Everything she had bought, from the stiletto heels and stockings to the lacey bra and panties, had certainly had the desired effect. He could barely take it all in. Had he died and gone to heaven? It certainly felt that way. George stood there, rooted to the spot, gazing in amazement at the sight before his eyes. Transfixed.

'It looks like you've got a bit of catching up to do, Mr Miller,' she said.

George didn't need a second invitation. His trance-like stare remained fixed on Debbie's beguiling curves as his hands started to tear at his own clothes. His blazer was cast carelessly onto the floor, his collar yanked apart and his tie wrenched off. His shirt lost a button in his haste.

'Slow down. Slow down,' she said, slowly walking over to him. 'There is no rush tonight. No schoolmasters or parents to worry about. Just you and me and our imaginations.'

She helped him remove his tangled shirt and put her arms around his waist. For the first time in five years their mouths were locked together again. Like two pieces of a jigsaw puzzle, they clamped tightly to one another as a perfect fit. She raised her arms and wrapped them around his neck, pulling his head closer to hers. His hands gently eased around her hips, then slowly lowered onto the pert little cheeks of her arse, softly caressing her buttocks. The feel of their flesh on each other's bodies bought back memories that were precious, exciting and very sexy.

They made love all night. Better than ever. It was as if they had never been apart. She felt she belonged to him and that he belonged to her. Dangerous assumptions, but she couldn't help it. As she watched his head bobbing up and down and in and out between her legs and felt his tongue slowly bringing her to another mighty climax, she wondered if they weren't really meant for each other. They had said they loved each other many times at school, but this was different. This was more real, more adult, more genuine. She stroked the back of his head with her right hand. She felt the orgasm rise in her. She clenched the pillow with her left hand and held his head tightly with her right. She arched her back, pushing her pelvis into his face. She moaned as his tongue conjured up yet another explosion of pleasure within her. Another mighty earthquake rampaged through her body.

As the feeling receded, she slowly released her grip on his head and the pillow. She looked back down at him kissing the inside of her thighs and smiling up at her. She realised that for better or worse, she was and always had been, very much in love with George Miller.

13

Sydney looked nice.

From the deep, comfortable recess of his sofa, George clicked the remote control and turned off the television. His "Groundhog Day" routine now included watching old black and white movies that were regularly screened during the afternoons. It passed the time.

It had been two weeks since George had been summoned to Bernie Roswell's office to discuss his future. That meeting had had a profound effect on him. It was clear that other people had been paying the price for his hedonistic lifestyle, doing their best to paper over the cracks and make excuses for him. They had been fighting his corner in the hope and belief he would change his ways and put all of his efforts into getting fit. But he had let them down, time and time again. These friends had done as much as they could for him and they were starting to show signs of the strain and personal cost to themselves. Things had to change. He had been given this last chance to prove he could behave and act like a mature human being. For the first time since his school days George was going to have to make a supreme effort. Not to attain anything, just to keep hold of what he had. Over the last two weeks he had been making that effort, staying in every night with only himself for company. He hadn't touched the booze, not even a glass of wine with his dinner and he had made every effort to strengthen and mend his damaged knee. He had been to see the physio every day and spent hours in the gym and swimming pool. He felt like he had all those years ago when Doug first signed him as an eighteen-year-old. He had to prove himself then and he surely had to prove himself now.

That evening, the team was due to play the first leg of its European semi-final at home to Milan. George was obviously not available for selection and would also miss the second leg in Italy eight days later. He would almost certainly not be considered for the final three weeks after that, assuming they got that far. It was such a depressing thought. Once again, he had successfully denied himself the chance of a major trophy, a medal and a night of glory, not to mention a silver-framed spot-lit photograph, that would remind generations to come that he had ever existed.

The small carriage clock on the shelf by the television told George it was nearly five o'clock. He would soon have to leave and make his way to the club. It was all part of the team spirit and sense of family. For the unselected players, attendance was compulsory, unless they had a note from the doctor or physio. For the backroom staff it was a chance to see the game from the director's box and rub shoulders with some of their heroes. George had seen far too many games from the director's box over the recent months.

It was an exciting time to be part of the football club. All hope and anticipation for the season were now being channelled into these two semi-finals. They were the difference between a disappointing season and a hugely successful one. The prestige and financial rewards for winning were colossal. In the pubs and bars and in the restaurants and cafes, the talk was of little else. Everyone had their own opinion and everyone thought themselves as qualified and as knowledgeable as the manager and players they were discussing. By the day of the match, you could almost taste the atmosphere. It was reminiscent of what the older supporters referred to as "the good old days". Twenty years earlier, the club had enjoyed a successful decade both domestically and in Europe, but that was all in the past. After that "golden generation", the club had sunk back into the depths of mediocrity. A place in which they were convinced they did not belong. But now the buzz was back. Maybe this time it would kick-start the club into another famous run of success. Maybe this would awaken the sleeping giant.

The ground was only about half an hour's drive from George's riverside apartment.

He had bought the flat soon after signing for the club. As a boy he had been fascinated by the Thames. His parents used to take him and Graham on boat trips from Greenwich up to Westminster when they were younger. George had always liked the thought of living near the river and because of his success in football, had been able to afford this magnificent penthouse riverside dwelling. He also owned a large house in Buckinghamshire where he would host lavish parties in his beautiful garden and a smallholding in Scotland that he would use when he needed to get away from everyone and lose himself fishing, or on the golf course. But the flat in London was his favourite place to be. It was where he did most of his living.

He stared out of the large, picture bay windows overlooking the river. His apartment was on the fifty-second floor and at nearly 600 feet high, on a clear day he could see for miles. Magnificent views of the city and beyond. All of London's iconic landmarks laid out in front of him. The Gherkin, the Eye, the Shard, Buckingham Palace and the Mall. The powerful river with all its aquatic traffic and of course, the jewel in the crown, Tower Bridge. There can't have been many better views to be had of London.

The early afternoon sunshine had disappeared and the golden glow of the city had faded. It had turned into a dark, drizzly evening. The twinkling diamonds that had been dancing and sparkling on the surface of the water, giving the river life and soul from the reflected rays of the sun, had vanished. The river was grey, the sky was grey and the buildings were grey. Except for the occasional red London bus weaving its way through the streets, the entire vista was as monochrome as the film he had been watching earlier.

George took the last sip from his cup of tea and picked up his coat. He hunched his shoulders to lift it fully into place and plunged his hands into the pockets trying to find his car keys. They were not there. He searched and patted his inside pockets and found his wallet, but still no keys. He scanned the large room and spotted them on the shelf above his desk. He walked over and grabbed them. As he did, he saw the four postcards leaning up against the wall. They were postcards Debbie had sent him. They had promised they would keep in touch with each other after their fortuitous meeting in a Newcastle hotel seven years earlier, but once again they had lost contact. Debbie had sent George the postcards over a period of about eighteen months, to his parents' address. Each one was from a different location. One was from Bali, one from Hawaii, another was from the Seychelles and the final one to arrive was from Sydney, Australia. None of them had a forwarding address, so he was unable to reply. He picked up the one with the Sydney Opera House on the front. He wondered if she had stopped sending them because she had met someone, maybe fallen in love and started a family. On the front of the card was an arrow, drawn in blue biro, pointing into the blurred sea of buildings in the background and a message saying, *I live here.* That was as close as George had come to knowing exactly where she was. He turned over the card and read the back. He knew what it said. He had read it a hundred times before.

When's your next game in Australia? I'll book the hotel. Come and have some fun Down Under. It's the greatest place on earth. Miss you. Love always. Deb xx.

George smiled. They had both got exactly what they had always wanted out of life. He had his football and she was being paid to travel the world. He was very happy for her and knew she deserved all of her success, but in a selfish way he would have loved her to have been there with him. He had always missed her, but never so much as now. With his social life confined to TV, mineral water and early nights, he would have given anything to have had Debbie with him. When he was with her, he needed nothing else. No drinks, no clubs, no other company. Life was fun and exhilarating. He knew she had been in Australia all those years ago, but where was she now? He gently put the postcard back in its place and gave it a loving smile. He had never been to Australia. Maybe he would try it. Maybe during this summer break. Sydney looked nice.

14

Alone again.

George arrived at the club just after 5.30pm. The match was due to kick off at 7.45 that evening. The weather was still gloomy and the day was still grey, but there was a palpable feeling of energy in the air. As usual he made his way across the car park and headed towards the offices to report in. He would have nothing much to do before the game, but the management liked to know he was there. As he walked towards the main entrance, George noticed a number of people striding purposefully and hastily, all in different directions, all heading towards one task or another. He waved and said hello to those whom he recognised, but most of them seemed unaware or unbothered by his presence. When he did manage to catch someone's eye, they invariably greeted him with a brief smile and a twitch of the hand, as if waving would take too much time and effort. Everyone had something to do, somewhere to go, or someone to see. Everyone except George.

He knocked on the door of the briefing room. Without waiting for an answer, he opened it and walked in. Bernie was sitting on the corner of the table shuffling sheets of paper. He glanced up at George over the rims of his half-moon glasses and then returned his concentration to his papers.

'Hello, George. How's the knee? Don't suppose you fancy a game tonight?' He peered over the rim of his spectacles again and gave him an inquisitive smile.

'Not too bad thank you, Mr Roswell. I only wish I could.' Bernie's eyes were back on his papers.

'Good. Good,' he muttered. George couldn't tell if this was referring to his knee, or whatever he was reading from his notes. He wasn't even sure Bernie had heard his answer. The room fell silent. George stood at the door for a moment, not sure what to do. Bernie continued to shuffle his papers and make small, grunting noises. George thought it best to leave. Bernie obviously didn't have any time to spare for a conversation with him.

'I'll just go up and see the doc for a moment. Won't be long,' said George needing to find a reason to leave. Once again Bernie muttered

'Good. Good,' he said, without raising his eyes. George turned and left the room, closing the door on his engrossed manager. He made his way towards the doctor's room. Walking along the hallway he could hear muffled shouting and laughing from the players out on the pitch. They were warming up and doing some light jogging.

George knocked on the doctor's door. There was no answer. He pushed the door open just in case. Sometimes the doctor had been known to take a little nap now and again. But the room was empty and the lights were off. He made his way up the corridor towards the treatment area. He had spent more than enough time in there over the past few weeks. He knocked and went in.

'Hello, George,' said the physio.

Gordon had been the head physio for a couple of years and had a good relationship with most of the players. He and George had got to know each other pretty well over the past weeks and months. He was massaging the legs of Duncan McGinley, a young Scottish player of whom a lot was expected. George could hear someone in the hot room, presumably waiting their turn for a rub down.

'How's it going?' asked George.

'Oh, you know what it's like on days like these. Never enough time to do everything or see to everyone.' Gordon turned his eyes back to the shiny, oily thighs of McGinley and sunk his fingers deep into the flesh.

'Well, I'll leave you to it. Good luck tonight Duncan,' said George. Duncan didn't turn his head, but let out a faint moan in reply.

George wondered what to do next. He looked down the corridor and heard the scuffing and scraping of studs on concrete and the echoing voices of their owners. The players were streaming down the corridor towards him. As they squeezed past, George wished them all good luck, but he was like a ghost, an invisible presence to them. They were so wrapped up in their own thoughts and conversations. They would be heading for a shower and a massage then their team talk about tactics and finally they would start preparing, in their own individual and superstitious ways, for the game. Everything was done as a team. Unity and togetherness, all for one and one for all. Nothing else and no one else mattered except the team. It was a magical feeling of brotherhood and solidarity. Magical that is, if you were part of it. George watched them disappear into the changing rooms, arms around each other's shoulders. He had been part of that brotherhood many times and loved the feeling. It was you and your mates taking on the world. Being on the outside felt very lonely.

Bringing up the rear was Doug, carrying two huge string bags full of footballs, one in each hand. George walked down to meet him and took one of the bags off him.

'Thanks, George. How are you?'

'I'm okay, I guess. How were they out there today?'

'They all look great. Unfortunately, there just isn't enough of them. So many injuries. It's killing us. I wish you were fit, George. We really need you right now.' Doug had meant it as a friendly compliment, but George couldn't help but take it as a scathing condemnation. As soon as he had said it, Doug realised that was probably how George would have interpreted his well-meant praise. There was a moment's silence as they both looked at each other. George lowered his eyes and felt nothing but guilt.

'You know what I mean, son' said Doug almost apologetically. George did know. He knew that Doug would never say anything to hurt him, but George could see the desperation in Doug's eyes at the scant resources of manpower they had to play with.

'Have you got time for a quick cuppa?' George asked hopefully.

'Sorry, George. You know the score. I'd be struggling for

time if the kick-off was at 10.45, let alone 7.45. I'll catch up with you after the match and we'll have a chat then.'

'Okay. Sure thing.' Doug took the bag of balls from George and waddled down towards the changing rooms. As he opened the door, the voices and laughter of the players spilled out and filled the narrow corridor. He heard the door slam and all was silent. Alone again. It had been nice to have a chat with Doug, albeit a brief one. Up until then, he had been muttered and grunted at and waved away by people who just didn't have time for him. He decided to find the one friendly face that would surely be glad to see him. He headed back towards the stairs that would take him up to the lounge outside Bernie's office. Brenda was certain to be there. She would make a fuss of him. Make him some tea and make enough small talk to kill the time before the game started. As he reached the second floor, he could hear Brenda's voice. He peered around the open door to her office. She was on the phone, speaking in a lovely, clipped voice. She glanced up and saw George. Immediately her face burst into a glowing smile. She actually looked pleased to see him. She waved with her free hand. George took that as an invitation to enter her office. She was talking to someone about accommodation. Probably for the second leg in Italy. Administration wasn't a side of football that George knew much about. He just turned up, played, got on planes, coaches or trains, checked in and out of hotels and occasionally went to do a press conference if he had to. Everything was arranged and organised for him and his teammates, probably by Brenda. George waited patiently for her to finish. He had never actually been inside her office before; this little capillary of the club's beating heart.

As Brenda talked, George slowly walked around the small room inspecting her chattels. It was homely. She had a couple of framed photos of kids on her desk. *Probably nephews and nieces,* he thought. A picture of what George assumed was her mum and dad and a small vase of not-quite-so-fresh yellow flowers. There were a couple of outfits on hangers draped in cellophane hooked onto the picture rail and a pair of trainers tucked behind the door. It was certainly a "lived in" office, without being untidy. He doubted if anyone would be able to find anything amidst all the paperwork and post-it notes scattered across her desk and over her screen. But he also guessed that Brenda would probably be able to lay her hands on any required item within seconds. She said goodbye and put the phone down.

'Hello, George. What are you doing up here? I'm afraid Mr Roswell isn't about at the moment.'

The truth that no one had time to speak or listen to him and he felt like a stranger in his own club would have been difficult for George to admit, both to Brenda and to himself.

'I didn't come up here to see Mr Roswell, I came up to remind myself just how beautiful you were,' George said placing both hands on her desk and looking straight into her eyes. He could see she had already started to blush. Her eyes widened. Just as she opened her mouth to speak, the phone rang again.

'Hang on a minute. Let me just answer this. Mr Roswell's office. Can I help you?'

The conversation went on and on. Every now and again Brenda looked up almost apologetically. He waited patiently again until the phone went down.

'Sorry, George. It's just so busy today with the match and everything. Now, what were you saying?'

Brenda leaned towards him. She was desperate for him to repeat what he had just said about how beautiful she was. George returned to his position resting on her desk. Their faces were only inches apart.

'Well, I just wanted...' The phone's annoying tones interrupted him yet again. With a look of incredulity on her face, Brenda mouthed "Sorry", as if it were her fault.

'Hello, Mr Roswell's office. Can I help you?'

George took a deep breath. He had never found it so difficult to have a conversation. He wandered out of her small office and into the wide-open space of the lounge. He looked at all of the photographs he had seen two weeks earlier. They were still there smiling, dancing, holding trophies, leaping for headers, or in the midst of a spectacular save. Immortal and eternal fame.

Brenda got up from her desk and wandered into the lounge to join George. She walked right up to him and looked into his eyes.

'Sorry, George. What were you saying?'

Brenda's voice had an air of resignation about it. She doubted now if she would hear the same words George had said earlier. That moment had gone. The phone hadn't stopped ringing all day. She would have loved to have taken it off the hook, or just ignored it and taken her chances with the irresistible George Miller. But she couldn't. She wished she hadn't been quite so conscientious.

'Officially that's me done for the day, although I did say to Mr Roswell I would stay on for an extra half an hour. But the phones shouldn't ring anymore in theory,' Brenda said hopefully, raising both hands with crossed fingers in front of her face. George smiled at her. She really was very sweet.

'Are you going to the game tonight, Brenda?'

'Yes, of course I am. Why?'

The phone's perfect timing destroyed the conversation yet again. Brenda looked angry and scowled into her office at the phone, pretending to ignore it.

'Why do you ask?' she said, looking increasingly more agitated with every ring.

'You had better answer that,' George said with more humour than anger in his voice. Brenda grudgingly trotted back to her desk and answered the call.

'Mr Roswell's office. Can I help you?'

The clipped, charming and inviting voice had gone and been replaced by a surly, curt, demanding and brusque tone. It was Bernie telling her she could shut the office down.

'Thank you, Mr Roswell. Good luck tonight,' she said in the more alluring of her telephone manners. When she returned, George asked her if she would like to watch the game with him.

'Oh, yes please. I'd love to, George. Thank you.' Her smile had returned and was even wider and brighter than the one she had greeted him with when he first peered around her door.

'I do have a couple of things to sort out first, but I should only be about half an hour.'

'Good,' said George. 'I will meet you in the players' bar.' Brenda agreed, but had to answer the phone again as George was leaving. As he walked past her office door, he waved and blew her a kiss. She responded with the same and let out a small, high-pitched squeak as she did so.

He decided to head straight for the players' lounge and try and stay out of everyone's way. As he walked, he saw the club doctor scurrying across the car park towards him with a briefcase in his hand, eyes fixed to the floor and moving at an impressive pace.

'Hello, Doc,' said George. Without even lifting his eyes or slowing down, the doctor whooshed past him.

'Can't stop now. See you tomorrow,' and with that, he was gone. It was plain to George that the only conversation he was going to get was from Brenda. He would wait for her and try and enjoy the evening and her company.

On entering the bar, he saw a couple of his teammates already there. Igor Kovanovic, a huge Croatian defender, and Pascal Mingard, a Frenchman who would, and should, have played upfront with George if they had both been fit. Both Igor and Pascal were injured in what George considered to be "the line of duty". Unlike him they had picked up their knocks on the pitch, during a match. That was part and parcel of being a footballer; it went with the territory.

15

Poisson baise dedans.

He sat down with Igor and Pascal.

'How is your knee, George?' Igor asked.

'Oh, it's fine. Shouldn't be long before I'm back in full training.' The three of them compared the varying state of their maladies and talked about the game to come.

'What is that you are drinking, George?' asked Pascal.

'Mineral water,' answered George.

'Water!' exclaimed Pascal. *'L'eau!!* I thought you were allergic to the stuff. Didn't you once tell me that …what was it now?…*Poisson baise dedans.* Yes, fish fuck in it!' George ignored them as they both roared with laughter at Pascal's joke. He sipped his water. As they laughed, Brenda appeared at the door. Her eyes scanned the room looking for George. Igor nudged George and nodding in Brenda's direction said,

'Hey, look who's here. The lovely Brenda. I wonder who she is looking for.'

George stood up and beckoned her over to their table. Igor and Pascal laughed again.

'Well, at least somethings haven't changed, eh George? You had me worried with that mineral water shit. I thought you were coming down with something. But you're obviously not too bad,' chuckled Pascal.

George bought Brenda a gin and tonic and the four of them chatted. Both Igor and Pascal were curious to discover whether George and Brenda were an item. They both kept steering the conversation onto relationships, but George was well ahead of them and seamlessly guided the chat in other directions.

Just before 7 p.m., Henry, the club steward, handed around the team sheets. George, Igor and Pascal all eagerly glanced down the list of names, but there were no great surprises that night. Bernie barely had enough players to put out a team. If you were fit, you were playing.

'I'm surprised Doug Fenner isn't on the subs bench tonight,' laughed Pascal.

George failed to see the funny side. If only he had been fit. If only he hadn't tripped and fallen in that nightclub. If only. If only.

Shortly after 7.30, they finished their drinks, wrapped themselves into their coats and braved the chilly night air to take their seats in the director's box. The floodlights illuminated the steady, drifting drizzle in the air. It was one of those miserable nights when most of the players would rather have been watching from the stands, but George would have given anything to have been down there on the pitch with the others. Brenda sat down and wriggled her bottom into the seat. George sat down next to her and they immediately linked arms. Brenda nuzzled her head into George's arm. On the surface, it was an exercise in keeping warm. Deep down they both felt it was of more significance. Both wondered how much.

'Is everything okay?' asked George.

'Yes,' purred Brenda, nuzzling her head a little deeper into George's side. 'Everything is just perfect.'

The match was hard and ugly, not what most would call a good advert for the game. There had been so much riding on the result that neither team had wanted to make a mistake. George's team won, one-nil, but the overriding feeling was that of relief, rather than celebration. They should have won by a bigger margin, but Bernie's makeshift forward line had misfired and squandered a number of good chances. George or Pascal would have had a field day if they had been playing. The concern was there for all to see on the faces in the bar afterwards. The Italians would be firm favourites to overturn the deficit and progress to the final. While George waited at the bar for their drinks, Bernie walked in.

'Congratulations, Gov.'

'Thank you, George,' Bernie replied in a low, gruff and unenthusiastic tone. Both of them knew the result was hardly a reason for celebration. The tension that had been so electric in the build-up was supposed to have been eased by a more commanding victory. But after that evening's result, the tension would only get worse. Next week they would have to go through it all again and George would still be just a spectator, left out in the cold once more. If only they knew it was as painful for him as it was inconvenient for them.

George and Brenda chatted. Small talk mostly. About their families and their lives outside the club. She was very easy to talk to and unlike a lot of people George knew, she was as good at listening as she was contributing to the conversation. She was fun and funny, with a great sense of humour. She was impish and naughty. They joked and laughed at each other's stories, very comfortable in each other's company. It was the most relaxed George had felt for a long time.

'I've just got to pop to the loo. I won't be a minute,' Brenda said standing up. George kept his eyes on her as she threaded her way through the sea of bodies on her way to the ladies. She looked as good from the back as she did from the front. As she edged past each group, most of the men's heads invariably turned to follow her meandering path, watching every curvaceous move of her body. George knew exactly what they were thinking. He should do. He had had the same thoughts about Brenda many times before.

George's new regime had made his life a little dull and boring. Staying in alone, with no drink. What if he was to ask Brenda back to his flat for a nightcap? He could do with some company. He could do with some female company. George was convinced that if he asked her, she would say yes. They could go back to his place and the fun could continue. It would be fantastic. He could drive her home, or back to the club in the morning and no one would be any the wiser. Brenda returned to the table.

'Same again?' she asked. George leapt to his feet.

'Don't be silly. This is my treat. Would you like another gin?'

'No, please let me buy you one. You've been so nice and so kind,' she pleaded.

'Okay then, just a mineral water, please.'

Brenda walked to the bar. Should he invite her home? It hadn't been something he had considered earlier, but now the seed had been planted, he was becoming quite excited by the idea. But would it be fair on her? She would almost certainly come back with him and give in to anything he suggested, but she would also probably expect more than one night of passion. Was it fair to use her as a stopgap, the filler for his empty time, a plaything to amuse himself with during his self-imposed confinement? She deserved more than that. He watched her smiling face as she returned with the drinks. The vivacious, attractive, sexy and seductive young woman he had been thinking of minutes earlier had suddenly become a vulnerable, innocent and fragile little girl. She *would* expect and deserve more than one night. Maybe there was more than one night ahead of them. Maybe there was a long-term relationship waiting to blossom. Although she was different in some ways, George could see a lot of Debbie in Brenda and that could only be a good thing.

While they talked, it dawned on George that any kind of relationship between them was doomed from the start. If they were to become involved with each other, Brenda's position as Bernie's PA would become untenable. She would almost certainly lose her job. There could be no guaranteed privacy or secrecy in any of Bernie's meetings or dealings. David Blackstone would insist she be replaced. A picture of David Blackstone appeared in George's mind and a shiver danced down his spine. What if David Blackstone saw it as an opportunity to finally get rid of him as well? What if the club valued Brenda's services as a secretary more than they valued his as a player? It would be him who would leave and Brenda would stay. That final frightening and degrading scenario made George's mind up for him. What had he been thinking about? Once again, the appendage in his trousers had temporarily held sway over common sense and rational thinking.

Brenda was now quite giggly and in her own mind preparing herself for a night of passion with the man she adored. The fact that they had got on so well and considering George's reputation, she was convinced that this was going to be the best night of her life. She was ready and eager to give herself to him completely. Their two empty glasses hit the table in unison.

'Right, if you're ready to go, I will drive you home, Miss Cousins,' George said getting to his feet.

'Home!?' Brenda said quizzically. She looked and sounded both surprised and disappointed. As soon as George saw the reaction on her face and in her eyes, he knew her answer would have been "yes", if he had proceeded with his lustful yearnings. He looked at her sad face. She said nothing. Just stared into his eyes, looking like any moment she would burst into tears.

'Well, I thought…it's raining and you,… erm…you probably, …' George stammered and stumbled, not knowing quite how to react or what to say. He had just told a small child that Christmas had been cancelled.

'Thank you,' said Brenda in a voice that had lost all of its sparkle. 'That would be kind of you.'

The atmosphere changed in a moment. The chirpy humour between them vanished in a trice. The smiles, the laughter and the intimate body language that had been obvious for the entire evening, were now gone. There was a coldness between them where there had been warmth. Brenda snatched up her coat and handbag, and marched towards the door, leaving George standing at the table looking a little bemused.

The fifteen-minute drive to Brenda's parents' house was a quiet one. Apart from a couple of comments from George about the rain and one about the number of red lights they had been caught by, the silence in the car was deafening. George glanced over at her a couple of times and thought he saw the beginnings of a tear in the corner of her eye. Brenda kept her stare fixed on the road ahead, not once turning to look at George. He pulled up outside the house and smiled at her. It was an unintentionally sympathetic smile.

'Thank you for a lovely evening and thank you for the lift home.'

The sparkle in her voice and the twinkle in her eyes had gone completely. She got out of the car and slammed the door in an almost petulant way. Without turning to look at George, she walked to the front door and disappeared into the house. George sat alone in his car for a moment trying to convince himself he had done the right thing. He was, after all, only being a gentleman. Brenda may hold him in even higher regard after this act of chivalry.

As he made his way through the orange-lit streets of south London, he looked down at the empty passenger seat. He could still smell her perfume in the air. He wondered what they would have been talking about if she were still there and heading for his apartment. There would have been a sense of mounting expectation in both of them, as they got ever closer to what would have been a night full of passion and pleasure. The excitement would have filled the car. But the passenger seat was empty and Brenda was gone.

George checked his mobile as he entered the flat. There were a few new messages. Graham had left a voicemail and sent him a text asking him to call him back. George called him, but it went straight through to voicemail. There was no answer on the landline either. Just the machine message. "Graham and Kerry are out at the moment. Please leave your name, number and message after the tone".

'Hi, Graham, it's George. Just returning your call. I'll call again tomorrow. Don't call back now as I'm just off to bed. Bye.'

Graham and Kerry had been together for the last five years and were very much in love. In some respects, George envied his brother. He had found someone he wanted to spend the rest of his life with. Graham and Kerry were probably out at some nightclub with friends, drinking, dancing and having fun. George cursed his confinement again. He clicked the remote control and watched the end of the late news. The sports' reporter confirmed that George's team had been very lucky and reaching the final would now be an uphill struggle. The TV cameras had picked him out in the crowd, while the newsreader bemoaned the club's injury problems. There was Brenda sitting next to him. Snuggled into him. Smiling and looking happy and contented. But she wasn't sitting next to him now and she probably wasn't smiling either. Feeling unwanted, unloved and once again alone, he clicked off the TV and went to bed. Maybe things would look better in the morning.

16

A desire for tea and a change of breath.

A heavy slap on the doormat heralded the arrival of the morning papers. In the still and quiet of Graham's flat, the noise cracked and echoed like a gunshot. The sound jolted him from his slumber. He slowly opened his eyes and peered through the narrow slits in his face. He felt like shit. He had never been good at holding his drink and always suffered horribly the next morning. It wasn't fair. His brother, George, could consume extraordinary amounts of beer, wine, spirits, anything alcoholic and still be fine and functional the next day. Graham's head was pounding. He blindly fumbled in the bedside drawer and eventually pulled out a couple of paracetamol tablets. With a gulp of water, the tablets slid down his throat and began their mission of mercy. He'd only had a few glasses of wine with his dinner, followed by a couple of brandies. He ran his tongue over the surface of his teeth. He could still taste the overpowering flavour of the cognac. It was as strong as if he had just drunk it. He took another sip of water and toyed with the idea of burying himself back under the duvet and drifting off to the pain-free world of sleep. It was a very tempting thought. He stared at the ceiling. What he really wanted was a cup of tea. He was usually gently awoken with one by Kerry before work. But Kerry was away on a business trip. Was his desire for tea and a change of breath stronger than the urge to stay in bed? Fancy having to make such dramatic and life-changing decisions so early in the morning. There was only one answer. His dehydration and foul-tasting mouth would not allow him to lay there a minute longer. It was time to face the challenges of the day, whatever they may be, head on. He slowly swung his heavy legs over the side of the bed and lurched his torso into a sitting position. All of a sudden getting out of bed didn't feel like such a good idea. His head was spinning and he felt a wave of nausea wash over him. His body convulsed in a shiver. He swallowed and let out a long, loud baritone belch. The taste of brandy; the smell of brandy; the thought of brandy! He rubbed his hands over his face and pushed his fingers through his mop of dishevelled black hair. He wished those paracetamol soldiers would hurry up and start fighting back. He gave his beard a good scratch, stretched his arms above his head and let out a little whimper. He stood up. He had made it. The hardest thing he had to do all day was now behind him. What next? Tea. Their flat was large and spacious. Apart from the two bedrooms, one at each end and the main bathroom between them, the rest of the space was open plan. The main room was about fifty feet square with polished wooden floors and original brickwork walls. He and Kerry had bought it a few years earlier. They had both been pretty successful in their business ventures and could afford what was a very sought-after central London residence.

Graham had fallen on his feet soon after leaving university. He had been introduced to a man called Paul Kerrigan who ran his own investment company, ploughing cash into new companies and helping them to take off. He would then sell his original stock back to the owners at a very attractive price and keep a percentage of all profits made in the future. Everyone a winner. Kerrigan led a lavish lifestyle, the envy of most, but particularly a young student just out of university. Graham saw the potential to have a slice of that lifestyle. He not only admired Paul for his business acumen, he also liked him as a man. He was jovial, generous and gregarious. He was one of those wealthy men who knew how to spend his money and have maximum fun with it. His maxim in life was, "Today is everything. Yesterday has gone, and tomorrow might never come. Do it now".

Kerrigan was also impressed with Graham. After taking him on and showing him the ropes, he soon saw a return on his investment. Graham was a hard worker, full of drive and enthusiasm. Kerrigan saw a lot of himself in Graham and he liked what he saw. He was also a big football fan and Graham was a link to the glamorous world of professional soccer. George's career was on the up and having George Miller's identical twin brother working for the firm was only ever going to be a good thing. Graham learnt fast and it wasn't long before he was one of the most successful and well-paid members of the company. Kerrigan always knew Graham's ambitions would mean a parting of the ways eventually and so it was no surprise to Paul when Graham walked into his office one morning and announced he would be leaving the firm and setting up on his own. The two men shook hands and parted the best of friends.

Success wasn't long in coming and after less than two years in business Graham had equalled and surpassed the turnover, wages and lifestyle he had left behind. He had plush offices in the City of London and was employing over twenty people. He considered himself a success.

Kerry had also done well. The fashion world had taken a shine to Kerry and Kerry had made the most of it. The design and marketing of high-end fashion was a very lucrative, but at the same time, incestuous, cliquey and cut-throat world. If your face fitted, you were fine, but you could go from being the most celebrated star and talk of the town, to being yesterday's news in a blink of an eye. You had to ride the wave until it decided it was time for you to get off and some other dashing young thing would take your place. At that particular time, Kerry's wave was at its peak. Before Kerry had met Graham, the travel and glamour of the industry had been part of its allure. The expensive hotels and the best champagne, the beaches and the mountains, the sun, the sea, the snow and of course, all of the sexy people involved. All of the luvvies and the darlings; all of the movers and shakers. And the eternal question, what was going to be "The New Black"? But since Kerry and Graham had settled down, the constant travelling and living out of a suitcase had become a bit of a bind. It was keeping them apart at a time when they were desperate to be in each other's company as much as possible. Kerry was sometimes away for up to a month. It had been getting tougher and tougher. Recently, they had been going through what could only be described as a "sticky patch" in their relationship. Both of them wanted to rediscover the electricity and passion they had felt when they first met, but work, fatigue and routine had taken the sheen off their love lives and their daily, and nightly habits had become diluted.

The previous evening, the two of them had gone out to dinner. Kerry was travelling up to Manchester to stay with an old girlfriend before flying off to the States early the following morning. The job was in Santa Barbara and was due to take about four weeks. Although it was a great business opportunity, it couldn't have come at a worse time. This latest separation had cast a dark cloud over the evening. Neither of them really expressed what they truly felt, for fear of upsetting one another. They certainly didn't want to part on a sour note. The conversation remained on safe ground; nonconfrontational issues. It was a tough evening for both of them.

Just after 9 p.m., Kerry sadly announced, 'I guess I should be making a move. It's a three-hour drive to Manchester and I have an early start tomorrow.'

Graham reluctantly nodded in agreement. Kerry laid the napkin on the table, leant over and gave him a kiss.

'I'll be back soon. These few weeks will fly by, just you see. Be good and don't go chatting anyone up in football club bars.' It was an attempt at light-hearted humour and a reference to their first meeting. They both smiled, but neither of them looked happy.

'Take care of yourself and let me know when you arrive,' said Graham.

'Of course,' Kerry answered reassuringly, kissing Graham again. 'See ya.' Kerry turned around and without looking back, walked out of the restaurant. Graham drew in a deep breath and let out a long sigh. He was alone. He was going to be alone for at least the next four weeks, maybe more. As he stared into space, the waiter's body arched in front of his fixed gaze.

'Would sir like anything else?'

Graham refocused.

'Yes, please. Would you bring me a cognac?'

'Of course, sir.'

The waiter left Graham to his musings. He scrolled through some of the photographs on his phone, of him and Kerry smiling and laughing together. There were a few that included George too. They were happy times. Times he was desperate to revisit and happiness he yearned for. He knew he would regret the brandy in the morning. He always did.

Graham rinsed the remaining toothpaste from his mouth and spat it into the sink. He looked at himself in the mirror. His eyes were still not fully open. He puffed out his cheeks and exhaled slowly. He stared deeply into his own bloodshot eyes with an expression of regret, as if apologising to himself for feeling so bad. Another belch punched its way out of his throat. The brandy cut right through the freshly laid minty barricade of the toothpaste as if it wasn't there. It tasted foul.

'Shit,' he whispered. He walked back into the main room. It was a huge area and it felt very empty. Although the grand piano still stood proudly in its place and the other furniture did its best to fill the space, the void that Kerry had left was plain and obvious. The apartment seemed colder than usual. Kerry would normally have gone to work by now anyway, but the stillness and the quiet had lain undisturbed until Graham had walked into the room.

The loneliness was becoming more unbearable and this was only the first morning.

He went to the front door and picked up the papers. As he passed the kettle, he filled it with water and flicked the button on the back. On came the little blue light and it grudgingly started to splutter into life. He dropped the wad of papers on the table. The loud thud competed with the ever more frantic rumblings and gurglings of the kettle. It had just about reached its point of boiling orgasm. The button clicked off. He made his tea and took a sip from the steaming mug.

Graham liked to keep up to date with what was going on in the world and had most of the daily papers delivered each morning, from the uniquely pink to the other broad sheets and most of the tabloids. He liked to give himself a good hour or so to browse through both the important and the trivial events the world was experiencing, absorbing as much useful information and mindless crap as he could to ease himself into the day. Graham had a habit of starting from the back pages and working his way forward. Sport, then TV, a bit of gossip, the stock market and then the main events on the front pages. Political mayhem, the latest serial killer, a tsunami or volcanic eruption.

That day's back pages were largely devoted to coverage from last night's game involving George's team. Pictures of the goal scorer, the manager, even a picture of George sitting in the crowd, in some editions. Graham took a closer look. There was George wrapped up in his overcoat sitting next to a rather attractive looking blonde. He noticed they were arm in arm and looking very much like a loving couple. Graham smiled and wondered who the girl was.

'You could do a lot worse for yourself than her, Georgie boy,' Graham chuckled to himself. 'Same old George.'

The happiness and contentment portrayed in the picture was sadly not replicated by the accompanying article. The journalists were all fairly scathing of the team's performance and each one concluded that reaching the final was now going to be an uphill battle. As always, scapegoats needed to be found and as always, the manager and the players were ripe for the role. Graham read each article in turn. They were mostly written by people who had never played the game. People who earned money writing about the inadequacies and failures of better men than themselves. People who had never felt the intense pressure of a big game, or the weight of expectation pressing down on their shoulders from thousands, sometimes millions of fans. The same people who had never felt like they had been hit by a train after a fearsome tackle from the opposition midfield enforcer. People whose ability with words was not affected by victory or defeat and who would squeeze every last dramatic drop out of either, with no repercussions or consequences to themselves. Graham didn't have a very high regard for most of the so-called experts on the game. He had seen over the years how the same people had built George and others up into almost demi-gods, only to shoot them down and castigate them at every possible opportunity. In some of the articles, George was being criticised for letting his team down as a result of his cavalier lifestyle. Some even suggested that he looked happy to be sitting in the warm dry stand with his friend and not out in the wind and rain battling with his comrades. One by one, the newspapers were flung unceremoniously across the room, disintegrating in flight and floating down to the ground, dismembered and chaotic.

Graham finished his tea and clicked the kettle back on. As he looked over the corpses of the scattered newspapers, twitching in the gentle breeze from the open window, he noticed the little red light flashing on the answerphone. There were two messages. The first was from George. He had left it the previous night while he and Kerry were at dinner. Graham listened to the message and thought George sounded a bit down. Unusual for him. George was very much a "glass half full" kind of person. The second message was from Kerry who had phoned earlier that morning from Manchester.

"Hi, darling. I'm at the airport. I guess you're probably still asleep. I tried your mobile and left a message on there as well. I will see you in a few weeks and I promise we will spend some time together. Why don't we go away somewhere nice and hot for a couple of weeks? Think about it. I'll see you soon. Love you. Bye".

17

Big brown eyes.

Just hearing Kerry's soft, gentle voice made Graham feel warm and happy. Kerry had only been gone for twelve hours, but already he was feeling lonely. He remembered how easy it had been to fall in love. How natural and exciting it had been and how wonderful life had seemed when they were first together. The memory of their first meeting was something they had discussed on many occasions. It was a story that never failed to put a smile on both of their faces.

They had met at a football match, about five years ago. Graham had started playing semi-professional football soon after leaving university. Having chosen to further his education at the expense of a career in sport, he was keen not to let football drift out of his life altogether. He certainly had a talent for the game and if you believed what Doug Fenner said, Graham was at least his brother's equal. Upon returning home from university, Graham was courted by a number of non-league clubs. His skill, technique and ability were head and shoulders above most of the people he played with, and against. Playing also kept him fit. He would often joke with his brother that even given George's professional full-time training regime, Graham the businessman and part-time footballer was probably the fitter of the two. It was a theory with which George seldom argued. George had always done just enough to get by. Graham, on the other hand, had always pushed himself. He always wanted to improve, to see how far he could extend himself. If he had chosen a life in sport, with his extra drive and commitment he might have become even more successful than his brother.

After one particular game, Graham wandered into the club bar as usual to have a few drinks with the opposition and his teammates. There was a dull drone as the many conversations blended into one another. Occasionally the drone was punctuated by a loud and raucous laugh, or someone's voice shouting above the din to order another drink. As Graham approached the bar, his eyes immediately locked onto a pair of big brown eyes across the other side of the room. The stare was almost magnetic. Unable to break it, Graham eventually smiled and got a smile back. It was Kerry who finally broke the stare, when drawn back into the conversation the group was having. Graham felt intrigued and excited. He picked up his beer and slowly made his way over. He edged and squeezed his way through the ruck of bodies, holding his beer high in the air to avoid spilling it. He noticed a teammate of his was in the group. He inched his way towards Jim Beattie, but couldn't stop staring at the beautiful, inviting brown eyes. Each time he did, he saw they were looking right back at him. Once he reached Jim's side, he stopped.

'Alright JB? Well played today.'

'Thanks, Graham; you too.' The others in the group had stopped talking and were all looking at him. There was a momentary silence which the dull drone of the bar seemed unable to fill. Finally, Jim spoke.

'Graham, let me introduce you to an old friend of mine, Stan Andrews.' A large, rotund man stuck out his hand and Graham shook it. He had a booming voice that punched its way out from behind a thick, somewhat overgrown and slightly greying beard and moustache.

'Nice to meet you, Graham.'

'You too, Stan,' replied Graham, happy to have been included in the group. Jim continued.

'This is Albert. A business associate of mine from Paris, and this is Kerry.' Graham shook both of them by the hand, nodding at Albert and giving Kerry a smile.

'This is the famous Graham Miller. Not to be mistaken for his lesser-known sibling George. Sometimes we think Graham sends George along to play instead of him, but then we realise that it's just Graham having a bad day.' They all chuckled.

'Don't listen to him, Stan. He's just upset because George makes a habit of scoring against the team he supports so he takes it out on me,' Graham retorted.

'Well, I'm not surprised they can't tell you apart. You are the spitting image of your brother,' said Stan patting Graham on the shoulder. 'Now, can I get any of you a drink?'

'Vodka and tonic, please,' said Kerry, presenting Stan with an empty glass. The others told Stan what they wanted and he made his very undainty way to the bar.

From the conversation, it was obvious that Albert

and Kerry were together. But from their body language, it seemed that things were not altogether harmonious between them. Graham listened and observed.

'How long are you here for, Albert?' Jim asked.

'Only a few days. I have some personal matters I need to clear up and then I will head back to Paris either Monday or Tuesday.'

As he spoke, he glanced at Kerry but did not hold eye contact for more than a second. There was a sadness in his eyes and a slight tremor in his soft, French voice. Graham saw his chance and joined the conversation. He looked at Kerry and once again, the magnetic hold locked their eyes together.

'And what about you, Kerry, are you leaving for Paris too?' Kerry looked at Albert whose stare remained fixed to the floor.

'No, I live in Berkshire, just the other side of Reading. Albert is staying with me while he is here. We have a few things to sort out. I have never really wanted to live anywhere else but this country and Albert is a staunch Frenchman who couldn't imagine living anywhere but Paris. Isn't that right, Albert?'

It was almost too much information thought Graham and for a brief moment felt a twinge of sympathy for Albert.

'*Oui.*' Albert nodded while still looking at the floor. Stan returned with the drinks oblivious to the slice of soap opera that had just been acted out.

'Here we go. Vodka and tonic for Kerry, cognac for Albert and a pint for you Graham. Cheers, everyone,' Stan said, raising his glass in a salute.

'Blimey, Albert, cheer up. It looks like someone's run off with your sense of humour.'

He slapped Albert on the back jolting the Frenchman forward.

'It might never happen, you know,' Stan chuckled. Albert forced a smile, totally lacking in sincerity and raised his glass towards Stan. He took a small sip of his brandy, but his eyes were vacant.

Stan, Albert and Jim began to talk about a business venture they were considering together, which gave Graham the chance to talk to Kerry. They talked about everything and nothing. Football, fashion, politics, music. They even touched on the subject of relationships and partners. Kerry confirmed Graham's suspicions regarding Albert. He had come over from Paris to collect his things and say farewell. They had been seeing each other for a couple of years, but the problems presented by the miles between them had made the romance difficult. Kerry insisted on continually telling Graham what a wonderful man Albert was. How considerate and attentive he had been. But ultimately Kerry's words were more of an epitaph than a glowing résumé; less of a commendation and more of a eulogy. Graham was volunteering information about himself; information he hadn't told anyone before. Laying his life out for Kerry to peruse. Kerry was doing likewise. Within the hour, they knew more about each other than they did some of their closest friends. The attraction between them was something new to Graham. He had never felt anything quite like it before. It felt like they had known each other forever.

Graham noticed Albert occasionally glancing over at

them. Whether he was checking on Kerry, or on him, he couldn't decide.

Albert finished his drink and looked at his watch.

'I'm sorry, gentlemen, but I have to be going. I have a lot of things to do tomorrow.'

He looked at Kerry. 'I can catch a taxi if you want to stay.'

Kerry shot a quick glance at Graham, then looked back at Albert.

'No. That's okay, I will leave too. You're right. We have a lot to do tomorrow. Anyway, a cab from here would cost a fortune!'

Albert pulled on his coat and said his goodbyes.

'I will just go to the toilet and then meet you outside,' he said to Kerry. He turned to Graham and gently added, 'Goodbye, Graham. I hope you have a long, successful and happy life.'

He shook Graham's hand, clasping it with both of his. He smiled and nodded. Graham knew it was unlikely he would ever see Albert again and was touched by his dignity.

'Thank you, Albert. It was nice to meet you too. I hope you have a safe journey home.'

Albert turned and walked out of the bar. Graham then turned to say goodbye to Kerry, but the self-confidence that had been in abundance just minutes earlier, seemed to have deserted him.

'I was wondering if you would like to,.. um,.. maybe if you're not too busy,.. I mean, if you would like to,.. er,.. next time you're in town, or,.. that is, if you'd care to have a drink or something,.. er,.. maybe, unless you have other plans of course …'

He was floundering and stumbling like a love-struck, nervous, fourteen-year-old. Kerry cupped both of Graham's hands.

'That would be great. Yes, I'd love to,' Kerry smiled, putting Graham out of his misery.

'Here is my card.' Kerry handed him a business card.

'I'm obviously going to be a bit tied up for the next few days,' Kerry gestured towards the door through which Albert had just left.

'But if you give me a call towards the end of next week, I'm sure we can work something out. Anyway, I had better go. Albert will be waiting and he has never been very good at waiting. It's been lovely to meet you, Graham.'

'You too,' Graham replied. They were still holding each other's hands. For a brief moment, they began to lean in towards each other. They had both wanted to kiss, but for some reason, the handshake seemed enough. They grinned, as if having read each other's minds. There would be plenty of time for kissing and much more later.

Graham sat at the bar, ordered himself another pint and found himself wishing away the next few days.

He wondered if Kerry and Albert were talking about him on their way home and if so, what were they saying? Would the conversation have been awkward or aggressive? He hoped not. He hated the thought that he would be the cause of any uncomfortable or rancorous exchanges between them.

He couldn't wait to see Kerry again. It would feel like an eternity until the following Friday. Thursday was, of course, "towards the end of the week". There was no need for him to suffer an extra day. He would call on Thursday. Wednesday night would be better. More time to make plans. He would definitely give Kerry a ring on Wednesday afternoon, just before lunch.

18

Coffee?

Saturday night had planted the seed of expectation in him. The thrill he had felt when first seeing, then meeting, talking to and arranging a rendezvous with Kerry was still making his body buzz. The time since then had been nothing short of purgatory.

Never had Graham had to wait so long for Wednesday to come around. Sunday, Monday and Tuesday had taken weeks to pass. The more he tried to wish the time away, the longer his agonising wait seemed to take. By Wednesday morning, Graham was convinced the second hand on his watch was labouring unusually hard to fight its way around each circuit. Had it been the same for Kerry? Had the thought of meeting up again blocked out all other thoughts? Had the time been dragging in a similar way just the other side of Reading? Graham looked at his watch. It was just past midday. He could wait no longer. 12.04 was now officially *towards the end of the week*. He scrolled down the list of contacts in his phone, until he came to the most recent entry; Kerry. There was no smiling picture to go with the number as yet, but that would surely change very soon. He touched the call sign. As he did, he took in a deep breath like a drowning man coming up for air. It was ringing. Two, three, four times, each ring increasing Graham's anxiety and pulse rate. Maybe Kerry was in a meeting or otherwise engaged. Maybe there had been unforeseen complications with Albert. Maybe Albert was still there. The thought of any obstacle coming between them now, or having to wait even longer to gaze into those deep, gorgeous brown eyes, was unbearable. At last, a voice answered.

'Hello.'

'Hello, Kerry,' said Graham.

'Yes, this is Kerry. Who is that?'

The elation of hearing Kerry's voice again was slightly tempered by the lack of recognition.

'It's Graham. Graham Miller from the football club last Saturday.'

'Oh yes. Graham. How are you? I'm sorry. I've been expecting a number of calls regarding business and couldn't work out which of my clients you were. Everything has been quite chaotic over the past few days as you can imagine, what with Albert and work. I nearly called you yesterday but didn't know if it would be convenient for you, so I decided to wait for you to call me and stick with the plan. I'm so glad you've called so soon, I thought I was going to have to wait until Friday.'

Graham was thrilled that Kerry had been thinking of him, but a little peeved that he had gone through twenty-four hours of unnecessary angst.

'Did Albert get away alright and did he have a safe journey home?'

Graham's question was disguised in courteous curiosity. In reality, he was asking Kerry if the coast was clear. The disguise was a thin one. Kerry smiled, knowing exactly what the question meant.

'Yes. He left on Monday morning. We sorted everything we had to and both of us decided it would be sad and painful to prolong the parting. He is a very sweet man and I was, and am, very fond of him. It just wasn't meant to be. I think he has taken it a little harder than I have, but he will be fine. Anyway, let's not talk about Albert. I'm sure you didn't phone to talk about him.'

It was the perfect answer. Graham couldn't have scripted it any better if he had tried. Albert was gone and Graham felt at ease. As Albert had departed out of one door in Kerry's life, so Graham had entered through another. They were both single and unattached but would hopefully not remain that way for much longer.

They spoke on the phone for nearly half an hour. Graham suggested they meet for dinner that evening in Soho. Kerry agreed. As soon as he had hung up, Graham phoned his favourite restaurant in the West End and made a reservation. His wait was nearly over, but he once again found himself wishing the time away. It was just before one o'clock. He had five hours to kill before he would have to leave. He began to busy himself in the bathroom, grooming and preening himself. A shower, a shave, another brush of the teeth and a gargle with the mouthwash. What to wear? Should he be smart or casual? He wanted to give the right impression. He didn't want to come across as too stuffy, but then he didn't want to look too scruffy or casual. He looked at himself in the full-length mirror of his wardrobe. The boxer shorts were on. It was just the rest of his outfit he was worried about. Trousers, shirts, ties and jackets were taken out, put on, then cast aside. The discarded clothing that had been his first dozen attempts to look right were strewn about the bedroom. Suits were too formal and jeans not formal enough. Eventually he settled on some dark blue trousers, a white shirt with no tie and a dark blue blazer. He looked at the finished article. He was finally satisfied that he was ready. He looked again at his watch. Three o'clock. He still had another three hours to wait. He watched some television, played some music, he even tried to do a bit of work, but his mind wasn't on it. His concentration was somewhere else.

At last, his watch told him it was six o'clock and time to leave. After one last nervous look in the mirror, a comb of the hair and a final inspection of himself, he left the sanctuary of his flat for what he hoped would be the beginning of a new and joyous chapter in his life.

Kerry arrived at the restaurant a couple of minutes after Graham. This time, the greeting was not a handshake but a full embrace. The chemistry between them was just as good, if not better than it had been at the football club the previous Saturday. There was no tentative small talk, or fitting conversations around other people. It was just the two of them. They both asked questions and volunteered answers. They spoke about their families and their upbringing, where they went to school, their lives at university and their ambitions for the future. Graham wanted Kerry to know everything about him: to see him as an open book with no secrets. He certainly didn't have as an extensive portfolio as his brother when it came to relationships and lovers, but he wanted Kerry to know everything about his past. Kerry was being equally open about past boyfriends and lovers. Albert was mentioned a couple of times, but with the reverence that would be used when talking about a recently deceased relative. The time passed quickly. The more Graham learned about Kerry's life and character, the more besotted he became. He had never had a more open and frank conversation with anyone in his life. No stone was left unturned and no skeletons were left in the closet.

The meal was coming to an end. The sweet trolley had long since been and gone and the wine was all but drunk. Graham was keen for the evening not to end and wondered if he should invite Kerry back for a coffee, but that could be misinterpreted. The evening had been such a success and he didn't want to force the pace. It was now obvious the two of them had a future together. He didn't want to destroy any chance of a lasting, meaningful relationship because of his lustful impatience. He would wait for Kerry to make the first move. After all, Kerry had just finished one relationship and may not be ready to jump headfirst into another one. He wasn't going to ruin it before it had a chance to blossom. He would wait. Bide his time. Kerry would decide when the time was right. It would be worth it in the end.

Graham sat back in his chair, content at his decision and drank the last of his wine. If there were to be a few more days, even weeks, of celibacy then so be it.

'Would you like a coffee before we leave?' Graham asked.

Kerry's hand reached across the table and gently cradled Graham's hand. Their fingers entwined naturally. Kerry leaned across the table and quietly said,

'I would love a coffee, but not here. I would love to invite you back to my place, but it's quite a long drive. Plus, my flatmates have some friends staying over from Turkey and it's a bit chaotic. I don't think we would get much privacy.' Kerry squeezed Graham's hand a little tighter, 'And we would like some privacy. Wouldn't we? Would you think it rude of me if I were to invite myself back to your flat for a coffee? That is, if you don't mind and it's not inconvenient.'

Graham nearly dropped his empty wine glass. He was aghast. A shiver ran down from his head to his toes and then back up again, like a charge of electricity. He was suddenly aware that his jaw had fallen open. He shut his mouth and did his best to compose himself. Just as he had relaxed into the idea that their courtship would be a gentle and gradual affair, he had suddenly been told to ready himself for action. 'Er..um..No..I mean yes. That would be fine. Great. Yes, that would be great. That's a wonderful idea. We will do that. I... I should have thought of that myself. I'll get the bill and we can go.'

Graham twisted in his seat, caught the eye of their waiter and waved his wallet gently in the air. The young man nodded, then disappeared. Kerry was keen to split the bill, but Graham insisted on paying it all.

Finally, after what seemed an age, the waiter returned and gave Graham the bill on a small silver salver. He had already decided it would be quicker to pay by cash. He took some notes out of his wallet and slapped them on the silver tray. With as much dignity and poise as their urge to leave would allow, they left the restaurant and headed for the car park.

'I'll follow you,' said Kerry. 'Don't lose me now, will you?'

'Don't worry,' beamed Graham, 'I won't lose you. I promise.'

That was the last thing he was going to do. On the drive back, Graham spent more time looking in his rear-view mirror than he did out of the windscreen, making sure that Kerry was right behind him. It only took about twenty minutes to get to his flat and with a huge sigh of relief he pulled up outside and saw Kerry's Mini park just behind him. Graham sat there for a moment, daring to pinch himself. Still looking in the rear-view mirror he saw Kerry get out of the car and start to walk over towards him.

'Please don't let this be a dream,' he whispered to himself. It wasn't a dream. It was a dream come true. The two of them held each other's hand and walked to the door. Graham opened it and invited Kerry inside.

'Very nice,' said Kerry looking around from side to side. 'Very nice.'

Kerry turned and looked at Graham, their faces only inches apart.

'I'm loving what I'm seeing,' Kerry added.

Graham pushed the door shut. They were alone together for the first time. He softly planted a kiss on Kerry's lips. They looked deeply into each other's eyes, smiled and kissed again. Graham eased the back of Kerry's head towards him. The kissing increased in intensity. Their mouths opened and their tongues played with each other. Graham gently bit Kerry's bottom lip and held it between his teeth. Kerry bought the embrace to a stop and pulled away slightly.

'Shall we leave the coffee until later?'

Graham just nodded and they resumed their mouth play. They made their way towards the bedroom. Within minutes the two lovers were as tangled in each other as it was possible to be, their naked bodies there to be touched, caressed, tasted, explored and enjoyed. There was no need for imagination now. Everything was there to see; everything was available. They were there to give and receive all the pleasure and love they could. How had they managed to exist without each other? They had been together for one night, but it seemed like they had known each other forever. Forever! That was still to come. But would forever be long enough?

19

The Grizzly Adams look.

Graham took another sip of tea. They were fond memories. The excitement of that first date and the weeks and months after, still made the hairs stand up on the back of his neck. They were so much in love. They still were, but their lives were now more about routine than spontaneity. Recently they had been spending less and less time together and now there was this infernal separation. Graham longed to give Kerry a hug and a kiss and snuggle up in bed together. To draw the curtains and spend the entire day beneath the duvet like they used to. What was it Kerry had said in that message? Graham listened to the voicemail again.

"You have two saved messages". George was up first and Graham heard the sadness in his voice once again. It was unlike George to sound so glum. Graham wondered what could be troubling him, but it was Kerry's voice he wanted to hear. Kerry came on to repeat what Graham had heard earlier. A holiday. Some time together. He listened to the message as if he were hearing it for the first time.

He loved the sound of Kerry's voice. It was soft and sweet, caring, soothing and reassuring. He wished the message had gone on for longer and promised even more. He felt a calmness come over him. Things would be fine. When Kerry returned, they would both make the extra effort that their relationship deserved. Graham's smiling eyes fixed on a photograph on the table. It was a picture taken a few years earlier. Graham on the left, George on the right and Kerry in the middle. All three were beaming happily at the camera. It had been taken on a holiday to the Canary Islands. The three of them and a girl called Mariana had decided to go away on a last-minute break. Mariana had taken the photograph. She was a nice girl. Pretty face, long auburn hair and a real head-turner in her bikini. She had a pronounced accent, Hungarian if Graham's memory was correct. She had only known George for a couple of weeks before they decided to go on holiday. It obviously hadn't been the real thing between her and George as she disappeared shortly after they returned to England. She was quickly replaced by an equally gorgeous brunette a few days later. Graham took a closer look at the photo in its silver frame. Graham and George both had their arms around Kerry's shoulders. It was a happy-looking group.

The photographs taken on that trip were the first ones of the brothers in which the viewer could easily identify who was who. All of their lives they had been identical in every way. From childhood through their school days and teenage years up until then, everybody, including John and Paula, struggled to know which twin was which. The amusement it afforded the boys when they were at school continued into their adult life. But it also had some drawbacks. Graham was constantly stopped in the street by young boys and fathers wanting his autograph. He was also regularly propositioned by beautiful young girls. Graham would invariably come clean and explain that he was in fact George's twin brother. This however did little for Graham's self-esteem, as the boys, their fathers and the young girls always looked so disappointed when they discovered he wasn't the "real thing". He had been a disappointment to so many strangers over the years. There were times when he decided to go along with it and pose for a photo or sign a shirt or programme as George. He had his brother's signature off to a tee. He felt he was helping his brother with his workload and his PR. Likewise, George would sometimes extricate himself from an awkward situation by announcing that he was in fact Graham. It could be exciting as well as dangerous to walk down the street looking like George Miller. Finally, Graham had decided to do something about it. Both men were clean shaven and kept their hair fairly short. Graham saw an opportunity to reinvent himself. He let his hair grow and after a few weeks without shaving, a bushy beard and moustache started to fill his face. For the first time ever, there was a clear and visible difference between the Miller twins. With each day and each week, the evidence from the bathroom mirror showed Graham transforming into a totally different person. A single entity. Graham had mixed emotions when staring at his hairy reflection. There was a sense of liberation and self-approval. He could see himself as an individual person and not one of a matching pair, but there was also a sense of desertion and maybe even betrayal. It felt like he was breaking the mould. Turning his back on what they had been and what they still were. Rejecting what they would have become. Bringing the curtain down on their successful double act. The hair and the beard grew in both length and popularity. Friends and family alike were pleased. Secretly, John and Paula were pleased. Even George seemed to like the new look and was happy with *his* newfound independence. But most importantly, Kerry liked it. So, the Grizzly Adams look stayed from then on. For the first time since they had been born, Graham was Graham and George was George and there was no doubt which one was which.

Graham smiled at the photograph and placed it back on the table. He ran his fingers through the bushy growth on his chin. It had certainly been a defining point in their lives. They were now just twin brothers.

For all the visual aid that the beard brought, John and Paula had been noticing small differences between their sons since they were about sixteen. Not so much physical, but in their personalities and their characters. As the boys approached the end of their school days, John and Paula saw the gap between the two boys widen. George the extrovert, Graham the introvert. George was loud and always had something to say, whereas Graham was more considered, quieter, and kept his thoughts to himself. It was therefore no surprise to either John or Paula when Graham decided against joining Doug Fenner's club with his brother when the time came. Doug was a little disappointed. He saw as much in Graham, if not more, as he did in George. But Graham had worked hard and achieved some good exam results and had decided to continue with his education at university. He had applied for and been accepted into Norwich University.

George was pleased for him, although he thought he was completely mad. Graham however was as eager to start the next chapter in his life, as George was to start his.

20

A change of course.

Graham's days at university were happy ones. He revelled in the new start. The protective cocoon of eighteen years, the routine, the solid foundation of home and family had gone. He had to fend for himself in an alien environment just like everyone else. It was an exciting time.

Graham blossomed, becoming more outgoing and vivacious. He started to show more of the traits that would normally be associated with George. He had never intentionally played second fiddle to his brother, it just sort of happened that way. George was always the one who would draw people's attention. He was the jester and the storyteller. Graham never felt the need to challenge that and subsequently, seemed to blend into the background. But at university, on his own, his demeanour and character took a more demonstrative path. Graham quickly made lots of friends. His outgoing personality and his generous fun-loving nature made him popular with both students and staff. He was also the target for a number of young ladies who were eager to be associated with such a handsome and likeable young man, just one of many aspects in Graham's life that was starting to change. He thought his brother would be proud of him.

He had a number of relationships in the first couple of years. It was almost part of the curriculum. People would fall in and out of bed with one another, mostly because it seemed like a good idea at the time. It was more about expression, recreation and liberation, than love or commitment.

Graham's relationships came to nothing. There had been a number of girls he really liked, but there was never the spark to sustain them. They were more about the sex than anything spiritual or emotional. He enjoyed them while they lasted, but he knew he needed more. He found the whole "girlfriend-boyfriend" scenario, uncomfortable. He found it difficult to put the effort and commitment into a relationship he knew would be fleeting, so the rather promiscuous society of university life made it easier for him to dip in and out whenever he liked. He worked hard and he played hard, as did most of the students. Sex was a way of letting off steam and sometimes meant no more than that.

Of course, the academic side of university life was what Graham had signed up for. He loved the work, but the social side of life was equally important. Philosophy, politics, economics, religion, were all subjects debated deep into the night, by some who knew what they were talking about, and some who didn't. At parties and gatherings, a seemingly endless supply of vodka, cider, or anything remotely alcoholic, was mixed with thinly rolled joints and opinions that just might, one day, change the course of history. Most of these earth-shattering ideas and beliefs would drift out of the windows along with the thick grey herbal smoke and be gone until the next time, when they would be repeated as new.

With a little help from his family Graham had been able to afford an apartment just outside the university grounds. It was close enough to be able to walk to and from, but far enough away to render a modicum of solitude and seclusion. During the week it provided the solitude that Graham craved. He was able to bury himself in his studies, away from all temptations and distractions. He worked long hours and was comfortable in the silence of his own company. But from Friday night until Sunday evening his apartment transformed itself into the hub of the social world. There was a constant stream of visitors, some carrying bottles or cans, some with Indian or Chinese takeaways. It became the meeting place for his large circle of friends. Whatever the evening had in store, it generally started from Graham's apartment and whatever transpired, it invariably ended up there. Graham didn't mind. He rather enjoyed the kudos.

It was at one of those parties that Graham's life was to radically change course. A gathering of about thirty people had slowly built up over the evening. There had been plans to go into town and have a few drinks in the local pubs, but the weather was so foul, the assembled masses were happy to stay where they were. The open windows were testament to how heavy the rain was lashing down, the thunder and the lightning adding extra drama to the evening. At about 2.30 a.m. the sound of the rain smashing against the windows eased, then stopped. It was the chance most of them had been waiting for, to return to their own beds without getting soaked. Graham watched as the human flotsam and jetsam leaked out of his front door and into the street. Some were staggering and some needed assistance from their friends. As the loud attempts at whispered "Good nights" drifted into the night air, Graham shut the door. He was alone. He cast his eyes over the devastation. It was a complete mess. Everywhere he looked he could see empty beer cans and bottles. Silver tinfoil cartons once full of biriani and jalfrezi, were now bristling with stubbed-out cigarette ends. Pizza boxes with the remnants of partially eaten crusts lay on the floor and tables. The combined smell of everything that had been drunk, smoked or devoured, clung to every surface in the flat. Although the windows had been wide open, he knew the smell of "party" would be evident for a few days to come. He pulled the windows shut and decided to leave the cleaning up until the morning. It had been a long night and he could do with his bed. On the way to his bedroom, he saw some feet protruding from behind the sofa. He wasn't alone after all. He peered over the back of the sofa to see who they belonged to. Rachel and Denzel. They were snuggled together and didn't look like they were going to wake up for some time. They did look sweet though, with their legs wrapped around each other. Even drunks could sometimes look cute. He pulled the throw off the sofa and laid it over them, tucking them in like a mother would her children. It wasn't unusual to find bodies scattered around the flat the morning after a party. People would fall asleep where they dropped. On one occasion, Graham had discovered someone asleep in his bath. At first it had given him quite a fright. He had only noticed the sleeping form while he was sitting on the toilet. Lucky for him and the semi-naked girl in the bath, she didn't wake up.

Graham took one last look at the desolation and turned off the light. Out of sight, out of mind. He closed the door to his bedroom. There was only one thing on his mind and that was sleep, a long and deep sleep.

In the still and calm of his room, Graham quickly became aware of someone breathing; like the slow rhythmical sound of the sea lapping over a shingle beach. In, and out; in, and out. Once his eyes became accustomed to the dark, he could make out a shape in his bed. Someone had probably thought they would grab half an hour's sleep after too much beer and failed to wake up. It certainly wasn't the first time Graham had shared his bed with an unidentified guest. Fortunately, the bed was big enough. Indeed, there had been one occasion when four souls had taken refuge beneath his sheets. Graham undressed and slid into bed as quietly as he could. He glanced over to see who he was sharing with, but the mystery person was so well cocooned in the duvet, it was impossible to see. He would no doubt find out in the morning. Every waking second was now a moment of sleep lost. He rolled over onto his side, trying not to pull too much of the duvet off the sleeping beauty beside him. The slumbering body let out a small high-pitched grunt and wriggled slightly, burying itself even deeper into its hibernation; then the sound of the waves washing over pebbles returned with its metronomic, tidal rhythm. Graham smiled. Life was great. He was convinced he had made the right decision when opting for university over football and was proud of himself for doing so. With a self-satisfying grin on his face, he slipped into a beautiful, restful and contented sleep.

Graham's senses began to stir. How long had he been asleep? Was it morning already? Surely not. Even through his closed eyes, he could tell it was still dark. He was between sleep and consciousness. His brain was awake, but his body was still sleeping. Had he woken from a dream? He felt his body in a heightened state of excitement. If it had been a dream, he wanted to return to it straight away. Keep his eyes shut, relax and drift back to whatever fantasy land he had just left. But it wasn't a dream. His body was slowly and surely catching up with his brain. The excitement and arousal that had sparked him into premature consciousness was now soaking through him. The tingling pleasure was growing and becoming more intense with every second. As the last remnants of drowsy sleep left him, he opened his eyes, blinking several times. He was now fully awake. He lay there rigid and still for a moment, trying to make sense of what his senses were telling him. It was beautiful. He could feel a moist, warm massage being lovingly applied to what felt like the biggest erection he had ever had. The caressing touch of lips, the wriggling flicking stroke of a well-lubricated tongue and the faint sense of carefully guarded teeth moving slowly and sensually up and down, on what was now the focal point of his existence. He felt the soft kiss of someone's nose brush his belly and the warm zephyr of exhaling breath circulate around his thighs as his full length was swallowed. The rest of his body was numb. There was no more feeling to go around. Every nerve ending had deserted its post and had gathered in his groin. The lips drew back almost losing touch with the heavy bulbous end of his penis. The tongue once again teasing the very tip for a moment, rolling from side to side, before the mouth plunged back down again engulfing him and sending another shockwave of pleasure through him. Graham rolled his eyes to the left. He could see that his mystery bed partner was now no longer asleep. He looked back down the bed. The duvet was breathing up and down to the rhythm of his pleasure. He lay there still, enjoying every second. He slowly eased his legs a little wider apart to allow full access. He felt a hand gently squeeze his balls and start to play with them. Even his curiosity to discover who was perpetrating such bliss was outweighed by the electric pulses that were coursing through his body. He felt himself plough even deeper into the heavenly cavern, feeling the back of the throat and beyond. He started to arch his pelvis in harmony with his oral delighter. He had to know. He lifted the duvet and gradually peeled it back. The head that was giving him so much ecstasy didn't stop, unconcerned at its imminent exposure. The rhythm remained constant. Up and down, in and out. Intent and committed to bringing the action to a conclusion. Graham looked down on the mop of long black curly hair that was moving between his legs. Without slowing, the head turned and looked Graham straight in the eyes. Even in the murky darkness of the night, Graham recognised the face staring back at him. Fabio Bragga. For a split-second Graham felt his body snap to attention, as if 1000 volts had been blasted through him. It was a little unexpected to say the least. Fabio was a nice bloke and a good friend, but this? What was this? Fabio smiled. He smiled with his eyes. His mouth was full of Graham, and busy. He could see the confusion in Graham's face. He winked at him. Graham nervously smiled back. Fabio continued with his work, his hand becoming increasingly animated, squeezing and pumping on the shaft and gently cupping his balls. Why didn't he stop him? Graham thought to himself. Why was he just lying there, letting it happen? Fabio's mouth was lavishing wave after wave of extreme pleasure. That's why. Graham closed his eyes and relaxed again, giving in to Fabio's efforts. It was far too good to stop and Graham had now reached the point of no return. He began to arch himself up and down with more force, pushing himself harder into Fabio's face. The entire length of his twitching manhood disappearing between Fabio's lips over and over again. Graham lowered his left hand and stroked the back of Fabio's head, gently regulating the speed and depth of penetration. Fabio seemed happy to be manipulated in that way. He smiled again at Graham, glad to obey. As the climax arrived, Graham held Fabio's head with both hands, threading his fingers through his thick black curls. Fabio had stopped moving. All of the thrusting was coming from Graham's groin. Faster and faster and harder and harder he drove himself into Fabio's open mouth. His grip tightened. Graham snapped to attention. He felt his body spasm and every one of his muscles tightened. Fabio's head remained still, held in place and caressed by Graham's firm hands. Graham gushed and pumped his pleasure deep into the back of Fabio's throat. The ejaculation seemed endless and Fabio was glad to take it all. Graham groaned with joy as each burst of fluid shot out of him. Eventually his buttocks unclenched. His body returned to its relaxed state and his grip on Fabio's head loosened. With his freedom returned, Fabio went back to work on Graham's slowly deflating organ, squeezing out and licking up the last few drops of evidence. Graham lay there unable to move. As Fabio finished off, Graham tried to come to terms with what had just happened. Was there anything to come to terms with? They were both adults and they both knew what they were doing. It had been magnificent for him. Even Fabio seemed to have enjoyed it. What was the problem? Why did he feel an overwhelming sense of guilt?

Fabio eased himself back up the bed, retaining a gentle hold on Graham with his left hand, and looked at him.

'I'm sorry. I just couldn't resist. I woke up and saw you. I don't know what or who you were dreaming about, but you were so hard and it seemed a shame to waste it. I hope you don't mind,' Fabio said with a cheeky grin, licking his lips.

Graham shook his head, still unable to speak. He leant over and kissed Fabio on the lips. Fabio's tongue immediately entered Graham's mouth. Graham's tongue responded. He felt like someone else was pulling his strings, controlling his movements and his actions. But he didn't mind. He felt happy and at ease.

'No, I don't mind,' he said finally, as he pulled Fabio's face towards him and kissed him again. Graham reached down with his hand. Fabio was rock hard. He played with him for a few moments while they kissed and then lowered himself down the bed. It was his turn to please. With no hesitation or self-doubt, Graham took all that Fabio had and eagerly repaid the compliment. It surprised him to find that he derived as much pleasure from the giving, as he had from the receiving.

Fabio and Graham remained lovers for six months. They were never in love, but Graham enjoyed the experiences and the discoveries he made after Fabio had opened the door to a whole new world. He had a couple more relationships after Fabio, but they too were purely physical.

It had been a major turning point for Graham. From that moment he felt more at ease with himself. He stopped worrying about his awkwardness around girls. He knew he was more comfortable and more confident with his own sex and he learned to embrace it. He still wasn't sure if he was gay, or bisexual, but it really didn't matter. What he did know was that he felt liberated and free. He felt happy.

Once Graham had come to terms with his "sexuality", he knew he had to tell his family. It had come as a surprise to himself in the beginning, so how his mother, father and brother would react was anyone's guess. He knew it had to be done sooner rather than later. Although Graham wasn't famous like his brother, word could always spread and if the gossip columnists had nothing better to report on, it might seem like a juicy little titbit for them to print. He didn't want his family to find out that way. He knew it would be a difficult moment for both him and them. He tried to imagine what their reactions would be and if it would change the dynamic of their relationship. Would they be shocked? Probably. Would they be disappointed? Maybe. Would they be ashamed? God, he hoped not. How would it change things between them? Would George choose to distance himself from his brother? They had always been so close. Inseparable. What would John and Paula's reaction be? They had always taught their boys that there was no room in the world for discrimination or bigotry of any kind, whether it be racist, sexual or religious, but that was easy to say. It was a generalisation. How would they feel when it actually affected them directly? Would they think less of him? He couldn't bear the thought that the bond he had with his loved ones would be jeopardised by his actions. He believed what they had as a family was as good as anything could ever be. Any change to the status quo would only be damaging. There were so many possible outcomes racing through his mind. None of them were particularly good. But it would have to be faced and dealt with.

21

A metaphorical hand grenade.

Graham called Paula and invited himself down for Sunday lunch. He had carefully picked a Sunday when he knew George would be free of any footballing commitments and suggested to Paula that it would be nice if he were there too. He had some news he wanted to tell them all. Something he wanted to tell them as a family, so maybe George could come alone. Just the four of them. Paula thought that was a lovely idea. And so, the date was set, the cast would be assembled and Graham would drop his bombshell. Judgement day. Probably the most difficult, uncomfortable and unpredictable day of Graham's life so far.

Paula had mentioned to John and George that Graham had some news he wanted to share with them. George was intrigued. Had Graham met a beautiful girl, fallen in love and decided to get married? Was Paula going to have to buy a new hat or an outfit for an impending wedding? Maybe the girl was pregnant. Maybe there was another tiny member of the Miller clan ready to be announced. Was that the news?

Maybe he had decided to travel or emigrate. Australia, New Zealand, America. Paula and John wouldn't be very happy about that. The more George mused about what his news might be, the more extreme his ideas became. He was desperate to know and came close, on a couple of occasions, to phoning his brother and asking him; even for a clue. But he managed to fight the urge. He didn't want to spoil Graham's surprise. He would just have to wait until Sunday like everyone else. John wondered whether Graham had decided to quit university and take up Doug Fenner's offer and become a footballer like his brother. Paula had had the same thoughts. The wealth and fame that George had already acquired was enough to make most people envious. Paula hoped not. She was very proud of her university son. He was living her dream. When she was young, she had always dreamt of going to university, but in those days her family's financial situation hadn't allowed it and she never had the opportunity. She had been genuinely thrilled when Graham had chosen to carry on his education after school. She was, of course, very proud of George, but somehow, she had a little more admiration and respect for Graham because he had taken, what she perceived as, the tougher road to fulfilling his potential. They were all anxious and excited to hear what Graham's news was.

Graham let himself into his parents' house as quietly as he could. As he stood silently by the door, he could hear voices and laughter coming from the kitchen at the end of the hallway. He paused for a moment and tried to gather his thoughts. He listened to the jollity. Everything was as it always had been. The sounds, the smells, the atmosphere.

The warmth of the perfect family home. Was he about to change that ideal forever? He was carrying a metaphorical hand grenade and was about to lob it into his wonderful family's life. He had been bracing himself for this for several days. Rehearsing repeatedly in his head how he would tell them. How he would break the news to them in the least shocking way possible. He had tried to picture their faces and reactions. Over the past few days, he had been thinking of nothing else. He had begun to see himself as the villain, an outcast and a leper.

He started to walk towards the kitchen. It was now or never. The three voices became louder as he approached. Three voices of the three people that meant more to him than anyone, or anything, in the world. He stood in the kitchen doorway. He watched John and George laughing and joking, trying to outshout one another. John picked up a tea towel and threw it at George. He missed and the tea towel wrapped itself around the back of Paula's head as she stirred the pans on the hob. With the tea towel comically draped over the back of her head and covering half her face, she turned around and scolded the two of them. She waved a wooden spoon at her husband with all the loving menace she could, in a manner Graham remembered from when they were children. Paula had always claimed she had three children and the biggest child of them all was John. They both looked suitably reprimanded and sorry. Then they both roared with laughter again. Graham stepped into the kitchen. There was no turning back now. He plonked the bottle of red wine down loudly on the granite worktop announcing his arrival.

'Ahh, here he is. The man with the mystery,' George said jokingly.

'Hello, Son,' said John.

'Hello, darling,' said Paula, breaking away from the pots and pans. She walked over to him.

'Hi Mum.'

He kissed her and gave her a big hug. His legs felt like jelly. He was using all of his energy just to try and smile. But he knew it wasn't a very good smile.

'How's things then, Son? What have you been getting up to?' asked John. Before Graham could say a word, John continued. 'And what's this big announcement you've got for us? Come on, spit it out. You've got us all wondering.'

Graham couldn't ever remember feeling so uncomfortable or so isolated. All of his plans about how and when he would broach the subject had been dashed. Unknowingly, his father had taken away what little control he had, by his enthusiastic eagerness to find out what his news was. The spotlight was on him straight away. All three of them were looking at him and waiting for him to speak. He felt the breath in his lungs build up as he inhaled. He opened his mouth, but no sound came out. His throat was suddenly bone dry. He stood there for a moment like a rabbit caught in the headlights, frozen with fear.

'Leave the poor lad alone. He's only just walked through the door,' Paula said waving the wooden spoon in John's direction again. 'Now go on, all of you, out of the kitchen.'

Graham felt the deep breath slowly escape through his nostrils and a shiver of relief at his temporary stay of execution. John and George left the room.

'Get Graham a drink, John, and you can get me one too,' Paula shouted after them.

'How are you, love? It's nice to see you. Go and sit down. Lunch is nearly ready,' she said with a motherly smile. Graham joined John and George in the dining room. George was telling his father about a Portuguese winger the club was trying to sign. John was all ears, but Graham couldn't really concentrate on his brother's voice. He felt sick. He knew he wouldn't be able to eat anything. Even the smell of Paula's lovely lunch was making him want to vomit.

By the time they sat down at the table, it was clear to all three of them that something was wrong. The "happy family" atmosphere had gone. There was a feeling of apprehension in the air. The conversation was stifled and uneasy. John, Paula and George shot worrying glances at each other. All the colour had drained away from Graham's face. He was pale and washed out. He looked scared and helpless. He looked like a lost child. He couldn't make eye contact with anyone and kept his stare on his food. Whatever the announcement was, it wasn't about marriage, pregnancy, emigration or football. The silence was only being broken by the scraping and clinking of knives and forks on the plates. John decided to take the lead, but just before he could speak, Graham stood bolt upright. The sudden movement and the clank of cutlery and glasses, as Graham's legs hit the table, took all three of them by surprise and each one of them reeled back in their chairs with shock. The boldness of the move had also taken Graham a little by surprise. This was it. He still hadn't taken his stare away from his plate and gazed at his lunch for a few more seconds, before raising his eyes and staring directly at the three agog faces looking back at him. He clasped his hands together as if he were praying and covered his mouth with them. He certainly had their full attention now. John's mouth was still a little agape from the suddenness of Graham's move. Graham swallowed. His Adam's apple felt like a piece of flint in his throat almost cutting through the flesh. He took an even deeper breath and lowered his clasped hands onto his chest.

'Mum. Dad. George.' He looked at each of them in turn as he addressed them. The flint in his throat was still razor sharp. As he began to speak, Paula noticed the beginnings of a tear forming in each of Graham's eyes. They both swelled quickly, and just before he spoke, they plunged down over his cheeks.

'I want you to know that I think I am' … he paused … 'No. I want you to know that I am gay. I am gay.'

Silence engulfed the room. They were all still looking at him, as if they expected him to say more! More! There was no more. That was it. The deed was done. It had been as simple as that, but what now? The silence felt like it went on forever. All three of them had rather stunned looks on their faces. Graham stood in front of them. The tears were flowing down his face and dripping off his chin. He unclasped his hands and put his arms down by his side. He lowered his head and returned his stare to his food, waiting for their reaction. As the emotion took hold of him, he felt his body start to shake. He didn't know how much longer he could remain standing; he felt on the verge of collapse. Paula was the first to move. She stood up and wiped her mouth with her napkin then threw it onto the table.

'Is that why you look so awful? Has telling us worried you that much? Are we really that scary? Come here and give your mum a hug.'

She opened her arms and Graham fell into her embrace like a ragdoll. What little emotion he had managed to keep inside him, poured out. He wrapped his arms around his mother and wept like a small, helpless child.

'Fancy making yourself ill over something like that. For a minute there you had us all worried. I thought you were sick or something.'

Paula clasped the sides of his wet face and looked him square in the eye, the tip of her nose touching his, the glistening evidence of Paula's own emotions showing on her face.

'What did you expect us to do, stop loving you? You silly boy.'

Graham tried to force a smile. He was sobbing and shaking. He felt his chin and bottom lip quiver uncontrollably as the next tide of tears swept down his face. John and George joined in the hug and the family scrum was complete. They squeezed each other tightly. When they released their grip and looked into each other's eyes, they all had tears on their faces. George wiped a tear from his cheek and winked at Graham, then gently patted the side of his face. No words were needed. Graham finally managed the elusive smile he had been searching for.

It had been a reaction he had not even dared to consider. It hadn't seemed possible before, but it might even have made the family stronger. Nothing would ever break this family up or come between them.

Whenever Graham thought of that Sunday afternoon with all its emotion, tension and love, it always brought a lump to his throat and a tear to his eye. It was a reminder of just how lucky he was. He had been lucky in both life and love. He had met and was living with Kerry, the man of his dreams. He was successful, comfortable and happy. Life was good.

He decided to go and have a long swim to wash away the hangover, the smell of cognac and his sense of loneliness. Kerry's absence was painful, but Graham knew that once he returned from this trip, they would get back to how they were during those wonderful early days. He would call George when he got back from the pool. It was time he saw his brother again. He had sounded a little deflated on the message. They would go out for a few beers and cheer each other up.

A couple of hours in the pool would set him up nicely for the day. It normally did. Everything would be alright after that.

22

San Diego.

Graham dried himself off with the huge, soft white towel he had taken with him. He had been in the pool for just under two hours. It had been a very invigorating swim. He gave his face and hair one last rub and picked up his mobile phone from the locker. In the time he had been in the pool he had received forty emails, several texts and a voicemail. His phone always seemed more active when he was away from it. He scrolled through the messages. Some junk, some business. As they flashed by like the closing title credits on a low-budget film, Graham noticed George's name whizz through the screen. He packed away his towel and headed for the exit. He paused in front of the large mirror by the door and ran his fingers through his mop of hair. He looked himself up and down, smiled courteously and nodded at his reflection, just as he would have done to a stranger. His reflection smiled and nodded back. He felt good.

Sitting back comfortably on his sofa with a hot cup of tea, he began the task of going through his correspondence in detail. The swim had washed the last remnants of his hangover away and the smell of shower gel on his body had taken over from the smell of last night's brandy. He felt fresh and alive. He could concentrate and focus on things that a few hours earlier would have proved far too daunting for him. Graham went straight to the message from George.

"Hi Graham. Hope you're okay. Don't know what you're up to over the next few days, but if you fancy meeting up somewhere it would be good to see you". He sounded a lot better; more upbeat than his last message. There was more of a smile in his tone. Graham contented himself that his brother, for now anyway, was okay. He would plough through the rest of his emails, then call George once he had finished.

One of the last emails Graham saw was from a client of his in America. The American company had some work for him if he was interested. The only drawback was they would have to meet face to face. Most deals were now done over the Internet or via conference calls. Technology had made the need for business travel almost obsolete. The "Carbon Footprint Brigade" had triumphed in their ongoing war against globetrotting executives criss-crossing the planet in search of the next multi-million-pound merger. Not great news for the airlines, but it suited Graham. In the early days, he had regarded business trips as perks of the job. Mini working holidays where he could see the world at someone else's expense, but since meeting Kerry, he had developed a growing resentment towards them. Time away from home meant time away from Kerry. The message was quite clear though.

"It is imperative you come here for a number of meetings to secure what should be a very beneficial outcome for all concerned".

The company was based in San Diego. Graham craned his neck and looked over his shoulder to the large, imposing, framed map of the world hanging on the wall behind him. His geography was pretty good and he knew where San Diego was, but San Diego wasn't where his primary interest lay. He rolled himself off the sofa and got to his feet. He took a closer look at the map. His eyes went straight to the west coast of the USA. There was San Diego. A drive up the coast heading north through Carlsbad onto Long Beach and through LA, then continuing past Ventura would take you straight to Santa Barbara. It was just over one inch on the map, just over 200 miles in reality. Graham traced the route with his finger. His brain started to compile a plan. He smiled and tapped Santa Barbara twice. It was too good to be true. A business trip that would actually bring them together. He could fly out tomorrow and spend what he imagined would be a week, maybe two, in San Diego completing the deal. Then drive up to Santa Barbara and spend some time with Kerry. No more counting off the hours and days until his return. No more sitting in the flat feeling lonely and sorry for himself. He would go out to the States and end their separation. Graham stared lovingly at the map as if Kerry was looking back at him. His heart began beating a little faster. He softly ran his index finger across Santa Barbara again and felt the relief and happiness flood back into his body.

He hurriedly made the arrangements for his trip. After he had successfully booked his hotels, flights and car he slumped back into the numerous cushions scattered across the sofa. He closed his eyes and drew in a long, deep breath through his nostrils, then after a short pause, exhaled slowly through pursed lips. He had told the CEO that he was really looking forward to seeing her again. They had made plans to dine out, even see a show or two. But he was looking forward to the meeting that would take place 220 miles to the north, about a week later, even more. He clasped his hands behind his head and tried to imagine the look on Kerry's face. He thought of all the things they could do during the evenings. The bars, the restaurants, the clubs and the theatres, but more exciting than anything else, they would be able to hold each other and be with each other. That was the thought that sent the nicest tingle through his body. What was going to be a tough and unbearable separation, had now transformed into an exciting and glorious time of expectation.

Graham's dream-like trance was broken by the buzzing of his phone from the other end of the sofa, jolting him out of his fantasy world and making him spring to life. He picked up the phone. It was George.

The brothers spoke for over an hour. George explained to Graham what a boring existence he was leading. He told Graham that all the fun had been sucked out of his life. Everything he loved was now forbidden and everything he hated was now compulsory. Graham was impressed.

'Sounds like you really have turned over a new leaf this time. Even if it isn't by choice; or permanent.' They both laughed. As the conversation continued, Graham realised his brother was fine after all. He was bored witless, but fine. It was just the angst of having to knuckle down and do things that were ultimately foreign to him, like hard work.

Graham told George about his business trip to San Diego and how he had just booked all the flights and hotels. George was a little confused by the excitement in Graham's voice. He knew his brother resented the idea of having to travel away from home and spend time apart from Kerry, but when Graham got around to explaining the second leg of the trip to Santa Barbara, George understood where all the passion and urgency was coming from. Graham explained how he and Kerry had been going through a difficult time in their relationship. How, for the first time since they had met, inertia had crept into their daily lives, but how they were both committed and excited about putting things right.

'And now we don't even have to wait until he gets back.' Graham announced gleefully. 'It starts as soon as I arrive in Santa Barbara. A new beginning. Even better than before. I really can't wait.'

George hadn't heard his brother sound so upbeat for a long time.

'That's great news. I'm really pleased for you. I'm sure you'll have a great time. Say hello to Kerry for me. Maybe we can have that beer when you get back. You can tell me all about it then.'

'Sounds good to me,' Graham said. 'Take care, George, and look after that knee.'

'I will. It's all but wrapped up in cotton wool these days. See you when you get home.'

Once the call was finished, both of the brothers sat back and thought for a moment. Graham was relieved that

George was okay and obviously only grumpy about his new, although almost certainly temporary, lifestyle. Graham chuckled to himself and said out loud, 'It won't do you any harm at all, George.'

George smiled as he thought of Graham and Kerry meeting in Santa Barbara. They were a great couple and loved each other very much.

And so, in an apartment in central London one brother hurriedly and excitedly ran around packing his suitcase and looking for his passport, while in another apartment on the south bank of the River Thames, another brother sat alone with a mineral water, watching a black and white movie.

23

The hamster's wheel.

The following days passed very slowly for George. The repetitive nature of his life made the time drag. Each day was a rerun of the day before and a prelude to the day to come. His life was like a hamster's wheel, frantically pedalling, but going nowhere. "Groundhog Day", some people called it. The only rays of sunshine and happiness came courtesy of Graham's texts and photos. It looked like he was having a wonderful time. The deal in San Diego had gone through nicely and would open up all sorts of opportunities for Graham's company. Messages then started to arrive from Santa Barbara. Everyday George would receive pictures of them eating dinner or going to the theatre, or sometimes just relaxing on the beach. Graham had even taken the time to send him a postcard. Graham knew that George loved a postcard. It read:

Hi George. Let the fun begin. Am with Kerry and things couldn't be any better. Loving life. Back soon for that beer. Gx.

The postcard was placed on the shelf above his desk, next to the ones he had received from Debbie Morris some years earlier. They sat well together. A microcosm of happy memories and good feelings. The warmth he felt when he looked at Debbie's cards was always tinged with a feeling of regret. He had let her slip through his fingers not once, but twice. He had always hoped their paths would cross again. He was certain that if they did, he would not let her disappear from his life a third time. There was rarely a day went by without Debbie Morris occupying some part of George's thoughts.

The only event that had broken the monotony of his existence during that time had been the second leg of their semi-final in Milan. On the evening of the game, George settled down in front of his TV to watch the combat. He always found it a more nerve-wracking experience watching games on the television. He had no input as a spectator and could do nothing to influence the outcome. When he was playing, even if he was having a bad game, he felt part of the organic structure and process.

It had been a terrific match. It was end-to-end stuff. It was as exciting as the first game had been dull, both teams going at it hammer and tongs. George, along with most spectators, was on the edge of his seat from start to finish, constantly jumping up and down with every footballing thrust and parry. When the final whistle sounded, the score was 1-1. A draw, which was enough to see George's side into the final. George raised his arms in celebration and relief. He watched as the players, his mates, embraced each other and congratulated themselves. There were huge smiles and even a few tears. Doug and Bernie shook each other by the hand, and patted one another on the back in a more formal and statesmanlike fashion. Even the chairman, standing next to David Blackstone, was applauding enthusiastically up in the stands. It had been a magnificent night for the club. They had climbed a massive mountain to get to the final. But their reward was an even greater challenge. The "Mount Everest" of challenges. The final in Barcelona's, Camp Nou, stadium would be against what most pundits regarded as the best club side in world football. The mighty Madrid. While the players and fans continued to lap up the atmosphere in Milan, George's mind started to wander. Was there any real chance he would be available for that game or was it just a pipe dream?

The day after the game George began his regular routine. Another visit to the "hamster's wheel". Pulling his car into the club he saw that there was already a sea of cameras, journalists, OB trucks, generators and gazebos. The press and media circus had arrived early, waiting for the return of the victorious team. They were due to arrive back at the club shortly before lunchtime. As George got out of his car, he could feel the excitement in the air. He saw a number of heads turn in his direction. They were checking to see if anyone important had arrived. George prepared himself for the media scrum to surround him and demand his thoughts and opinions on what had been a great night. He was used to having cameras and microphones thrust in his face. But no one came. Next to the journalists and TV presenters another area had been roped off for the fans. There was already a large number of them there too. George looked across towards the ever-increasing mass of people.

Not even the fans had noticed him. Maybe they had and just weren't interested in his views. He could have been the postman or the cleaner for all of the interest he had been shown. He was invisible to them.

As he neared the offices, he saw Brenda fly out of the doors. She was running towards the security guards, standing by the roped-off areas. She had some papers in her hand. Her tight knee-length skirt was making running rather awkward. Along with her high heels, she looked quite comical, George thought. Tight skirt and stilettos were not ideal attire for jogging. She was taking tiny little pigeon steps as fast as she could go, only able to move from the knee down. The high heels looked extremely precarious too. Long, thin and definitely not designed for anything more energetic than a stylish stroll. If one of them were to snap, or she lost her balance even slightly, she would doubtless come a serious cropper. George mentally prepared himself to rush to her aid if the need arose, but it didn't. Her competence and confidence on those spindly supports was far better than he had imagined possible. George thought he had caught her eye and waved, but he got no response. She kept on running, without even acknowledging him. Bloody hell! He was invisible. George took one last look before he went through the doors into the main building. The fans, the press, even Brenda were all oblivious to his existence. He started to feel gloomy again. Suppose Brenda had noticed him but didn't want to talk to him? He hadn't seen her since the evening of the first Milan game. He knew she had been upset when they parted, but surely, she couldn't have been that cross with him. It started to feel like a very lonely world.

Apart from the hullabaloo created by the impending

trip to Barcelona, the days after the semi-final settled back into the usual routine for the players and the staff. George's routine still included the gym, physio and the swimming pool, but he had also been allowed, and encouraged, to do some training on the pitch.

He could feel his knee getting stronger and stronger every day. He pushed himself harder and harder. He even surprised himself at the effort he was making. He had started to work with the ball at his feet. It was great to feel the grass under his boots and the touch of the ball on his instep. Breathing in the fresh air and working outside felt wonderful. It was like being let out of prison. Both Bernie and Doug were pleased with his progress, his attitude and his enthusiasm. He was a couple of weeks ahead of schedule thanks to all the extra effort he had been putting in. All the tough times he had endured over the past few weeks were now proving to have been worthwhile.

There was a huge contrast to the dilemma Bernie had faced for the first match against Milan to the one he now faced for the final. Then it was a question of whoever was fit, played. Now, they were blessed with so much choice, the questions were all about who would be left out. For the first time in a long while Bernie had an almost full squad of fit players, all eager to be part of the manager's plans.

As the days ticked by, the feeling at the club became increasingly positive and upbeat. They would undoubtedly start the game as underdogs, but now with their big guns ready to fire, they would be able to give it their best shot.

At last George started to train with the first team. He suddenly became part of the family again. Part of that "band of brothers". Laughing, joking, supporting and encouraging one another. He realised how true the saying was that "You never appreciate what you have until you've lost it".

He had been part of the "Brotherhood" for years, a big part of it. But he had never really cherished it. Having been on the outside for what seemed an eternity, his return to the fold felt magnificent. He felt like an eighteen-year-old again, experiencing it for the first time. He looked around and realised what he had been missing. He promised himself he would never take it for granted in future. All the wise words he had heard over the years from the likes of Doug and his dad came back to him. And they all rang true. It had taken him a long time to wake up and realise how lucky he had been. He wasn't going to forget those lessons and he was going to make sure he appreciated every second from then on.

Walking off the pitch and heading to the showers, he wondered if he really was in with a chance of playing some part in the game against Madrid. He was raring to go, but would he be given the opportunity?

24

Don't forget your boots.

George received a message from Graham telling him he would be flying home from Los Angeles on Saturday. He would be on the overnight flight arriving at Heathrow Sunday morning. Graham sounded very excited.

I've got so much to tell you. Let's meet up as soon as possible. I will call you when I get home. What are you up to on Monday? Graham's enthusiasm was almost childlike. George would be repeating his routine of gym, training and swimming during the day, but his evenings, as they had been for some considerable time, were pretty free. The following week the players had been given Tuesday off to spend with their families. They were then due to take part in a final training session on Wednesday before flying out to Barcelona on Thursday. A day's training on the Camp Nou pitch on Friday would be followed by the big game on Saturday evening. The timing was perfect. George messaged him back.

*Monday would be great. Come over to mine. You can
stay if you want. I've got Tuesday off so we can have a
good chat then. Have a safe flight. Gx.*

Things had gone well for Graham in America. The business
part of the trip had been a huge success and would open
up an entirely new avenue of trade for his company. The
personal side had gone even better. Kerry had been
overjoyed to see Graham in Santa Barbara. It was a very
emotional meeting. They had gone out to dinner on that
first evening and poured their hearts out to each other.
They expressed their love for one another and their desire
to return to the passionate, carefree ways they had enjoyed
when they first met. Sitting outside the beautiful Stonehouse
Restaurant, holding hands, looking into each other's eyes
and planning the future, reminded them of their first date.
The excitement was back. There was an eagerness to pay the
bill and leave as soon as possible. They both knew how the
evening would end. Coffee wasn't even mentioned.

Kerry would be returning home about ten days after
Graham. It would be the fresh start they needed. Everything
had turned out for the best and the future was clear, simple,
and wonderful.

George still inhabited a world of hard graft and
abstinence. He had made good progress, but was still
unsure if he figured in any of Bernie's plans. As much as he
wanted to play in Barcelona, he knew his real victory was
keeping to his regime and proving all his detractors wrong.

After training on Thursday, George had been asked to
pop into Bernie's office for a chat. He was a little surprised.
He hadn't done anything wrong. The only occasions he

had been summoned in the past were for reprimands, or to explain himself after accusations or rumours concerning his private life. It felt strange walking up to see the manager with no fear or guilt hanging over him.

It was a windy, cold May afternoon and without his big coat, the chill cut right through him. As he made his way over to the offices, he plunged his hands deep into his trouser pockets and hunched his shoulders against the Arctic blast. His walk skipped seamlessly into a trot and then into a jog. He smiled as the cold breeze burnt his cheeks. He had never jogged over to Bernie's office before.

He closed the main door to the building behind him and the howling, gusting noise of the wind was silenced. All was quiet and serene inside and it was a lot warmer. The only sound was the echoing of George's footsteps as he vaulted up the stairs, two, sometimes three at a time. Once he had reached the second floor, he began to hear the tap-tap-tap of Brenda's long fingernails typing on her keypad. He crept up to the door and popped his head round, waving his hand and wriggling his fingers. Brenda didn't even look up from her screen. With her earphones in and her brain totally engaged in the task at hand, she had shut the rest of the world out completely.

George had had no contact with Brenda since they parted company after the Milan game just over three weeks earlier. He knew she had been upset at the abrupt ending to the evening's proceedings. He had felt both sorry and righteous about his actions that night. Once he had found himself back at his flat on his own, he wished he had brought her home with him, but ultimately, he knew he had done the right and proper thing by taking her back to her parents' house. He hoped she hadn't taken it so badly that she was ignoring him. She was very sweet and he did enjoy their little flirtatious meetings every now and again. He continued to peer around the door and carried on wriggling his fingers. He started to feel a little bit silly, but he persevered. She would have to look up soon.

'Hi, Brenda,' George said loud enough to ensure she would hear him through her earpieces. It was loud enough to make her jump and sit back in her chair. Her startled face looked angry at the interruption and for a split second George feared the worst. A moment later, once she realised it was George, a softer, more inviting face stared back at him and she quickly broke into a smile.

'Hello, George,' she said, immediately stopping her typing and pulling the earphones out. She stood up. 'I have been wanting to talk to you for a while.'

Her smile had gone and her face looked sad and apologetic.

'Why, what's wrong?' George asked.

'Well, it's just,… I mean I wanted to,…' She was struggling to put her thoughts into words. 'I wanted to say sorry.'

George frowned quizzically at her.

'Sorry! What for?'

Brenda walked out from behind her desk and stood directly in front of him, her head slightly bowed and her arms straight down by her side, like a naughty little girl confessing to some dreadful deed.

'For the way I behaved the night we watched the football together. I was so rude at the end and you had been so nice to me. I just wanted the night to go on forever. I was having such a wonderful time. I thought we were going to…' She paused and started to blush. 'Well, anyway, I felt awful about it in the morning. I hated myself the next day.'

Her head bowed another notch. George couldn't see her face, but he could hear a slight trembling in her voice.

'I was going to call you, but I didn't know if I should or not.'

George put his fingers under her chin and tilted her head up until she was looking into his eyes. He could see the beginnings of a teardrop forming. He eased his thumb up to her eye and softly brushed it away.

'I'm really sorry, George. I think I must have had a few too many gins.' She spoke as George cleared away the last vestiges of moisture from her cheeks.

He smiled down at her.

'Don't be silly,' he said gently, his hand still cradling her face.'I never gave it a second thought. I'm glad you enjoyed it. I certainly did. We even made some of the back pages of the newspapers. There I was in the crowd, snuggled up to the prettiest girl in London.'

Brenda's face broke into a smile again. She flung her arms around him and pushed her face into his chest. She loved being complimented by George. He embraced her, holding her with his left arm and caressing the back of her head with his right hand. She squeezed him tightly. Brenda would have stayed like that forever if she could.

'Come on now,' said George, 'let's have no more tears.'

He eased her away, holding her by the shoulders.

'I'm here to see Mr Roswell, Miss Cousins. Would you kindly inform him that Mr George Miller has arrived?' He said it in a very businesslike tone. Brenda reluctantly relinquished her hold on him. She rubbed her eyes, straightened her blouse and pinched her skirt back into place. In an equally businesslike voice, she replied,

'Certainly, Mr Miller.'

George turned and followed her out of her office. He could see she had already knocked and opened Bernie's door.

'Mr Roswell will see you now.'

She held the door open with an outstretched arm inviting George to enter. She stood in the middle of the doorway, ensuring he had to squeeze past her to get in. As he did so, she took in a deep breath, forcing her chest to expand and her breasts to rub gently against him. The contact sent a shiver of excitement rushing through her body. He kept his eyes fixed on hers. She had that cheeky little grin on her face that George loved so much. Brenda's eyes stayed fixed on George.

'Thank you, Brenda. That will be all,' came the fatherly voice of Bernie.

'Yes, Mr Roswell,' she replied without taking her eyes away from George's stare. George watched her walk back to her own office. He was sure there was an exaggerated wiggle in her hips, just for his benefit. He shut the door.

Doug was in the far corner of the office looking out onto the grey, bleak afternoon. He looked relaxed and calm. He had his hands tucked casually into his pockets and he was quietly whistling to himself. He looked like he didn't have a care in the world, but then Doug normally looked like that. He had an unflappable serenity about him that put everyone at ease. George couldn't ever remember him raising his voice, swearing or losing control, even when things got tough. Bernie was pretty similar, although he had been known to throw the odd "F" word into his half-time talks if he thought it was merited. They had been in the game long enough to know that ranting and raving at players rarely did any good. They preferred the arm around the shoulder approach. They were both thoroughly decent men, working in a cut-throat, money-driven industry.

'How's the knee, George?' asked Bernie. Doug finished his whistling and sauntered over towards them both, hands still deep in his pockets. 'Doug tells me you are not far off being ready to return.'

'It feels good, Mr Roswell. Good and strong,' George said positively.

'Good. Good.'

Bernie was perched on the corner of his desk and was fiddling with a pencil. There was a moment's silence. George felt he needed to fill it.

'I'm very grateful to you and Doug …er…Mr Fenner. I know you have stuck by me when I really haven't given you any reason to. I want to repay your loyalty and confidence in me in any way I can.'

Bernie nodded his head, listening intently to what George was saying. He jumped to his feet, slammed the pencil down on the desk and wandered over to a whiteboard at the far end of the room. It had columns of names written on it in various colours. George could see his name up there in the green column. He wondered what significance the various hues held. Bernie glanced at the names on the board and without looking back, began to speak.

'We have a number of players back from injury now and a couple available after suspension. It looks like we are going to be spoilt for choice.'

He carried on perusing the board and another silence

filled the room. George looked at Doug who was now sitting on the same corner of Bernie's desk the manager had just vacated. Doug shot him that look. The smile and the wink. The comforting and reassuring sight George had become used to over the years from his mentor. Bernie spun around, looked straight at George and laughed.

'Ironic, isn't it, when you think about it? We could hardly put eleven fit players on the pitch against Milan in the first game.'

He looked at George as if he expected some kind of explanation. George was unsure what he should do or say.

'Sit down, George.'

Bernie pointed to one of the chairs by his desk.

'I want you to make the trip with us to Barcelona. I can't promise you anything. As you can see, I have a lot of options now. But I want you to come along and be part of it. The youngsters all look up to you. You've worked hard and I think you deserve at least that. I'm still a long way off deciding who will be picked for the game on Saturday week. I have choices now in every position. Good problems to have, but it means that some people are going to be disappointed. I'm telling you this, George, because I didn't want to get your hopes up too high. I'm not saying there is no chance. Never say never, eh? I just want you to be part of the family again, at the very least.'

Bernie rose from his chair and Doug sprung up from the desk corner. Bernie walked around his desk and patted George on the arm. He offered him his hand and George shook it.

'All of your hard work has not gone unnoticed upstairs either, I can tell you.' Bernie made a slight nod with his head in the direction of David's office above.

'Keep the faith, George. There are a lot more miles in that knee of yours, I'm sure.'

'Thank you, Mr Roswell. Thank you for being so straight with me. I promise I won't let you down.'

George shook Bernie's hand, then reached out and shook Doug's. He gave him the look again. As George turned and headed for the door, he heard Bernie's voice pipe up again.

'Oh, George.' He turned to look at his manager.

'Yes, Mr Roswell?' Bernie was smiling.

'Don't forget your boots, son. Just in case.' George smiled back at him and let out a small chuckle.

'I won't,' he said.

The door shut behind him. He was back in the large, airy space of the lounge. He had mixed feelings about what had just happened. On the one hand, he was overjoyed that Bernie and Doug were pleased with his efforts and progress. He was thrilled that they had decided to take him along on the trip to Barcelona and that he would be part of the family again. He was pleasantly surprised that Bernie had left the door open for him to play some part in the game, but having got so close, he now wanted to play even more. For weeks there had been absolutely no chance of him even being fit enough to travel. Now he was fit enough to travel and possibly even play. He desperately wanted that possibility to become a probability.

Brenda came bounding out of her office as soon as she heard Bernie's door close.

'Everything alright, George?' she asked.

She was standing very close to him.

'All is fine and dandy, thank you, Miss Cousins. No reprimand, no scolding and look, no rapped knuckles.'

He held out his hands to show her. She immediately

grasped them in hers and pulled herself towards him, pressing his hands firmly into her bosom.

'Oh George, I was so worried I had upset you. I'm so pleased we are still friends. We *are* still friends, aren't we?' She squeezed his hands tighter and forced them a little harder into her breasts. He smiled.

'Of course we are. Why do you think I keep getting into trouble? It's only so I can come up here and see you.'

He leant forward and kissed her forehead.

'See you soon,' he said. 'I'm sure it won't be long before I have to report back up here again.'

Grudgingly, she released her grip on his hands. They had felt nice pressed up against her. She wondered if he had felt her beating heart, pounding with pleasure.

'Bye, George. If I don't see you before you go, good luck in Barcelona.'

George's drive home was made in a trance. It was a route he had taken hundreds of times before. The car pretty much knew its way back by now.

The outcome of his battle to win a place in the team, or some part of the action was still in the balance, but the battle to win his way back into Bernie and Doug's trust and affection had been fought and won. It would be the icing on the cake if he could somehow repay them both by contributing to a successful outcome on Saturday week. It would mean so much to them, to the club, to the fans and of course, to him. This was the moment he had worked so hard for. Harder than he had ever worked for anything. And he was on the verge of achieving it. Life was good.

25

Lauren Perrier Rosé.

George returned home after the day's training session on Monday. He felt great. His body felt stronger and fitter than it had for a long time. He had been sharper, quicker and more decisive than he could ever remember. His knee was in good shape. He still wore some strapping around it, but that was only a precaution. He knew in his heart he was ready to play. He was as good as new, probably better.

The trip to Barcelona was now only a few days away. There was one more session at the club's training ground on Wednesday before they flew out on Thursday. They would then train on Friday, before the game itself on Saturday. So, he had two more chances to impress and maybe, just maybe, get his name on the team sheet for the final. He truly believed he had done as much as he could to show the management he was ready. He would be keeping everything crossed and hoping for a piece of the action.

George had arranged to meet Graham that evening at 6.30.p.m., at the same club he had taken Lisa to several weeks earlier. He was looking forward to seeing his brother and curious to find out just what Graham was so keen to tell him. It had been obvious from his voice that he was bursting to impart some earth-shattering news. Graham's news was always rather dramatic.

Their meeting would have to be a low-key affair due to his "appointment" in Barcelona. So, an early start and an early finish seemed like a good idea.

George relaxed in the bath, very content with life. He had everything he could have possibly wanted. Wealth, fame, a great apartment, a wonderful family and a career that was now back on track. The only missing piece of the jigsaw was someone to share it all with. He had dated many beautiful and glamorous ladies, but the more he thought about it, the more he warmed to the idea of settling down. He would find a nice girl. Someone who would love him for "who" he was, not "what" he was. Images of past girlfriends passed through his mind like a police identity parade. Even Brenda's smiling face, looking up to him and clutching his hands to her bosom came into his head. But none of them gave him the warmth or sense of permanence he craved. There was only one image, one name, that could make him shiver with excitement at the same time as feeling the warm glow of contentment. Debbie Morris. She had been the first and only girl to really own his heart, but she was lost somewhere among the billions of people on planet Earth. Whereabouts unknown. He had tried to find her via the numerous social media sites, but all his efforts had proved fruitless. The trail had gone cold after that last postcard from Sydney. She could be anywhere.

George looked at himself in the mirror. He wasn't

trying to disguise himself, but he didn't really want to be recognised. He was wearing his large coat with the collar turned up. He had his favourite Detroit Lions American football cap on and a scarf wrapped around his face. It was still bitterly cold outside, so nothing looked out of place or over the top.

The cab driver dropped him off right outside the club and within seconds he was inside. He knew the owner and most of the staff. He regularly phoned ahead to let them know he was coming and would normally ask for a particular table to be reserved. It was the one set back into an alcove, away from the bar and the dance floor. The one which provided an element of privacy. He declined the offer of the cloakroom attendant to take his coat and scarf. He would keep himself wrapped up until he reached the relative sanctuary of his table. There were only a few people in. Mostly suits, sitting at the bar having a beer after their day's "wheeling and dealing". Some of the staff busied themselves cleaning tables and rearranging the chairs in preparation for the rush in a few hours' time. The club usually started to fill up about 9.30 and was generally heaving by 10.30. George knew he would be long gone by then.

'Can I get you anything to eat or drink, sir?' A waiter's voice interrupted George's people-watching.

'A mineral water, please,' George replied, glancing at the young man without looking him straight in the eye.

'Yes, sir.'

He was new. George hadn't seen him before. The club was known for attracting "A-listers" from the world of film, sport, music, even politics. Because of that, it also attracted members of the press looking for a story. The staff were under strict instructions not to appear starstruck or ask for autographs or photos. The management prided itself on its reputation for discretion.

Two minutes later, the familiar sound of his brother's voice boomed into the quiet little alcove.

'George! How are you?' Graham was grinning from ear to ear. He bounded over, arms spread wide ready to embrace his brother. In his urgency, he ran into one of the chairs, knocking it over and then tumbled onto the table in an undignified heap. It hadn't been the quietest or most graceful of entrances, but they were together. They hugged.

'How was America?' George asked.

'Oh, it was fantastic. Better than I could have ever dreamed.'

'The business or the pleasure?' George asked cheekily. Graham laughed and they sat down.

'Both,' he said. 'I have got so much to tell you. I've been absolutely bursting to tell someone.'

'Wow. Sounds like big news,' George said. 'Are you …?'

George didn't get a chance to finish his sentence. Graham cut straight across him.

'Listen, George. Listen, I have to tell you.' He reached out and grabbed his brother's hands. He pulled them closer together and sat forward on his chair.

'While I was out there with Kerry, we did a lot of talking. Man, did we talk. We talked about everything. We remembered what we had in the beginning and we decided we want that now and forever more.' His hands gripped George's a little tighter with every sentence. He paused for a few seconds. He looked like he was just about to explode.

'Kerry and I have decided to get married.'

Graham's face lit up with an excited and radiant smile. They stood and embraced again.

'I'm so pleased for you! I really am. That's wonderful news!' George beamed.

The waiter arrived with George's mineral water, placing it on the table.

'Can I get you anything, sir?' he asked Graham. Graham looked at the mineral water and frowned.

'Yes please. Would you bring us a bottle of Laurent Perrier Rosé and two glasses, please? That *is* your favourite, isn't it, George? We have some celebrating to do,' he said triumphantly. George looked a little concerned, but convinced himself that one glass wouldn't do any harm.

'Yes, we have. It's not every day that your twin brother tells you he is getting married,' George said, shaking Graham's hands with all his might. The waiter said no more and left to get the champagne.

The crystal glasses made a beautifully pure ping as they touched.

'Cheers. Here's to you and Kerry. Couldn't happen to a nicer couple.' They raised their flutes and sipped at the bubbles.

'No one else knows. Not a soul. I haven't even told Mum and Dad. I want to tell them once Kerry gets back. He messaged me last night and hopes to be back Wednesday week. I thought we could all go over there and break the news together. But I simply couldn't keep it to myself anymore. I had to tell you.'

'Well, I'm very glad you did,' said George. 'Cheers!' They both took another sip. George was enjoying the taste. He hadn't had champagne for some time. He hadn't had any alcohol for some time.

Graham was in full flow. He was talking non-stop about the ceremony. Where it would be, who would be there, what they were planning to eat and how the evening was going to pan out. Everything from the band and seating plans to the menus and flowers. George was a mere spectator as Graham rattled off detail after detail of their planned nuptials.

The waiter approached the table again. The machine-gun fire of Graham's voice paused briefly as the waiter asked, 'Can I get you anything else, sir?' The first bottle was nearly finished and Graham was showing no signs of slowing down.

'Another one of these, please,' said George. He felt fine. He had always been able to hold his drink and one more glass wouldn't hurt him. He would let Graham finish the rest.

The waiter returned and placed the full bottle on the table. Graham didn't even pause for breath this time. George didn't know if it was the champagne or the excitement, but Graham seemed a little bit pissed already. It didn't matter. He could sleep it off at his place tomorrow. Both of them had a free day. Graham emptied the remnants of the first bottle into his glass making sure he got the very last drop out of it. He then picked up the full bottle and continued pouring. He went to fill George's glass, but George put his hand over the top.

'I'm alright for the moment, thank you.' But Graham's reactions were by now a little impaired and he splashed some champagne over his brother's fingers.

'Oops. Sorry,' said Graham slamming the bottle back into the ice bucket. He carried on talking about the church service. His voice was beginning to slur. George had drunk two and a half glasses and decided that was enough. Graham, however, seemed intent on polishing off the rest.

The time had flown by and the club had started to fill up. The music was louder and the lights on the dance floor had started to gyrate and flash in time with the bass and drums pumping out of the PA system. Although they were tucked away in their little haven, they now had to raise their voices to be heard. Graham stood up.

'I need a piss,' he shouted, getting gingerly to his feet. He wobbled off towards the gents. George caught the eye of the waiter. He thought Graham had had enough to drink and the time had come for them to leave. He picked up the two empty bottles in one hand and waved at the waiter with the other. When the waiter was close enough to be heard, he asked George if he wanted another bottle.

'No thanks. I think my brother has had enough. Can I pay for these, please?' The waiter took the two empty bottles from George.

'Yes, sir. I will be right back with your bill.' George looked around the club. It was filling up. When they had arrived, it was easy to pick out each person there as an individual. Now there was just an anonymous sea of faces. The dance floor was throbbing, the bar area was packed and every table was taken. Everybody looked like they were having a good time. He looked at his watch. 9.45. He had never left a club this early in his life before!

'Here you are, sir. I hope you enjoyed your evening.'

George paid the bill and left a handsome tip, as he always did.

'Thank you, sir,' the young waiter said as he checked the payment slip.

'Thank you very much, sir!' He looked at George with wide, surprised eyes, having seen the large gratuity George had added to the bill.

'Enjoy the rest of your evening.' As the young waiter backed out of the alcove, he nodded and smiled at George. It had taken him the entire evening to pluck up the courage to say something to him.

'And good luck on Saturday, Mr Miller.' George smiled at the boy.

'Thank you.'

He saw Graham walking back from the toilets. He was staggering a little and using every possible piece of handrail and furniture to steady himself on his way. George picked up Graham's coat and held it open, ready for him to slip his arms into. Graham tentatively climbed the two small stairs up to the alcove. He half turned his body to put his left arm in, but his foot clipped the top step and he stumbled forward. His flailing arms tried to find support from somewhere, anywhere, but there was none. As he frantically groped at thin air he slammed into the table, just as he had done on his entrance and fell forward towards his brother. Instinctively, George moved to catch him, but it was too late. Graham was going down in stages. It was like watching a tower-block demolition. He crashed into the table and then into George. The full weight of Graham's shoulder smashed into George's knee. *That knee!* George buckled under the impact and they both ended up in a heap on the floor.

'Shit. Shit. Shit,' shouted George through clenched teeth, as he felt the pain shoot through him.

'Bloody hell. Sorry, George. I think I might have had a little too much champagne. Are you okay?'

George's hands were now wrapped around his knee and his face was grimacing in pain. Graham was about to make a joke out of it, when he realised the seriousness of the situation. George was in real trouble.

'Oh, fucking hell. Is it your knee again?' George just nodded.

'Help me up and let's get out of here quickly. We can put some ice on it when we get home. I'm sure it will be okay.' Graham picked George off the floor and helped him to stand. The noise level in the bar was loud enough to have camouflaged the little commotion they had caused. A number of heads turned in their direction, but for the most part it had gone unnoticed. George tried to put his weight onto his right knee and winced. He could just about walk on it if he used Graham for support. With his coat on, collar up, scarf wrapped around his chin and his cap pulled down over his eyes, he thought they should be able to get out without any further fuss. Now he really was in disguise. Holding tightly onto his brother he limped down the few stairs and across to the bar. Keeping his gaze firmly on the floor, they headed towards the exit as anonymously as they could. Outside, George leant up against the wall while Graham hailed a taxi. The throbbing in his knee was increasing in intensity. He desperately wanted to believe he hadn't done anything too damaging to the joint. An ice pack and some rest overnight might do the trick, but in the back of his mind, in the "reality department of his brain", he knew it was probably more serious. The immediate future didn't look quite as rosy as it had done a few hours earlier.

Graham came over and offered his arm.

'Come on. I've got a taxi.'

They climbed in and made the short journey back to George's apartment. Nothing was said in the cab, nor in the lift up to the fifty-second floor. Graham took the key and opened the door.

'How's it feeling now?' he asked. By the sound of George's wincing and grunting and the expression on his face, Graham already knew the answer.

'I'm sure it will be okay,' said George with absolutely no conviction whatsoever. He collapsed onto the sofa still wearing his full disguise. He took off his hat and scarf and asked Graham to get the large bag of peas out of the freezer. When Graham returned, George had taken off his coat and was undoing his trousers. As they were lowered, they exposed his red, swollen knee. George crashed back down onto the sofa and feared the worst. The cold shock of the frozen vegetables on his leg did little to take away the pain. Both brothers looked at the problem, but neither knew what to say.

The excitement, celebration and jubilation of the last few hours had gone. The atmosphere was now flat and sombre. Eventually Graham, who had sobered up remarkably quickly, spoke.

'I'm so sorry, George. This is all my fault. I don't know what to say. I really don't.'

The damage had been done. Blame was not going to change anything or make it better. It was, after all, an accident. George listened to his brother's apologies. As devastated as George felt about the evening's events, he realised it was as much his fault as anyone else's. It was his idea to buy the second bottle of champagne and keep the party going.

'Hey, don't worry about it. It's done. I'll keep the ice on it overnight and we can see how it is in the morning. If it is still bad, then I will have to tell Bernie I slipped getting out of the bath or something like that. I really don't think I was in the shake up for the game on Saturday anyway. I was just going along for the ride, so nothing has really been lost.' George said the words. He even made them sound convincing. But he knew in his own mind he had made a huge mistake and he was utterly deflated.

26

Screwed.

There wasn't much sleep to be had at the Miller residence that night. Graham's mind was a battlefield of contrasting emotions. Kerry, the wedding, their future; and on the other side there was George, his knee and *his* future. George too was tossing and turning in his bed, the pain from his knee reminding him of the mess he was in every time he moved. He knew that any remote chance he had of playing a part in the game on Saturday was now gone. He had to accept that, but what about Bernie and Doug? He could just about manage his own disappointment, but what about theirs? He would have to tell them a lie. A believable and feasible lie. A lie that would retain their trust. On this occasion, the truth was out of the question. Even though it had been Graham who was drunk and had fallen and he had been sober and not to blame, the picture the truth would paint would have catastrophic repercussions for everyone involved. Because of his past record, he would be judged and condemned by both club and public, friends and enemies alike. There would be no mercy or consideration given to any defence or mitigating circumstances he could come up with.

He had been up several times in the night to replace the ice pack. With each trip to the freezer, he tried to convince himself that the dull throbbing ache in his right knee was beginning to recede, but by the time he climbed back into his bed he knew the pain was no better.

Both brothers were up by 7.30. Graham made the tea.

'How does it feel this morning?' he asked, without much hope of a positive reply.

'It bloody hurts,' said George. 'It does feel a little better than it did last night and the swelling has gone down a bit, but there is no way I will be able to do anything on it. I doubt I will even be able to travel with the boys to Barcelona.'

Neither of them could think of anything to say. Graham almost started to talk about Kerry and the wedding, but thought better of it.

'I'm going to try and take a shower,' George announced.

'Do you need a hand?'

'I think I can manage.'

George took a sip of his tea and stood up. With an exaggerated limp he made his way to the bathroom. Graham watched as he hobbled down the hallway.

'Shall I get the papers?'

'Yeah, if you like,' George shouted back with little interest.

Unlike Graham, who surrounded himself with the news everyday, George tended to avoid it. He had discovered to his cost that the press had very little to say regarding sport, or the people involved in it that was either true, complimentary, or constructive. He had of course supplied them with many of their front-page stories over the years. He had a love-hate relationship with the tabloids. They loved him. He hated them. As far as George was concerned, when it came to what the papers had to say, ignorance was bliss.

The shower was a struggle. Every twist and turn caused another stinging jolt of pain. He had been mulling over what he would tell Bernie. How he would break the sad news to him that after all of his hard work and dedication, he had been felled by a simple accident at home. He had to get his story perfectly sorted in his mind. Once he had done that, he could call Bernie and explain what had happened.

Graham let himself back into the apartment. He was holding a mountain of newspapers. He dropped them on the table with a loud splat.

'I bought some more peas,' Graham said triumphantly, as he removed the huge bag from beneath his jacket.

'Great. We'll all be okay now,' George smiled.

George was wearing a pair of shorts, sitting on the sofa with his leg propped up on the table, resting on a couple of cushions. The new bag of frozen peas was immediately set to work. Graham started to flick through the papers as he usually did. George's mobile suddenly buzzed into life. He picked it up and looked at the screen. *Doug Fenner.* What on earth could Doug want with him at this time in the morning? It was supposed to be a rest day for the players and it was highly unusual for anyone on the management side to interfere with the players during their downtime. George frowned at his phone, trying to think what Doug could want to talk about at such an early hour. Maybe something was wrong. Maybe Doug was calling because he had had an accident. They were very close and it wasn't beyond the realms of possibility that Doug would call him if he needed help. He answered the call as cheerfully as he could.

'Hi, Doug. How are you? Everything okay?' Doug didn't reply to any of the formal niceties.

'Tell me it's not true George. Tell me this is a mistake.'

His voice was full of emotion.

'George, don't do this to me. Not now. Tell me it's not true.' He was pleading; almost begging. George was totally confused. What was all the panic in Doug's voice for? What had happened? He didn't have a clue what he was talking about. His mind was racing to try and understand what he was hearing. George's dumbfounded face glanced up at Graham, with a bemused and confused expression. Graham had gone grey. He was ashen. He was standing there looking absolutely petrified. A wave of nausea came over George. What was happening? Within a matter of seconds, everything had gone crazy. Doug was talking nonsense and Graham looked like he had just seen a ghost. George looked at Graham again trying to make sense of it all. He was holding up one of the newspapers. There, on the inside back page, was a picture of George. He was standing in a club holding two bottles of champagne and waving his arms in the air. Below the main picture was a shot of him flat on his back clutching his right knee. The headline read, *Champagne George's Barcelona hopes float away on a sea of bubbles.* George thought he was going to throw up.

'George. George.' Doug's voice was now frantic, demanding an explanation.

'Tell me it's not true.'

He had to think fast, but even he was struggling to come up with anything that would explain the predicament he now found himself in. George opened his mouth and prayed his brain had thought of something to say. For reasons he couldn't even explain to himself, he said, 'Doug, calm down. There's been a mistake. It's not true. It's not what it looks like. Everything is fine. Just calm down. I promise you it's all nonsense.' He had told him what he had wanted to hear, but it hadn't calmed him down very much. Doug's voice had lost its normal softness. There was more of an edge to it now.

'What the fuck happened, George?' he demanded.

He wasn't used to hearing his dear old friend shout or use language like that.

'Doug, it's fine. I was out with Graham. He had some wonderful news he wanted to celebrate. He had too much champagne and got a little drunk. He fell over and that's all there is to it.'

'But, George, the article said you were carried out and unable to walk. For Christ's sake, if this is true, the shit is going to hit the fucking fan for all of us.'

George paused for thought. He had to carry on with the story he had started, but he knew it was leading him into a cul-de-sac with no means of escape.

'Doug. Graham got pissed, fell over and I had to help him down the steps. He doesn't hold his booze very well. I carried him out and we got a taxi back here. He is here with me now and feeling rather sorry for himself. Do you want to have a word with him?'

'No. I don't want to have a fucking word with Graham,' Doug snapped. It's you I'm fucking worried about.' The calming and soothing tones George was used to hearing were gone. He didn't recognise the voice on the other end of the line.

'Doug, I was on the mineral water. I am fine. Don't worry.'

There were a few seconds of silence, filled only by the sound of Doug's heavy, thoughtful breathing. George immediately started to think about the repercussions of what he had just said. A complete fabrication of the truth. Total bullshit.

'Are you sure you're okay, George? I can't make any more excuses for you. You know that.'

'I know. Listen, tell Mr Roswell and Mr Blackstone you have spoken to me and that everything is okay. Explain to them it was Graham who the reporter photographed and obviously mistook him for me. I will see you all tomorrow and you will see all is fine.'

Doug sounded a little calmer, but still not altogether convinced.

'Okay, George. If you're sure.' He hung up.

George looked over at Graham. He still had that ashen look on his face. George had taken a mighty leap out of the frying pan, but was plummeting irreparably towards the fiery furnace that would probably be the funeral pyre of his career. He was in deep, deep shit. Even the dubious and tenuous stories he was thinking of telling them, about slipping in the shower, were no use now. Graham walked around the table and sat down next to George. They both read the articles. George was being accused of premature celebrations before the team had even got to Barcelona. A frivolous and selfish party animal who had once again let his club and himself down. The script was all concocted. It had been written to suit the pictures. Pictures that even George had to admit were rather damning. The photographer had been in the club at the right time for him and the wrong time for George. A chancer. He had popped in for a drink on the off-chance of catching a glimpse of a celebrity or two. He was aware of the little dimly lit alcoves that were favoured by people who didn't want to be seen and had positioned himself at the bar directly adjacent to where George and Graham were celebrating. Seeing George was exactly what he had been hoping for. To get a shot of him waving two champagne bottles over his head was a bonus, but to snap the picture of George rolling around on the floor was the cherry on the cake. A great night for the snapper. Those pictures would make him a lot of money.

They read a couple of articles, but they all ran the same basic story. It was damning evidence for sure. No wonder Doug had been so agitated.

The situation George now found himself in was a frightening one. Not only had he fucked it up for himself, but he had lied to, and betrayed, Doug's and Bernie's confidence and trust. He had burned all his bridges. He was, up the proverbial "shit creek without a paddle" and his fucking canoe was sinking rapidly. What the hell was he going to do and what the hell was he going to say when he met Doug and Bernie face to face the next day? He was screwed. He was totally screwed.

27

Hello, George.

George changed the ice pack on his knee every hour and kept taking the anti-inflammatory tablets, but neither were performing the miracle required. Every time he stood and put weight on his knee, the pain shot through him. The reality was his career at this club was over. David Blackstone would make sure of that. The chances of any other top-flight club taking him on were slim too. No one in their right mind would want to invest in a thirty-year-old accident and injury-prone liability like him. He would be put on the transfer list and sold to the highest bidder, probably at a bargain basement price. Even worse, he might be used as a makeweight in some player-plus-cash deal to bring someone else in to replace him. He would end up in the lower leagues. A travelling novelty. A circus act. Being passed around from club to club, each one trying to squeeze the last drops of saleability from him. He would end up as a free transfer, playing in front of 800 people on a wet and windy Tuesday night in some footballing backwater most people hadn't even heard of. Twenty-four hours earlier his mind was on the Champions League Cup final with all of the glory and razzmatazz that went with it. A last huge hurrah that would have enabled him to retire in a few more years with the love, admiration and gratitude of the fans and the club. With dignity and pride in his achievements and success. Everything about his life was on the up. He had never felt more positive about his future, but now all those dreams were in tatters. Instead of honours and medals, all he had to look forward to was humiliation and shame. A slow and ungraceful slide into sporting oblivion. Ridicule and abuse from the supporters and public alike. In those few seconds, standing in that bar, everything had changed. His life had been completely turned upside down. The wounds he had inflicted on himself were almost certainly mortal. He would have to deal with that as the time passed. He tried to persuade himself that the stink from this would eventually blow over. That other bad boys would steal the spotlight and takeover the mantle of pantomime villain. It would soon be forgotten and in a few years he would be remembered as that lovable rogue; the cheeky chappie who liked a drink, who always had a gorgeous girl on his arm and was always fun to be with. All crimes and misdemeanours softened after a while. He would be asked to do TV punditry and quiz shows. Baking, dancing and cooking programmes; there was even *that bloody jungle* if he was really desperate. Retired celebrities rarely vanished completely from view. Actors, singers, sports personalities, even crusty old politicians, they were all at it. Apart from the nagging questions he would always be asking himself regarding what might have been, he would survive. He would come out the other side bruised but not beaten.

However, there was something even worse than *his* immediate plight to consider. Something even worse than the demise of his career. Doug and Bernie. What about them? They had stuck by him in the face of growing and sometimes unbearable pressure. They had trusted him and he had let them down. How would this reflect on them? Would David Blackstone feel the need to gain retribution for all the times they had ignored his views on George? That was something he couldn't influence. What he was struggling to come to terms with was that he had compounded the stupidity of the night before by lying. Trying to buy himself some time. He had panicked and made the situation ten times worse. They would both be furious with him and rightly so. They had given him one last chance to prove himself and he had blown it. George was genuinely fond of them both and it hurt him deeply to think of the damage he had done to his relationship with them. He had let them down in the most public of ways. Embarrassed and humiliated them. And now he had lied to them. Would either of them be able to forgive him or want anything to do with him in the future? He doubted it. The pain in his knee was nothing compared to the pain he was feeling in his heart.

The brothers sat opposite one another. The atmosphere was lugubrious. To add to the gloom, the day outside was another monotone, damp, miserable canvas.

Graham tried to lighten the mood by bringing up stories from their past, but smiles and laughter were rare commodities in George's apartment that morning.

'Do you see or hear anything from Debbie Morris these days?' Graham asked.

George recounted their meeting in Newcastle some seven years earlier but told him he hadn't had any contact with her since, apart from a few postcards.

'I wonder what she is doing at this very moment,' mused Graham. 'I've searched for her a few times on social media, but she doesn't show up anywhere. Maybe she is under a married name. Anyway, she has proved to be quite elusive. A bit like you, George. You never really went in for all that social media malarky, did you?' Speaking about Debbie did lighten the mood a little. George couldn't help but smile when she was in his head. They remembered "The Switch" they had played that enabled George to meet Debbie outside the school gates and how it had infuriated Frankie De Costa. And what of Frankie De Costa? Whatever happened to him? What was he doing now? Probably a ten to twelve stretch in Brixton Prison. Graham stood up, walked around the table and sat next to his brother.

'Why don't we see if we can find him? He should be relatively easy to locate with a name like De Costa.'

He picked up his pad and tapped in the name. A number of options came up on screen. More than they had imagined.

'My god!' said George. 'One Frankie De Costa was enough! There must be at least fifteen here.'

Graham scrolled through each one. Frankie De Costa, civil servant lives and works in Birmingham. Definitely not. Father Frankie De Costa, Anglican priest in Bristol.

'Don't think so,' said Graham. 'Wait a minute, what about this one?'

There was a picture of a man, about thirty years old, with a rather forced smile, a face that looked very much like a weasel and a very familiar glint in his eye. Sure enough, it was him. Same school, same age, same old Frankie. Graham scrolled down further to try and learn more about their old adversary.

'By the look of it he works in construction,' said Graham, but that was all they could find out. Neither of them wanted to get back in touch with him so they would have to make do with that. If only they could have found something on Debbie Morris, George thought. How he would love to see her again.

They chuckled and laughed at the old stories and for a short while managed to take their minds away from the mess they were in.

By the late afternoon the memories of the twins' antics and pranks had stopped and the TV was on. It was showing one of George's favourite black and white movies, *A Tale of Two Cities*. It had been a long day and they were both emotionally drained. Graham watched as Sydney Carton approached the guillotine, having taken the place of Charles Darnay.

"It is a far, far better thing that I do, than I have ever done; it is a far, far better rest I go to than I have ever known".

A grunt came from across the room. It was George; he had fallen asleep. He was lying on the sofa, head back and mouth open. In the film, Sydney Carton paid the ultimate price and Charles Darnay would reap the ultimate reward. The following day George would be paying a heavy price. Maybe not the ultimate price, but a price from which his career would not recover.

Graham clicked the TV off and wandered into the bathroom to take a pee. While he was washing his hands, he looked up at his reflection in the mirror. They were different now. He had a thick mop of black hair and a bushy beard of which he was very proud. He stroked the beard from his cheeks to his chin. He had grown accustomed to it. It had become an integral part of who he was. It defined him more than anything else. By the side of the sink, next to the toothpaste, were George's grooming tools. Everything he needed to keep his hair short and his chin clean. Razors, trimmers, foam, the lot. Graham looked at himself in the mirror again. He stared deeply into his reflection's eyes, almost looking for permission. He had made a decision. A drastic decision. He took one last loving look at his facial hair, took a deep breath, then went to work. It was a messy business. The trimmings and shavings went everywhere. It took him longer than he had anticipated. Once he had finished and tidied up the mess, he had been in there for about forty minutes. He took another look in the mirror. This time the man looking back at him was someone else. It was his brother. Even Graham was shocked. He could hardly believe it. For the last few years Graham had had his own identity. He and George were separate people, but now they were one again. There was nothing to tell them apart. He stroked his face where his beard used to be and rubbed his head where his black mop once sat. He smiled and greeted his reflection.

'Hello, George.'

From the lounge he heard George's waking voice.

'Graham. Graham, where are you?'

'I'm in here. Won't be a moment,' he shouted back. Graham steadied himself at the bathroom door. He opened it and strolled down the hallway towards the lounge. As soon as he came into view, a look of horror snapped across George's face. His eyes almost popped out of his head. He sat bolt upright as if an electric current had passed through his body.

'Oh my god!' he exclaimed. 'What the fuck have you done?'

Graham paused for a moment. *What had he done?*

'I've given us the option. I am George Miller. Identical in every detail apart from one. I have a working right knee.'

George's eyes were still bulging in their sockets. They stared at each other in silence for a few seconds, both shocked and amazed at the re-emergence of the "identical twin". Having had years to get used to the hirsute Graham, the reincarnation of the "doppelganger", had left them both momentarily speechless. After a few seconds of stunned silence, Graham spoke.

'George. I got you into this. The least I can do is give you the only possible option there is to get out of it unscathed. Think hard, Brother. If you don't want to do it, say now. There is no permanent damage done yet. Hair grows back. It's just an option, but from where I stand, it's the only one we have, apart from the truth.'

George did think long and hard. It was an option that hadn't even crossed his mind. It was ridiculous to think that a prank they pulled at school for their own amusement so many years ago, could possibly save his career and reputation now. When they were younger, they were identical in every way, but over the last twelve years they had become separate people. Their personalities and characters had changed. Their lifestyles had taken them on different journeys. It was undeniable that without the hair they still looked incredibly similar, but would that be enough to fool his team-mates and the management? He stared at his brother. He was staring at himself. Could it work? Did it really stand any chance of success? They both realised they were playing for high stakes. If they could pull it off, it would get them out of the deepest hole imaginable. If they failed, the consequences were unthinkable. It would mean a lifetime ban for George and criminal proceedings for both of them. When they pulled "The Switch" before, it was for fun. Getting caught was never something they were concerned about. It would have meant a dressing down from teachers, maybe even their parents, but nothing to be too worried about. If they were to try it now, the risks and the rewards were immense. They would be gambling everything. George would lose all of the respect and affection he had built up over the years. He certainly wouldn't be allowed to morph into the lovable rogue that would be invited into TV punditry or bake-offs. And Graham? He wouldn't escape unscathed. It would be an ugly and uncomfortable time for him as well. They would forever be linked to the scandal no matter how much facial hair either of them grew.

George's disbelieving stare remained fixed on Graham. It really was like looking in the mirror. He had forgotten just how alike they were. What if they could pull it off? It would solve all his problems. They could never tell anyone about it, not even their parents. Not even Kerry. They would have to take the secret to their graves. Could it really work? They had never been rumbled before.

For the rest of the afternoon they sat together discussing the pros and cons.

The more they talked about it, the more their excitement and adrenaline levels rose. Every question they raised seemed to have an answer; every possible problem, a solution. Graham would take George's passport, mobile phone and all of his personal belongings. Graham would leave all of his with George. Graham would have to avoid any unnecessary contact or conversation with his teammates. The less said, the less chance of any slip-up. He would have to keep as low a profile as possible. George would have to stay in his apartment until Graham returned. He should answer the buzzer to no one. Neither of them should answer their phones unless it was absolutely necessary. George would have to bring Graham up to speed with the players in the squad. Who they were, where they were from and everything he knew about them. Recent conversations he had had. In-jokes and nicknames. The names of players' wives and children. Anything he could think of that might come up in a conversation. It would be like a military operation. Planned down to the last detail. They were both excited and fearful. The more they talked, the more they convinced each other this crazy and ridiculous scheme could work, but talking about it was one thing, actually physically doing it was completely and terrifyingly different.

If they were to go through with it, Graham's first hurdle would be to go along to training the next day. To mix with the players and coaching staff for a few hours and prove to them that George Miller's knee was in good shape. If he could get through that without arousing suspicion, then they might just stand a chance. It *was* the only option they had.

28

All part of the plan.

Graham knew his way around the training ground. He had been a few times before with George, but those visits were made as an onlooker, a spectator, a guest. This time it was very different. He would normally have a chat with Doug, remembering old times. On more than one occasion, Doug had tried to persuade him to put his boots back on and come in for a try-out. He had always rated Graham very highly. George was the flamboyant maverick who could produce something breathtaking and spectacular, but Graham was solid, reliable and hard-working. On his previous visits Graham had been relaxed and jovial, talking and laughing with both players and staff. This time he was as nervous and on edge as he had ever been in his life. Driving through the gates, the security guards greeted him as Mr Miller. A victory, if only a small one. He had arrived early to avoid as much contact with the other players as possible. He headed straight to the changing rooms and put George's kit and boots on. As he stepped onto the grass, he could see a steady stream of other people arriving. Some he recognised, some he didn't.

'Hi, George. How's the knee?' someone shouted. Graham just waved in the general direction of the voice and gave a thumbs up. In the cold light of day, Graham wondered whether this was such a good idea after all.

The plan was to complete the training session, to prove to Doug that everything was alright and his fears over the newspaper articles were unnecessary. Graham would then return to George's apartment. They were still hanging on to the slight hope that another day of rest would have the desired effect, making it possible for George to travel to Barcelona with the others. If he could walk and act as if all was well, he could always claim a twinge once they were there or fake a slip between departure and kick-off that would render him sadly unavailable. This, however, was all about proving to Doug that the pictures and stories in the tabloids were false and that he was fit and raring to go.

Graham started to jog around the perimeter to warm up. This was not something George was known to do voluntarily.

Steve Denton was putting cones out in the middle of one of the pitches. Denton was Doug's right-hand man; the drill sergeant. Doug would bark out the orders from the sidelines and organise things, but his ageing legs found it hard to keep up with the rigorous workouts he imposed on his players. Denton was the one who cracked the whip. He was a typical Aussie. Hardnosed, straight talking and incredibly competitive. He was as irreverent as they came and didn't mince his words. If he thought you were slacking, he would tell you in his own inimitable way, whether you were a superstar or a novice. He did everything with a smile and a laugh, even when he was slagging you off. He was the one who would come out with the expletives.

"Fuckin' brilliant, mate! You're fuckin' world class!", or, "You fuckin' lazy bastard. Come on, get those legs pumping and earn some of ya fuckin' wages".

The players all loved him. As with most Aussies, what you saw was what you got and he didn't give a shit whether you liked it or not. He loved his job, he loved the club and he loved the players.

Denton looked up and saw Graham.

'Hey, George, here a minute.' Graham jogged over. He had only spoken to Denton a couple of times in the past. Another test.

'Hi, mate. How ya doing? Great to see you fit and well. There was a nasty rumour that you had fucked yourself up again.'

'They'll write anything to sell their mags,' said Graham dismissively. 'As you can see every word of it was true.' They both laughed. 'It was my brother who took the fall. He had drunk a little too much champagne and took a tumble.'

'Ah, yeah. Your brother. You two look alike, don't ya? I remember him now. Graham, isn't it?'

'That's right. Is Doug about?'

'Ah, no. Just me this morning. Bernie has meetings all day and Doug has been called away on some personal stuff. His mother's been taken ill and he's had to go and see her. He asked me to check on you and make sure everything was okay. He told me I should call him as soon as training finished and give him an update on everyone. Especially you. We're only going to do some light stuff today, so we shouldn't be putting too much stress on that fuckin' knee of yours. See you in a minute.'

Graham started his jogging again. By now most of the other players had changed and were warming up as well. There was the usual banter between them, but Graham kept his input to a minimum.

The training session lasted about two hours. There was nothing too strenuous and certainly no contact. They didn't want to accidentally lose anyone to injury at this late stage. As the players wandered back to the changing rooms, Graham decided to do a few more laps. It would keep him out of their way while they were changing. It was all part of the plan.

Graham was fit. Probably fitter than George and some of his teammates and the less eye contact or conversations he had with them, the better.

After about half an hour, Graham saw the players leaving the training ground. They shouted and waved at him.

'See you tomorrow, George. Don't wear yourself out.' Graham just waved and kept on running.

'George! George!' Denton shouted from the other side of the pitch.

'I've got Doug on the phone. He wants a quick word.'

Graham was slightly breathless. He took the phone from Denton.

'Hi, Doug, how are you? Sorry to hear about your mother. How is she?'

'I'm alright, thank you, George, and Mum is doing okay. Steve tells me you had a good session today. It sounds from your voice that you are still at it.'

'Well, I thought I would put in a couple of extra laps. Try to get the stamina levels up, you know.'

'Alright, but don't kill yourself. Don't overdo it, son. Listen, I'm sorry I couldn't be there today, but I'm glad you're okay. You had me and Bernie worried yesterday. When we saw those pictures and read those articles, well, you can't blame us for thinking the worst, can you? I can tell you, George, if those reports had been true the shit would have really hit the fan for all of us. Bernie had Blackstone ranting and raving on the phone, telling him you were finished at the club and promising to make an example of you. I can't tell you what a relief it is to hear that you are fit and well. I will see you tomorrow. Oh, and George.' Doug left a pause. 'Remember what Bernie said. Don't forget your boots. Just in case.' Doug let out a soft laugh.

'I won't' chuckled Graham.

Graham gave the phone back to Denton. The session had passed without incident. He showered and changed, then headed back to George's apartment. He had never liked the Maserati George coveted so much. Graham thought it pretentious and garish and wished he hadn't had to drive it, but it was all part of the plan, as was wearing George's clothes, watch, shoes and cologne.

On the journey, Graham stopped at a supermarket to get some basic supplies for George. He had forgotten he was now "George Miller, the famous footballer". Without the protection of his hair and beard, he had exposed himself to the celebrity-hungry public. He had become used to the anonymity his beard had provided, being able to go through life unmolested and unnoticed, but now that protection was gone. He was recognised by several shoppers who all insisted on having photographs taken with him and having various items signed. Someone even asked him to sign their box of cornflakes. He obliged them all in turn, thanking them for their good luck wishes and giving his opinion on the game to come. They all hung on his every word, like disciples listening to a holy man. After what seemed like an eternity, he finally got back into George's car and sped away from all of the attention. He was slowly becoming his brother.

George was eager to know how the day had gone. He had a thousand questions to ask. They sat down together and Graham recounted every detail, every word and every encounter he'd had. Once he had finished telling him everything, including his time at the supermarket, they both sat back into the sofa. George rubbed his hands together.

'Well, it would seem stage one is complete,' he said, rather melodramatically. 'Roll on stage two.'

Graham looked at George. He seemed almost excited at the prospect.

'How is the knee? Do you think you will be able to travel to Barcelona?'

The answer was the one he had expected.

'I can't really put much weight on it at all,' George replied solemnly. 'I guess we are in this all the way. Now they have seen me, …I mean you, train, they will expect me to be at least able to walk without a limp.'

The wheels were now fully in motion. What they had started would have to be played out until its conclusion. There really was no turning back. That realisation, simultaneously, sent a shiver of excitement and fear up both of their spines.

The brothers spent the rest of the day and most of the evening going over every possible scenario that might crop up. In-jokes with other players, nicknames, secret stories, tactics that had been learned, systems and plan Bs. Everything that George could think of, he wrote down and Graham tried to memorise. The heady cocktail of exhilaration, anticipation and sheer terror was enough to get both of their hearts beating a little faster than usual. They knew there was a very thin line between success and failure. Success would bring about the great escape George needed to ensure he had a future career. The ramifications of failure were so dreadful they didn't allow themselves to dwell on them for too long.

On Thursday morning, the cab arrived to collect George. The brothers embraced one last time and went through their checklists. Passport, wallet, phone, George's of course, and all the other paraphernalia that would normally accompany George on his foreign forays.

'What's Casey King's nickname?' George asked.

'Stella,' answered Graham.

'And where is he from?'

'Washington, USA.'

Graham batted the quick-fire, last-minute questions back with confidence. It was now or never. The green light had come on and it was time to metaphorically parachute into enemy territory.

'Good luck, Graham. And thank you,' said George. Graham didn't reply. He just smiled and shut the door. This would be the most nerve-wracking four days of their lives.

The cab driver was very chatty as they always were. He asked "George" how his knee was. Did he know if he was going to start the game? Who was fit, and who wasn't? What did he think of their chances? As Graham got out of the taxi, the driver stuck his head out of the window.

'Good luck, Mr Miller.' He paused. 'Good luck, George. Bring that trophy home.'

Graham nodded, smiled and waved at him as he drove off.

All the players and staff at training, the people in the supermarket, the car park attendants, security men and now the cabbie had all believed they were dealing with George. So far so good, but Graham knew there would be tougher tests to come.

He made his way to the conference room where the team and management were due to meet. As he walked across the car park towards the offices, he could hear someone shouting. A girl's voice. He scanned the horizon and saw a young lady waving at him out of a second-floor window. It was Brenda. He recognised her from her picture in the papers when she had been snuggled up to George. George had told him about Brenda.

'Good luck, George,' she said and blew him a kiss. Graham waved back and returned the gesture.

'Thank you! See you when I get back.'

By the time Graham reached the conference room, most of the other people were there. Doug saw him and walked over. He put his hand on Graham's arm.

'Sorry about all the panic, George, but it did give us a hell of a fright. Glad to see you're okay. We'll talk later.'

Doug patted the side of Graham's face and went back to join Bernie and David Blackstone at the front. Graham noticed David staring at him. He was looking at him suspiciously. Almost accusingly. Surely, he wasn't going to be the one to expose their plan. Graham contented himself that David's look was more frustration than anything else. A look from someone who thought they had got their man, only to discover he had slipped through their fingers. Graham smiled back at the slightly disgruntled face. *If only you knew,* he thought.

Graham spotted a chair at the back of the room and went to sit down. The briefing was standard and straightforward. Blackstone informed them in his "headmasterly" way of their responsibilities as ambassadors of the club. He told them what was expected and what was not expected of them. Graham felt sure that when David Blackstone talked about misbehaviour not being tolerated, he was looking straight at him. He was beginning to understand George's dislike of the man. Blackstone wished everyone the best of luck and sat down to a polite smattering of applause. Bernie then started to speak. He spoke about the opposition, their strengths and weaknesses. He talked about his team and their strengths. He was hoping to play the same system as he had in Milan. There would of course be a few personnel changes as so many more players were now available. Graham's stomach was rumbling. He felt nervous. He felt Bernie's eyes were on him when he mentioned changes. He started to think he was becoming paranoid. Even though he was sitting at the back of the room, it felt like everyone was looking at him.

When they were given the chance to ask questions, Graham kept his hands down and his mouth shut.

The players and staff filed out of the room and down the stairs. There were two large coaches waiting for them in the car park. The players and management boarded one and all the officials from the club boarded the other. They were off to Heathrow.

Graham sat down next to a window and placed his small bag on the seat next to him. There was plenty of room on the coach and he was keen to remain on his own for as long as possible. He shut his eyes and hoped people would think he was asleep. Most of the others were quiet and subdued as well, even the more exuberant ones amongst them.

Once the journey had begun and Graham was sure of his solitude, he opened his eyes and looked out. He watched the world going by. People, shops, cars and buses all going about their daily business. All of them looking like they didn't have a care in the world. And here he was, on the other side of the glass with the weight of *that* world on his shoulders.

The sight of low-flying aircraft coming into land suggested they were not far from the airport. Graham's peace was suddenly interrupted when Doug plonked himself on the seat beside him.

'Sorry to disturb you, George. Haven't had much chance to talk what with everything going on. How's the knee? Steve said you looked really good in training.'

'It's okay, Doug, thanks. It could still do with another couple of weeks before it is totally match fit, but I'm sure it will be fine for the start of next season.'

Doug looked a little disappointed with Graham's answer. Steve Denton had told him that George Miller looked fitter and sharper than he had seen him for a while and in his opinion, was ready to go. So much so that Doug and Bernie had been considering him for a starting role.

But the last thing either George or Graham wanted was any unnecessary exposure. If George Miller's name didn't feature on the team sheet that would be fine by them.

'Okay, George. Better get back to Bernie,' Doug said slightly mournfully. He wandered back down the aisle and sat next to the manager. As they spoke, Graham saw Bernie turn his head and look at him. Maybe Doug was relating his answer regarding his knee and his fitness and how he still felt there was room for improvement. Bernie looked away as soon as he saw Graham staring at him. He nodded his head several times as Doug continued to talk in what looked like a soft whisper into Bernie's ear.

The coach pulled up at the terminal and they all disembarked.

Their time at the airport was short and hectic. Check in, passport control, security, then on to the BA first-class lounge to await boarding. Each time Graham caught Doug's eye, he smiled and nodded in what he hoped was a reassuring way.

It was soft drinks, tea or coffee only on offer. The bountiful choice of champagne, wines, beers and spirits were all off limits to them. Graham sat down with a cup of tea and plugged in his earphones. Fifteen minutes later, they were being escorted onto the plane. Graham kept his eyes to the ground and his earphones in. He nodded and smiled at the pretty stewardess who welcomed him aboard and showed him to his seat. He sat down and looked out of the small window. Rain had started to fall. He watched as the men and women in their high-vis coats and vests shone out against the greyness of the day.

'How's it going, George?'

Casey King, or, "Stella" to his mates, had sat down in the next seat. Casey was the goalkeeper. A large and genial American. He was highly educated and could speak several languages fluently. He also had an impressive knowledge of the stars and all things astronomical, hence his nickname. Graham knew from his briefing that Casey was a very good friend of George's. He looked up at the huge bulk beside him and smiled.

'All good here, Stella,' he said. 'How about you?'

'Yeah, George, all great. Can't wait. How's that damn knee of yours?'

'Oh, you know, so-so,' Graham said, trying hard not to oversell it. 'I think I'm only here for moral support.'

'I don't know about that, George,' Casey said laughing. 'We need you. Proper old-style centre forward. Those foreign Johnnies hate it when we play with a real "number 9". I'll bet you get a crack at them at some point.'

Casey was being kind. Graham hoped his confidence was misplaced. He needed to be unseen, unheard and unnoticed. The more time he could spend anonymously the more chance he had of pulling it off.

Graham clicked his seat belt shut and closed his eyes again. He would spend most of the flight looking at the inside of his eyelids. That was also part of the plan.

29

Remember to sign "George".

To Graham's great relief, the rest of the flight was uneventful. The only contact he had was from the British Airways cabin crew who were offering refreshments. With his headphones in, he quietly, casually and politely declined. Casey had his earpieces in too and like Graham, was lost in his own world. At some point during the next two and a half hours, Graham must have dozed off. He was woken by the pretty, smiling face of the stewardess making sure his seat belt was fastened for landing.

Once they had touched down, their entourage was herded at great speed, like a flock of sheep, through passport control, baggage-reclaim and customs.

A large crowd was waiting to welcome them as they passed into the main airport building. Thousands of fans had already made the journey from England to see the game. They mingled with the locals, some of whom were also fans and some who just wanted to catch a glimpse of the footballing superstars on show. As they emerged into the arrivals hall, the noise level increased. The waiting crowds were cheering and calling out the names of their idols. Most of them were waving pictures and magazines they wanted signing. Graham didn't want to be aloof, but thought it best he stayed where he was, in the middle of the scrum as hidden from view as possible. The security guards were doing a good job of funnelling them towards the exit and their awaiting coaches. About fifty metres from the doors, a few of the players began to peel away from the herd and interact with the crowd. Graham suddenly became a little more exposed as his wingmen, Pascal, Igor and Casey, all drifted towards their adoring fans.

'George! George!'

Graham heard a young boy's voice calling. He couldn't help but glance over. There stood a boy, about ten years old. He was bedecked in the team's colours, with a replica shirt, baseball cap and scarf. He was eagerly waving a large colour print of George "in action" that had obviously been rolled up tightly during its journey from England. Once Graham had made eye contact, he felt obliged to go over and talk to him. He knew George would have done so. One of the things that made George so popular with the fans was his willingness to spend time with them and not to be too elusive. The boy was standing in front of a man who had his hands on his shoulders. Graham assumed it must have been his father. He was also dressed in a replica team shirt. Graham smiled at the boy. The father then joined in.

'Please George!' he shouted, holding his son's arm and helping him wave the curled-up picture. Graham broke ranks and wandered over to them. The excitement in the boy's face was magical. Even the father appeared a little in awe. Graham felt very important. He was making this boy's day just by signing his name onto a photograph. The lad handed Graham the picture and his father offered a pen. Remember to sign "George", Graham thought as the pen hovered over the print. Graham's ability to replicate George's autograph had been honed over many years. It was always a perfect copy. He signed it and passed it back.

'Thank you, Mr Miller,' said the father. The boy was busy looking at his prize, staring lovingly at his picture. Graham turned to rejoin the group, but within seconds he had a swarm of boys, girls, men and women pushing and shoving to get close to him, all wanting something signed. Mobile phones and small cameras were flashing constantly and the din of voices pleading with him to sign here or there seemed to get louder and louder. Ladies wanting him to sign their shirts were thrusting their chests at him. Children and adults totally in awe of him. This was a hell of a life his brother was living. Graham realised just how intoxicating it must be. He had always been aware that sportsmen and women were treated like demigods, but he was rather taken aback by the sheer hysteria and adulation being shown. It was no wonder, he thought, that so many celebrities had such massive egos. They were having them massaged at every turn. George had somehow managed to keep his feet on the ground over the years and had a reputation for being accessible and friendly and he was loved for it. Graham signed as many pictures, shirts, and ladies' breasts as he could, before he was bustled away by the security guards and onto the coach with the rest of the players. As they drove away from the airport towards their hotel, the crowds cheered and waved. He waved back at them. It was almost a regal wave. A wave that might be seen from the balcony of Buckingham Palace. What an adrenaline rush and that was just the airport.

Looking out of the window, he saw the local people going about their daily business, just as they had been back in London several hours earlier. Only here they were doing it in bright sunshine. It was a beautiful day. At last, the world had some colour to it.

Their hotel was a grand affair situated on the seafront; a tall and imposing building that oozed luxury. Inside, it was plush, swish and swanky. On his travels Graham had stayed in some very fine hotels, but this one was far more impressive than any he had been in before. The decoration, the lighting from the massive and imposing chandeliers hanging from the high muralled ceilings, the furniture, the huge paintings and the atmosphere all added to the grandeur.

The five-star rooms were from the seventeenth floor upwards. Graham was told he was in a room on the twenty-second floor, sharing with Igor. Igor was a good friend of George's and had been since his arrival at the club. The big Croatian defender had a reputation as a ladies' man and a playboy back in his home country. He and George had hit it off immediately. George had briefed Graham well about Igor. They were normally paired together on foreign trips.

There was a rooftop bar on the twenty-fourth floor for the exclusive use of the five-star guests. From there, the 360-degree views of Barcelona and beyond were spectacular, including the football stadium away to the north east.

After settling into their room, they were told they should be in the restaurant for dinner by 7.p.m. Graham lay down on one of the two king-size beds in the room and grinned. Worryingly, he realised he was actually starting to enjoy this. The nerves and trepidation he had felt at the beginning were slowly disappearing. He had seen and talked to both Doug and Bernie, albeit briefly, and they hadn't noticed anything odd. He had interacted with most of the players including Igor and Casey who knew George better than most and neither had suspected a thing. The fans at the airport had accepted him as George and the passport man had waived him through without a second glance. There were obviously going to be more tests ahead but surely, he thought, he was over the worst. The biggest danger now was his growing confidence and self-belief. He had to maintain his concentration and constantly remind himself of the dangers and consequences of any slip-up.

'Just be George,' he said to himself under his breath. 'Just be George.'

At dinner Graham sat between Terry Bridges and Pascal Mingard, two very contrasting characters. Terry, the captain, was a true leader. He was a local south London boy who had the club in his blood. Tough and as hard as nails, he was known for his ferocious tackling and hard talking. His long black curly hair gave him the appearance of a pirate, swashbuckling in every way. Straight talking, no nonsense and solid. He was the beating heart of the team and if he didn't think you were giving your all he would let you know in no uncertain terms, regardless of your standing or reputation. The one thing you always got from Terry was "everything". He led by example and would drag others with him if necessary. Pascal, on the other hand, was a softly spoken, quiet and typical Frenchman. He loved the finer things in life; fine food, fine champagne and fine wines. He always dressed in designer clothes and shoes, even managing to look more stylish than everyone else in his tracksuit and kit. He too was a bit of a ladies' man, but in a far more subtle way than either George or Igor. He had a style and class about him that was inherently Parisian, whilst possessing the looks of a Hollywood film star. He was lean and fast. Streamlined. If Terry was the tank in their armoury, Pascal was the jet fighter.

The banter during the meal was jolly and friendly. The atmosphere was relaxed and as far as everyone in the room was concerned, George Miller was back in the family.

As it approached ten o'clock, Doug stood up and suggested the boys head off to their rooms; like a father telling his sons it was time for bed. He wouldn't be tucking them in or reading them a story, but it was that time and to a man they dutifully obliged.

Graham sent a text to George. *Bit difficult to talk. Sharing a room with Igor. So far all going well. No one suspects a thing. Will call tomorrow when I get a chance. G.*

He clicked off the light by his bed and the room fell into darkness. He said goodnight to Igor and wondered what the next few days would bring.

30

Is it George, or is it Graham?

Training on Friday was hard, but invigorating. Graham relished all the physical challenges that were given to him. He ran hard and fast and put every ounce of effort he could into it. It felt great competing with professional athletes. He was surprised to discover that he was in fact fitter and stronger than some of the first-team regulars. In a sprint against Pascal, Graham was only just pipped at the post. The French jet fighter had had a run for his money. Graham panted and drew in deep breaths after the sixty-metre charge against the Frenchman. With his hands on his knees, he glanced up and caught Doug looking at him. Doug had a huge smile on his face and gave Graham a double thumbs up, nodding with excitement. Graham straightened himself up and nodded back. It suddenly dawned on him that by looking so good, there was a chance he might be putting himself in the frame for a starting place on the team. That was not part of the plan. He had been so wrapped up in his need to compete and test himself against these elite athletes, he had taken his eye off the real goal. He had rather shot himself in the foot. In his mind it had become a game to him, but it wasn't a game; it was a mission and he had to refocus quickly and get that mission back on track. It called for a change of tack. Ten minutes later, when Graham was sure Doug was watching him, he pulled up from his jog and started to rub his right knee. The grimace on his face suggested pain and discomfort. He didn't have to wait long before he saw Doug jogging over towards him with a concerned look on his face.

'What's up, George?'

Graham looked up to see not only Doug's concern, but massive disappointment in his eyes.

'Come on, let's get you out of here and put some ice on that knee straight away.'

Graham followed him off the pitch and into the changing rooms putting on a slight limp. He felt ashamed of himself for tricking the old man, but it had to be done. The entire masquerade had to be kept intact at all costs. Even at the expense of a dear friend's hopes and dreams.

'I'm sure it will be fine,' Graham said without trying to sound too convincing.

'At least you have a full squad to choose from. An embarrassment of riches.'

Doug nodded but couldn't hide the deflation of his spirit.

'True, George. But there is nothing like a bit of experience, especially in the big games.'

Graham spent the last half an hour of the session on the sidelines with an ice pack strapped to his right knee. He watched as the other players were put through their paces.

Casey King and Bryan Keller, the second-choice keeper, were being tested with crosses and shots by Steve Denton. Bernie was busy with another group that included Igor and the defensive players while Doug was barking orders at the rest of them.

It was a beautiful sunny day without being too hot. Graham sat back, clasped his hands behind his head and relaxed.

It was looking like their plan had a good chance of succeeding. Everyone he had seen and spoken to so far were content that they were dealing with George. The winning post was getting tantalisingly closer.

Dinner in the hotel that night was much the same as it had been the night before. There was a little more tension in the air and the frivolity and ribaldry were less evident. In twenty-four hours time, the game would be just about to start. One of the biggest games in the club's history. The nerves were beginning to show on the faces of both the players and the management.

Graham didn't know if it was coincidence or superstition that made everyone sit in exactly the same place as they had the night before. Once again, he was between Terry and Pascal, but the conversation was more subdued. At about nine o'clock, Bernie stood up and tapped his fork against his glass. The room instantly fell silent.

'Gentlemen, I don't have to tell you how important tomorrow's game is. It is a magnificent achievement to have made it this far considering what we have been through in the last couple of months, but finishing second is not what we are here to do. I know we will start as the underdogs and that suits me fine, but we will not be going into the game thinking like underdogs. I know we have the talent in this room to win tomorrow and I fully expect us to do so. If you believe in yourselves and your teammates and perform like I know you can, I really believe we will be taking that wonderful trophy back to London with us. I believe in you. We all believe in you.' He spread his arms and cast his eyes over the men and women sitting at the "top table".

There was a smattering of "hear, hear's" and tables being patted in response. Bernie continued.

'Get a good night's sleep and try to channel all of your concentration and focus into the game for the next twenty-four hours or so. Then hopefully the celebrations will begin. The bar is open, but soft drinks only, please. Show some restraint tonight and tomorrow we can all let our hair down. Well, those of you that still have some to let down, that is.'

Bernie raised his eyes as if to inspect his own balding pate. A ripple of applause and laughter circled the room. 'Goodnight, gentlemen. I will see you all at breakfast at 8.30.'

With that, Bernie, Doug and some of the other backroom staff disappeared to make their final preparations for the game.

Pascal looked at Graham.

'*Café*, George?'

'Why not?' replied Graham.

The bar was quiet. A few of the players had wandered off to kill some time, most had gone to their rooms. Pascal and Graham sat at a small table and looked out into the night. Barcelona was all lit up and looked wonderful. Their conversation centred mainly on the game, the opposition and of course, George's knee. Graham was finding it surprisingly easy to take on his brother's identity.

Conversations and interactions were now becoming almost second nature to him. He was quietly congratulating himself on how well he was doing as he sipped his coffee and gazed out at the twinkling city. All was peaceful and silent.

A loud booming voice from behind him shattered the tranquillity.

'George Miller. George Miller... Or is it really Graham Miller?'

In an instant Graham's blood froze in his veins. He felt a shiver run up his neck. He felt faint and dizzy; naked and exposed. The muscles in his chest tightened and he found it hard to breathe. He thought he was going to throw up. He didn't recognise the voice. He knew it wasn't Doug's or Bernie's and was pretty sure it wasn't one of his teammates. But it didn't matter whose voice it was. That one sentence had reduced him to a bag of nerves. All of the confidence and bravado that had been building within him since he drove through the training ground gates on Wednesday morning had been extinguished in an instant. For the first time since they had left London, Graham could feel beads of sweat forming on his face and neck and the terror of exposure consuming him. He wanted to turn around and confront his accuser, but he was too scared. Once again, the voice sounded. This time he could tell the person was standing right behind him.

'So, is it George, or is it Graham?' the voice quizzically asked again. Graham's face had turned bright red, his hands had become clammy and he had started to tremble. He could feel his heart beating louder and faster. Pascal looked at Graham with both concern and confusion in his eyes.

'George. It's me,' the voice continued, as a hand landed on Graham's shoulder with a thud. Graham nervously turned and looked up to see who it could be, with more fear in his body than he had ever felt.

'It's me. Your old mate Frankie. Frankie De Costa. You remember, from school.' Graham looked incredulously at the man now standing beside him. He wasn't sure who he had expected it to be, but Frankie De Costa was definitely not someone he had considered. He didn't know whether to laugh or cry. A weasel-like face with a broad grin stared back at him as he desperately tried to regain some composure.

'You remember me, George. Christ, we used to have some wild old times back in the day.' Frankie turned to the three men with him.

'We've got some stories to tell, ain't we George?' he laughed, patting Graham boisterously on the back.

Graham was still in a state of shock and couldn't think of anything to say. Of all the possible scenarios they had prepared for back in George's apartment, this was not one. After what seemed like an age, he managed to talk.

'Frankie. What are you doing here?'

Frankie went on to explain that he and his mates were over to watch the match. He told Graham they were all big fans of both him and the club. They had paid top dollar for the trip which included match tickets, five-star accommodation and hospitality. It had cost them all a lot of money and they were determined to get full value for their cash. Frankie had done rather well for himself since leaving school. He owned "De Costa Construction" and lived a pretty comfortable existence. He had smartened himself up over the years. Success had bought him nice clothes and he was bedecked in heavy gold jewellery. He was obviously still the leader of the gang even though Robbo and Baz had been replaced by a more executive-looking mob. Graham's heartbeat was slowing down and his urge to puke was receding, but he still felt uncomfortable and vulnerable. He could still feel the sweat on his neck and his brow and was unsure what to do or say. He introduced Frankie to Pascal. After a polite handshake Pascal took himself off to bed, leaving the old school friends to reminisce. Without an invite, Frankie and his friends sat down with Graham and ordered themselves some beer. Frankie then started to relive some of the antics from their school days. His version of events suggested that he and George were good mates. Always larking around. And every story told with a laugh and a smile. Frankie seemed desperate to prove to his friends that he and George were close. He reeled story after story off the cuff about their school days. Graham didn't have the stamina or the confidence to contradict anything he said. He just sat there and found himself nodding and agreeing with everything.

Frankie recounted one story with great humour. The occasion George and his brother Graham, who incidentally are identical twins, pulled "The Switch" on him. He told them how George had got his brother to stand in for him. To take his punishment for a prank that Frankie and George had been involved in. It all sounded very light-hearted the way he recalled it. There was no mention of the fighting or humiliation Frankie had suffered.

'Of course,' Frankie continued, 'I could always tell which one was George and which one was Graham. Bloody teachers and headmaster couldn't, but I always could. I always knew. There was something about you, George. Something special. No disrespect to Graham, but you had the edge. You were "The Man". Don't take this the wrong way, but I do think Graham did rather live in your shadow, didn't he? Anyway, what's Graham doing now?'

They spoke for another ten minutes, with Graham contributing as little as possible.

'Let's get a photo,' Frankie suggested.

The others readily agreed and the group stood up. Graham stood next to Frankie and the other three gathered around, all smiling and all with their arms on each other's shoulders. Another band of brothers. The waiter was called over and given the job of photographer. After the men had inspected the photograph on Frankie's phone, Graham took his chance.

'Well,' he said looking at his watch, 'orders are orders and I have to be tucked up in bed by ten.'

He dutifully shook hands with each of the men. It felt very strange shaking Frankie's hand. It was slimy and cold, like holding a toad. After all those years Graham could still find nothing to like about the man. Graham said goodnight and started to walk away. He had only gone about ten yards, when he heard Frankie's voice shout out.

'Graham.'

Instinctively, Graham turned around. He immediately felt the same fear and vulnerability that had gripped him earlier take hold of him once again. He could feel the look of panic and horror on his face.

Frankie roared with laughter.

'You haven't played the old "Switch" again, have you?'

Graham smiled as best he could, but it was a struggle.

He raised his eyebrows and shrugged his shoulders with as much mystery and mischief as his pounding heart would allow.

'You never know, Frankie. You never know.'

Frankie let out another roar of laughter. The four friends had all had a lot to drink and were content to accept that they had been in the company of the great George Miller.

'No. I know George Miller when I see him,' Frankie slurred. He pointed his finger at Graham. 'And that is the real McCoy. Good luck tomorrow, George. Maybe we can have a beer after the game.'

'Thanks, Frankie. Enjoy your stay.'

Graham turned and continued walking towards the lifts, determined not to turn around for anything.

It had felt strange being polite to Frankie. Would George have been so, if he had been there? Maybe not. But then if George had been there, there would have been no need for walking on eggshells. He hurried back to the sanctuary of his room. Igor was in the shower, so Graham took the opportunity to call his brother and tell him of the day's events. He had overcome everything that had been thrown at him so far, including the surprising and unwelcome appearance of Frankie De Costa. They were inching towards the finish line, but there were still some mighty fences to be jumped before they could consider the job done.

31

Not the moving type.

Debbie Morris had always assumed the Millers were not the moving type. She'd had their old landline number in her phone for years. *George home. George mobile.* She knew the mobile number was long out of date, but she just couldn't bring herself to delete it. She hoped the home number was still good. It was John and Paula's number. She hadn't rung it for over twelve years. She had kept it because it was a thin and tenuous link to the boy she loved, or at least his family. Having seen it scroll through the screen on her phone for years, she now decided it was time to give it a go. To see if John and Paula still lived at number 75. With more than a little trepidation in her heart, she made the call. It rang and rang. She was just considering if she should leave a message, when a voice answered. A man's voice.

'Hello.'

She paused just long enough to draw in a deep breath.

'Mr Miller? Mr John Miller?'

'Yes,' replied the man's voice. 'Can I help you?'

'Hello, Mr Miller. It's Debbie Morris here.'

There were a few seconds of silence. Debbie waited for his response nervously.

'Debbie. Goodness me! What a surprise! How are you?'

It had been many years since she had heard John's voice. There was a warmth about it. There always had been. Immediately she felt at ease.

'I'm fine, Mr Miller, thank you.'

John interrupted her.

'Debbie. I think you can call me John now, don't you? We're not back in the old school days.'

Debbie laughed.

'Thank you, John. I'm fine. And how are you?'

They exchanged pleasantries and talked about what they had been doing for the past twelve years. Debbie learned a bit about what George and Graham had been doing, but not in any great detail. John was obviously very proud of his sons, and keen to talk about their success. But she learned nothing about where they lived or any romantic interests. Knowing that Debbie hadn't called to talk about old times John finally got around to asking her.

'So, what is it I can do for you, Debbie?'

'Well, I was wondering if you had a number for George. I was going to give him a call and see how he is. See if he fancied meeting up and reminiscing over a bottle of wine.'

'I do have his mobile number here, Debbie, but he's in Barcelona at the moment. His team are playing tomorrow night in the Champions League final.'

'I know,' said Debbie, 'that's really why I am calling. You see, I am in Barcelona too. I have just finished a job here and will be returning home in a couple of days. I have been offered a job in Australia and will be flying out there at the end of the month to discuss terms and find accommodation. I was hoping I could talk to him and maybe even meet up before I go.'

Debbie spoke to John and Paula for about half an hour. They both sounded genuinely pleased to talk to her. She hadn't asked any more about George's love life and they hadn't volunteered any further information, so she let it lie. She now had his number and all she had to do was find the courage to ring it. She decided it would be best to leave it until after the game. She didn't want to distract him from his work. She thought about him for a moment as she gazed at the number she had written down. Yes, she did. She wanted to distract him more than anything else in the world. He had been on her mind ever since they had parted company in Newcastle all those years ago. Again, they had meant to keep in touch, but she was constantly flying from country to country and never really staying in one place long enough to put down any kind of roots. In her heart she wanted him so badly. She always had. No one else she had met had ever come remotely close to making her feel the way he did. There was a glow about her when she thought of him. A tingling sensation that passed all the way through her body. Certain areas of her body tingled more than others. Her memories of what they did together behind closed doors made her yearn for a repeat performance; to feel his touch on her body and the press of his lips on hers. She ached for him. She would call him tomorrow after the game. If he wanted to meet up, talk, or even arrange something for the following week that would be fantastic. If he couldn't, or didn't want to, then she was off to Australia to start a new and exciting life. Either way, the future was looking good, but in her heart she knew which one of the two outcomes she was hoping for.

32

History awaits.

It was the day of the game. The increase in nervous tension amongst the players was palpable. There was a businesslike atmosphere in the group. The jovial school-trip feel of the last couple of days had gone. Steely determination had replaced the cheeky adolescent smiles and giggles. There was nothing else to focus on except the match. It was looming large. The physical preparations had all been done. The mental preparations were now beginning in earnest.

Breakfast was a quiet affair, each man in their own little bubble with their own thoughts. The only people who looked relaxed were Bernie and Doug. They had had their discussions, worked out their team and spoken about plans A, B and C. They had agreed on their formation and their tactics. They had done their homework on the opposition and satisfied themselves they had left no stone unturned. Everything they could possibly have done had been taken care of. Now their job was to try and relax their men.

After what was for most of them a light breakfast, they were led into one of the hotels large conference rooms. It was very plush. A huge oak table surrounded by beautiful antique chairs sat in the centre of the room. There was a large whiteboard and an enormous television at the head of the table. As he had done before, Graham sat as far from the front as possible. Bernie stood up and the low hum of voices immediately stopped. He had tried to second guess Madrid's starting eleven and formation and went through the opposition, player by player, in as much detail as he could. Footage of earlier matches was played, highlighting some of the dangers they might face from Madrid's stunning array of sparkling talent. Defensive frailties, few and far between as they were, were exposed and any small chinks in their armour were replayed and examined.

After about an hour, Bernie approached the whiteboard. Computers and technology were great tools and had added so much to the analysis and understanding of the game. But Bernie was old school. There was nothing he liked more than explaining his methods with multicoloured pens and a pointer. He removed a piece of folded paper from his inside jacket pocket.

'Gentlemen. This will be our starting eleven.'

He turned to the board and wrote down eleven names. Casey King, Ben Brown, Gary Donaldson, Nolu, Igor Kovanovic, Christophe Burnett, Terry Bridges, Benik Abdou, Steve Gregory, Pascal Mingard and Barry Allder. He punched a full stop after Allder's name and turned to face the room.

'There may be a couple of you who feel disappointed not to have been included in this list. There may even be a couple of you that are surprised to be included. What you must always remember is that this is a team game. It is all about winning, nothing else, and I think this side gives us the best chance. The rest of you will be on the bench and may well be called upon at any moment. If I think someone is struggling, or not putting in a full shift, they will be replaced straight away. We have a great squad, full of talent and I sincerely believe we can beat this lot, but you will all have to be at your very best.'

Bernie then went on to talk about tactics and who would be marking who. Igor was given the most daunting task. He was responsible for tracking the opposition's most dangerous player, Anton Kinnet, who most people regarded as the best in the world. The big Croatian nodded at Bernie.

'Slice of cake, boss. I put him in my jacket for the game. I let him out when we done.'

A quiet ripple of laughter went around the table, easing the tension a little. Even Bernie smiled.

'Thank you, Igor. It's a piece of cake, I think you mean, not a slice and you probably want to put him in your pocket, not your jacket, but that's fine with me.'

Another outbreak of laughter lifted the mood further, especially when Igor replied,

'Slice? Piece? I put the whole cake in my jacket pocket, boss.'

Once the laughter had died down, Bernie wrapped things up.

'I think that's all for now, gentlemen. You know what you have to do for the rest of the day and now I hope you know what you have to do tonight. Stay focused and we will be victorious. Thank you.'

Bernie packed up his papers. The rest of the day had been meticulously planned out. They had work in the pool, massages, lunch, a sleep in the afternoon and then onto the stadium.

Graham hurried outside and sent George a text. *Not in the starting line-up. Rest of squad all on the bench. So far so good. G.*

George had been like a caged lion ever since Graham had walked out of his apartment on Thursday morning. He had nothing to do except go over and over all of the countless possibilities that might confront them. His mind was constantly swinging from positive to negative. From the fruits of success, to the damnation of failure. He knew there was a good chance they would succeed. Graham had got this far without being discovered. Surely, he could maintain the bluff for another twenty-four hours. But the closer they got to the finish line the more George felt the pressure. They had created a ticking time bomb that could explode at any moment.

George's knee was recovering well. He could now walk on it without too much pain or discomfort. He prowled around his apartment both willing Graham's phone to ring and dreading the thought. Positive news or updates made him feel part of the process, organically connected to his brother and the cause. But each time Graham called or sent him a text, his heart sank and his blood ran cold fearing the worst.

The news about the starting eleven was a relief, but George knew the rest of the players would all be eligible as substitutes, so they wouldn't really be in the clear until the final whistle sounded. All Graham would have to do after that was to keep a low profile. Go through the motions and get home. *That's all,* he thought. *That's still a mighty long way to go.*

George allowed himself a chuckle at the thought of Frankie De Costa turning up after all those years. From being arch enemies at school, it was now apparent that Frankie was a big fan. Or more likely just using his connection with him to impress his mates and business colleagues. George wondered if there were going to be anymore unforeseen distractions or interruptions. They had tried to think of every possible event that might present itself to Graham and how he should deal with them, but they certainly hadn't factored in Frankie's arrival. Were there to be any more surprises waiting to jump out and scupper their plans? He truly hoped not.

He planned to sit in his apartment and watch the game later that evening. He desperately hoped his team would win and lift the famous old trophy. For Doug and Bernie it would be another high point in their illustrious careers; for his teammates, who had worked so hard and played so well to get this far and for the fans. The fans were the lifeblood of the club. The only true constant in an ever-changing footballing world.

But George's real wish was that his brother made it home undetected and unsuspected. That was the victory he was praying for.

The players arrived at the ground nice and early. They walked across the pitch and absorbed the aura of the magnificent arena. They had all played in big matches, at big stadiums before, apart from Graham, but this was a truly awesome theatre. It felt bigger and more intimidating than it had the day before when they were training there. The stands seemed to disappear into the clouds. It was breathtaking even when empty. In a couple of hours' time there would be close to 100,000 people in there. That was going to be something very special.

Graham strolled across the beautifully manicured turf gazing up into the heavens.

'It's an amazing place, isn't it, George?' said Terry Bridges as he approached Graham.

'It certainly is.'

Terry patted Graham on the back.

'I'm glad you made it, George. We will need you tonight, I'm sure of that.'

Graham continued looking in awe at the surroundings, but didn't answer.

'History awaits,' Terry said with a smile and patted Graham on the back again.

The television coverage started at 7.p.m. George nervously pressed the remote control and the huge screen on the wall eased into life. He sat on the sofa with a mixture of fear, dread, anticipation and excitement. He was one of millions of people around the world who would be watching, all with their own views and thoughts on how the game would pan out, all experts in their own minds. George nipped the top off of a cold bottle of beer and took a large glug. Of all the information and knowledge floating around regarding the game, the players and the predicted formations, there was one fact which only two people on the planet were privy to.

33

Go your own way.

The atmosphere in the dressing room was electric. There was no joking or laughing. There was no smiling or small talk. Graham sat quietly in front of his locker and watched his teammates ready themselves. With their own varied habits and superstitions, each had their pre-match rituals. Some players would put on their kit in a precise order and some would listen to the same music on their headphones. Graham hadn't been briefed by George as to what he should be doing at that precise moment, but fortunately for him, everyone else was so wrapped up in their own little world, the pre-match rituals of George Miller were of no concern to anyone.

The dressing room was a bustling hive of activity. Pascal was sitting opposite Graham and looked like he was saying a few prayers to himself, making the sign of the cross numerous times and kissing his fingers repeatedly. Casey was checking the contents of the little bag he took onto the pitch with him. There were an awful lot of chewing gum packets being squeezed into it. Barry Allder, their young and gifted left winger, sat motionless, staring into space as if he were in a trance. With his blue shirt on his lap he gently stroked the white number eleven emblazoned on the back. Graham watched him and wondered what was going through his teenage mind. As he scanned the room he saw Terry. Terry had all his kit on except for his shirt, exposing his chiselled, muscular torso. He had the physique of a prize fighter. There wasn't an ounce of fat on him. Graham watched as he removed his four front teeth and placed them carefully into his locker. Terry had many battle scars to show for his life in football as well as a few from outside the game. He was definitely someone you wanted on your side. He had never taken a backward step in his life. However bad his scars or wounds were from an encounter, you always felt his opponent must have come off worse. He was the type of person who could inspire everyone around him and get an extra ten per cent from his teammates and colleagues when it was most needed. Terry saw Graham looking at him. He gave Graham a large grin and stuck his tongue through the wide gap his front teeth had just vacated, waggling it like a crazed Maori performing the Haka. Graham laughed and nodded towards his captain. It was a rare splash of humour. Terry winked back and carried on getting ready.

The final team talk from Bernie was short and to the point.

'Go out there and do your best. Try and enjoy it and believe in each other. The best team will win and you have it in you to be that team. Good luck to you all.'

Terry stood up and puffed out his chest. He suddenly looked bigger and even more menacing than usual. He made his way over towards the door and pulled on the blue shirt he loved so much. He tugged at the badge, drew it up to his lips and kissed it. The rest of the players fell in line behind him. They made their way out of the changing room and into the tunnel.

The noise outside was muffled as they waited to be led out by the officials. They were like Roman gladiators ready to be escorted into the Colosseum. The two teams lined up next to each other. There were no pleasantries or friendly handshakes and no smiles or conversations between old friends. Every player's thoughts were on the business at hand. As soon as they walked into the Barcelona evening, the noise hit them like a sledgehammer. The deafening roar from the spectators created a wall of sound. Blue and white flags in their hundreds were being boisterously waved. The cross of St George and the Spanish Bandera were also billowing in abundance. Music was blaring from the PA systems and flamethrowers were belching fire high into the air. A barrage of fireworks exploded above them adding to the cacophony of noise. Graham's senses were under attack. The sights, the sounds, the smells and the crackle of electricity in the air made him shiver. Apprehension and anticipation pumped through his veins. He had certainly never experienced anything like it in the past and was fairly certain he would never experience anything like it in the future. It was a truly awesome and hair-raising spectacle.

The sun had slipped behind the lip of the stadium and the heat was slowly draining away from the day. The floodlights were on adding even more drama to the occasion.

Graham followed the other players who had missed out on a starting place and sat down on one of the plush, padded and heated seats that made up the Camp Nou "bench". He looked out at the vista in front of him and thought of George. What would he be doing at that precise moment? Almost certainly watching the drama unfold on TV sitting alone at home. Graham wondered what kind of emotional turmoil his brother was going through. This match should have been the zenith of his career. It was the game he had been dreaming of and preparing for in his mind, for his entire life. It should have been the culmination of all he had ever worked for. His crowning moment as a professional footballer, but he was over 700 miles away and he was a part of the biggest con the game of football ever had perpetrated on it. Thinking of George reminded Graham of the mission they were on and the perilous and treacherous path they were walking. The nervousness he felt was not about victory, it was about survival.

Once the pre-match pleasantries and handshakes were over, the referee blew his whistle to start the game. From the first minute, it was an absolute cracker. There were chances at both ends. Posts and crossbars were hit. Both Casey and the opposition keeper were outstanding. For the neutral it was a pure delight, a footballing feast, but for the partisan supporter it was a nail-biting experience. As the game approached half-time, Terry Bridges received the ball in the centre circle. He ran forward and past a couple of half-hearted attempts to tackle him. From twenty yards out he swung his right foot at the ball. It was a pile driver. The Russian keeper never moved. It arrowed into the top left-hand corner of the net. A huge roar erupted from the fans waving the blue flags. Everyone on the bench stood and cheered. The sense of excitement and relief was palpable.

It was on. The dream had taken a step closer to becoming reality.

The referee blew his whistle for half-time and the players left the field. The euphoria in the dressing room was such that Bernie had to raise his voice to make himself heard.

'Calm down, gentlemen!' he ordered. 'You haven't won anything yet!'

More of the same was, unsurprisingly, the message to the players. Concentration, focus, teamwork and effort would win the day.

As they walked back out onto the pitch, Graham, for the first time, felt he was part of the machine. He was a member of this exciting family and he was sharing all their hopes and fears. He felt the warmth of the bond between them and the camaraderie of *his* band of brothers. He no longer felt like the intruder he really was.

Sadly, all the hope and happiness Terry's goal had given them, disappeared just ten minutes into the second half. Anton Kinnet had momentarily escaped from Igor's *jacket pocket*, tiptoed through the defence and equalised. It was a shattering blow so soon after the restart. Both Bernie and Doug became very animated, shouting at their players to refocus and put the disappointment behind them. It was only 1-1, and still all to play for. But things went from bad to worse for Bernie when Igor Kovanovic was involved in a nasty collision with one of the opposition players. After several minutes of being treated on the pitch, a stretcher was called for and Igor was taken away with a suspected broken leg. Bernie was forced to make substitutions much earlier than he had planned, to reorganise his defence. The euphoria of half-time seemed like a distant memory. They were fighting with their backs to the wall. The Madrid side was relentless and forced save after save from Casey King. The big American was playing the game of his life. He flung himself at everything they could throw at him. Even over the monstrous din of the crowd, Graham could hear Casey barking orders at his makeshift defence. He was like George Washington at Yorktown, organising his troops, standing fast and commanding respect. He was a Goliath.

With just under ten minutes to play, a tiring Pascal Mingard chased a through pass from Nolu, but pulled up grabbing his hamstring. He came to a limping, wincing halt and collapsed onto the ground.

'Ahh, shit!' Bernie's cry of desperation echoed off the sides of the dugout. He buried his head in his hands. 'I don't fucking believe it!'

The incredulity in his voice was that of a man who could see his dreams slowly, but surely, slipping through his fingers. Graham looked at Bernie. He looked deflated and crushed. Graham felt so sad for him. He knew how much this had meant to everyone and how hard they had worked to achieve what, only forty-five minutes ago, had seemed within their grasp. The anger and disbelief on Bernie's face had been replaced with a look of resignation and sympathy as he watched Pascal being helped off the field. As a spectator to the sad turn of events, Graham felt an enormous empathy for Bernie. But that was shattered in just four words. The manager, whose emotions had swung from disbelief through anger, frustration and resignation, now had his business face on again. He looked back over his left shoulder straight at Graham.

'George. Get out there!'

It was now Graham's turn to feel the wild extremes of his emotions. From feeling sad and sympathetic, he now felt horror and fear grip his entire body. His worst fears had just been confirmed. He was about to take centre stage, in front of a worldwide audience. So much for anonymity! Doug looked at him.

'Come on, George. I'll take you out.'

Graham got to his feet and followed Doug to the touchline. He couldn't feel his legs. They were moving him about, but he had no sense in them. He was sure he was going to be sick, right there on the touchline. Doug put his arm around him.

'Come on, George. This is your time. Grab it. You know, cometh the hour, cometh the man and all that.'

Graham felt a massive urge to suddenly come clean. To turn to Doug and say,

'Actually, Doug, I'm Graham, not George. There seems to have been a bit of a mix-up. Why don't you put someone else on instead?' He was that terrified. Doug patted him on the stomach and pushed him onto the pitch. Graham heard him say, 'Go on, son,' as he jogged past the wounded Pascal. They slapped hands.

'Bon chance, George.'

Since the charade had started, Graham had imagined that everybody was looking at him, even when he knew they were not. Now he knew they were. Millions of them. Hundreds of millions of them around the world. As he made his way onto the pitch, Terry jogged over to him. Graham waited for Terry to impart some kind of tactical briefing. To say something that would make sense to his muddled brain. Terry put his hand on Graham's shoulder.

'Like I said, George. History awaits.' He smiled and winked at Graham, patted the side of his face and then jogged away leaving him alone and isolated in a foreign wilderness.

This had always been a possibility, one the brothers had hoped would never materialise, but it had and Graham needed to deal with it. He felt like he had gate-crashed a party but knew no one there. He felt alone, insecure and scared. He felt out of his depth. The slow motion and surreal feeling of his entrance into the game was blown away by the referee's whistle. The shrill piercing blast heralded the chaotic movement of men all around him. Voices were shouting and people were pointing in all directions. His legs continued to move him around, but the feeling in them was still missing. The next few minutes were a complete blur. As if he were in a dream or a trance. It was what he had imagined an out-of-body experience must have felt like. He could hear people shouting out George's name, but was unsure what they wanted him to do or where they wanted him to go. As the game entered time added on, Graham realised he had another half an hour of extra time to get through. He had only been on the pitch for ten minutes, but he was already exhausted. The mental fatigue and strain had had much more of an effect on him than he expected. He was floundering. He felt like a fish out of water. He was confused and bewildered, finding it difficult to take in his surroundings or remember what he should be doing. With time almost up, he made his way into the penalty box, for what would presumably be their last chance in normal time, from a corner. He wandered slowly and unsurely into the mix of players. Everyone seemed to be pushing and shoving, trying to gain a bit of space. Again, all he could hear was shouting and all he could see were men pointing and jostling with each other. He felt lost in some kind of fantasy world where he didn't belong. All the training and tactical talks he had listened to so closely and tried to memorise in case a situation like this arose had evaporated from his mind. He just wanted it to be over.

The referee blew his whistle for the corner to be taken. The chaotic pushing, shoving and running in every direction immediately increased. Graham felt himself being dragged towards the centre of the penalty area by the almost tidal-like pull of the other players. He watched the ball as it made its curling passage towards the shoal of animated men. The ball seemed to be coming straight for him. Again, excitement and fear gripped him in equal amounts. Again, everything seemed to be happening in slow motion. He jumped to meet the ball. The ball had no interest in anyone else. It was cruising right towards him.

Just make good contact, he pleaded with himself. He craned his neck in anticipation, ready to snap his muscles with all his might and head the ball with as much power as he could in the general direction of the goal. But instead of contact with the ball, Graham felt an almighty thump between his shoulder blades. He felt the air burst out of his lungs and he crashed to the ground. He wasn't quite sure what had happened. Had he missed the chance? Had he missed the ball altogether? He looked up from his prone position. The sound of the whistle cut through all of the other voices and noises. The referee was pointing to the penalty spot and was engulfed in a scrum of opposition players, all remonstrating with him. Graham buried his face back into the lush turf. He hadn't done much in the few minutes he had been involved, but he had won his side a penalty which could and should, win them the match. He prayed it would bring an end to the game and his nightmare.

After a few minutes, the referee regained control having booked two of the Madrid players. Graham was back on his feet and began to walk towards his teammates waiting patiently around the "D". Terry Bridges held the ball in his hands and had a steely look in his eye. Graham was just about to wish him good luck when Terry thrust the ball into Graham's midriff.

'Here you are, George. I told you. History awaits.'

Graham's momentary feeling of relief and safety instantaneously disappeared. He instinctively grabbed the ball as it hit his gut.

'But, Terry!'

Terry wasn't listening and cut straight across Graham's voice.

'No buts, George. Pascal is off and you are our regular penalty taker. You won it. You score it.'

Terry was not a man you argued with. Graham couldn't decide which was scarier; taking the kick, or remonstrating with his captain. Terry tapped the side of Graham's face, winked at him, smiled and then walked back to join the others. *What the hell must George be going through right now,* thought Graham? A situation his brother must have dreamt about ever since he was a young boy was now taking place. The perfect scenario for a player in his prime, with self-confidence to burn. George would have absolutely relished the chance to be in Graham's position right then. Graham couldn't think of anywhere else he would least like to be.

To score was to win the cup. Time had all but run out. This would be the last meaningful kick of the game. How many times had they played out this scene when they were kids? How many times had they placed the ball on the spot and casually smashed it between the sticks, making the goalkeeper run back and retrieve the ball when they had been in the park? But this wasn't the park and the goalkeeper wasn't their dad. The prize wasn't just bragging rights between brothers, it was footballing immortality. Graham put the ball on the spot. Fear was not a feeling he had felt a great deal of in his life, but since they had started this crusade, it was a feeling he had become accustomed to. He had never felt so scared in his entire life.

The goal looked very small and the keeper looked enormous. He could feel his legs now, but he only felt them shaking and wobbling. He could hear his heart beating in his chest. The goalkeeper walked out to face him, to try and unsettle him. Graham stood his ground. The keeper scowled and looked down into Graham's eyes, his six-foot seven-inch frame towering over him.

'You will miss this one, Miller. You don't have the balls anymore,' he said in his deep, husky Russian accent.

The comparatively miniature referee squeezed between them and handed off the keeper, pushing him back towards the goal, like breaking up two heavyweight boxers. The Russian backed slowly away keeping his steely eyes fixed on Graham. The world had once again gone silent. Graham could hear nothing and all he could see was the goal. There were only two people in existence at that very moment. The prowling, waspish Muscovite and him. Graham looked at the giant as he jumped up and down, waving his arms above his head, trying to make himself even larger than he was. He was snarling and growling. He reminded Graham of Frankie. Well, Frankie had never succeeded in intimidating either him or George and neither would this Russian leviathan. Graham sneered back at him. He even managed a smile. A smile full of contempt.

George had always favoured hitting his penalties to the goalkeeper's right whereas Graham had always preferred the left. Had this colossal jack-in-the-box between the posts done his homework? Did he know about George's preference for the right-hand side? Graham took a long deep breath through his nose, then slowly exhaled it through pursed lips.

'Go your own way,' he whispered to himself.

The whistle blew. He took one last look at the animated goalkeeper then focused his attention on the ball in front of him. His legs started to propel him towards it. His instep caressed it to the keeper's left. As the ball sailed towards the goal, Graham looked up to see the keeper's massive frame diving away to his right, but with his eyes still firmly fixed on the ball, watching it on its way to glory. The net bulged with the impact and the ball nestled into the bottom corner of the goal. The silence was banished with a vengeance. The stadium erupted in an explosion of cheers. Graham was left standing there with a dumbfounded look on his face, as he was mobbed by his entire team. They all collapsed in a heap on the floor. Graham felt no elation, just a massive sense of relief. The final whistle sounded seconds after the restart. They had won.

Doug and Bernie had tears in their eyes. They were on the pitch, congratulating every one of the players in turn. Bernie shook Graham's hand.

'Well done, George! Well done, son!' he said with a huge smile. Doug said nothing. He just wrapped his arms around Graham and hugged him as hard as Graham had ever been hugged. Doug's tears were flowing freely. The embrace between the two men was an accumulation of years of friendship, love and trust. Doug tried to speak, but couldn't manage any words.

Graham had never seen so many photographers and flashlights before. Cameras and microphones were being poked into the players' faces for any comment or opinions. Graham desperately wanted to avoid any sort of coverage but realised that because of his part in the proceedings, it was inevitable he would be sought out and asked for his reactions and feelings. He tried to keep his comments as brief as he could, thanking Bernie and Doug for their support and trust, saying it was *their victory*.

The hustle and bustle continued for a few minutes, before they were ushered together to go and collect their medals. Terry brought up the rear and lifted the trophy. He raised the cup towards the fans, beaming at them with his toothless grin. A huge roar went up from the masses of blue and white-clad spectators. Graham thought of the young boy and his father from the airport. He wondered where they were sitting and how pleased they must be.

This was the world he had passed up when he decided not to pursue a career in football. Did he regret it? At that precise moment he really wasn't sure. It was difficult to imagine another line of work where you could feel so much adrenaline and so much emotion. He was loving it. He would absorb it all for now and enjoy every drop, but there was a life waiting for him when he returned home. A life with Kerry. He was sure that would generate just as much excitement, happiness and passion.

Back in London, George watched the drama play out. He saw Doug's and Bernie's emotions flow from their eyes. He watched as his teammates and his brother celebrated and danced about. There were the statutory photos of the team behind the sponsors advertising hoarding, with the cup, all bouncing up and down and waving their arms in the air. Magnums of champagne were being sprayed in every direction, some of it even into mouths.

George wiped his cheeks. He was 700 miles away, but his tears were flowing just as freely.

34

A bloody school reunion.

By the time the coach had dropped them back at the hotel, it was gone eleven o'clock. The mood in the camp was vibrant and everybody was keen to celebrate. A private party had been arranged in the exclusive rooftop bar. The players had been told to enjoy themselves *within reason*. There were no concerns about up-and-coming fixtures, or training schedules, so the champagne and celebratory beverages would be in plentiful supply. The words "within reason", had been included at David Blackstone's insistence, to remind them they were still ambassadors of the club. Blackstone was adamant their shining victory shouldn't be tarnished by any drunken or debauched behaviour. The morning papers should be full of pictures and reports that reflected their magnificent achievement and nothing else. They were due to leave the hotel at 9 a.m. the following morning and it was expected they would all be looking their best for the media coverage of their return to England.

On arrival at the hotel, most of the players made their way straight up to the party. Graham, however, was desperate to talk to George and discuss all of the evening's events. The privacy of his room would be the best place for that. George answered Graham's call immediately.

'We did it! We only bloody did it!' George exclaimed. For the first couple of minutes, Graham didn't manage to say a word. George fired question after question at him without giving him a chance to answer any of them. Graham smiled as he listened to his brother. As well as the excitement of winning, it was as much about the relief of clearing what they both saw as their last big hurdle. Compared to all the dangers and pitfalls they had been faced with and overcome, the next and last phase of the operation should be plain sailing. Eventually, Graham cut in and attempted to calm his brother down. He reassured him that no one had seemed remotely suspicious of him or his identity. The plan had worked beautifully. Better than either of them could have dreamt. Even with the unforeseen challenges that had presented themselves along the way, their ultimate goal was still achievable. It was a huge weight off both their shoulders. All Graham had to do now was blend into the background and get home. In just over twelve hours Graham would be back in George's apartment and they could really start to celebrate and relax. He could resume his own life and his own identity. The beard and the mop of hair would return and things would mercifully get back to normal. George would be a hero and Doug's and Bernie's trust and faith in him would have been repaid with interest.

'I had better go,' Graham finally said, 'there is a party

going on upstairs and I think they are expecting you to put in an appearance. I'll see you tomorrow.'

Graham put George's phone back in his pocket. He took a big deep breath and prepared himself for the last lap.

Up on the roof the party was in full swing. A three-piece band was playing in the far corner doing their best to be heard over the excited conversations of the revellers. Waiters were scurrying about filling glasses with champagne and delivering trays of beers and exotic-looking cocktails. It looked like he was the last to arrive. As Graham stepped out of the lift and into the warm breeze of the Barcelona evening, a smart grey-haired man in a suit and tie approached him. He was looking at Graham as if he was a long-lost friend. Graham smiled back, but hoped the man would carry on past him and disappear into the elevator.

The man offered his hand.

'You must be George Miller,' he said. Graham braced himself for another unexpected examination.

'Yes, I am,' answered Graham, shaking the man's hand.

'It is very nice to finally meet you in person,' the elderly gentleman added in a clipped Italian accent. 'We have never met before, but I have followed your career with great interest. I watched you play many years ago and have had you watched on more than a few occasions since.'

There was a quizzical look on Graham's face as he tried to prepare himself for yet another surprise scenario. The tell-tale signs of panic started to blossom within his body. His heart started to beat faster. He could feel the beads of perspiration beginning to form on his face and his stomach start to churn. The elderly gentleman could see his confusion.

'I am an old friend of Mr Fenner and wanted to congratulate him on this evening's victory. My name is Enrico Morotoni. About fourteen years ago a friend of mine suggested I should take a look at a couple of brothers playing for their school. He told me many good things were being said about "The Miller boys". I had some free time, so I came along. I always make notes after every game I watch, whatever the level. When I realised I might be seeing you I looked up my observations on that match. The notes said it was a poor game with nothing really to commend it, apart from the Miller twins. My notes also suggested I keep a close eye on you both. I asked if it would be possible to see you play again and maybe talk to your representatives, but was told nothing would be happening in that department for at least another two years. I must admit I was a little disappointed at the time.'

The quizzical look on Graham's face had faded away and had been replaced by a look of amazement, and relief. So, this was Mr Morotoni. Finally, after all these years, he now knew what he looked like and where he was from.

'You took the penalty very well tonight. You showed no nerves at all. That is the true sign of a great professional.'

'Thank you. I have had a lot of practice.'

'I was surprised your brother Graham didn't follow you into the world of professional football. He looked to be just as talented. What is he doing these days?'

Graham explained what his brother "Graham" was up to and why he had chosen a different path. Finally, he was speaking on a subject he was very knowledgeable about.

'Well, Mr Miller, I will not keep you any longer. It has been wonderful to finally meet you. Congratulations on your win tonight and of course on your career in general. I have to admit it saddens me a little to know that you and your brother slipped through my fingers all those years ago. But it would seem things have turned out well for you, anyway.'

He shook Graham's hand again and excused himself. Graham shook his head, a little bewildered. The past was coming back to haunt and taunt him. Just when he needed a trouble and incident-free glide to the finish line, another character had turned up in the most unlikely of situations. He looked up to the heavens, clasped his hands together in prayer and whispered, 'No more surprises. Please.'

He caught the eye of Casey King. Casey smiled and beckoned him over. Graham walked towards the large American. He was talking to Nolu. On his way over to them, he had his hand shaken and his back slapped numerous times. His small part in that evening's proceedings had guaranteed he was not going to be able to just blend into the background, but then George would never have *just blended*. He would have revelled in being the centre of attention. So, he must play the part of George to the full and to the end.

'Good evening, gentlemen,' he said when he reached his teammates.

'*Ah Die twee helde*', said Nolu vigorously shaking Graham by the hand.

'What's that?' Graham asked.

Nolu repeated what he had said. '*Die twee helde.*'

Graham looked at Casey who raised his eyebrows and shrugged his shoulders. Even Casey wasn't fluent in Afrikaans. After a pause Nolu translated for them.

'The two heroes', he said as he held out his arms towards both Graham and Casey. They laughed.

'Not me,' said Graham, 'I was only on the pitch for ten minutes. There is your man of the match right there,' pointing at Casey.

Graham had been given a glass of champagne as soon as he set foot on the roof. Within ninety seconds, it had been refilled.

They spoke about the game and what it would mean to everyone involved and the club in general. They spoke about Igor. The news was not good. As they had suspected he had broken his leg and would be spending the night in the local hospital. It was the only stain on what had otherwise been a spotlessly perfect day.

Graham's glass was continually topped up by every passing waiter. He had no idea how much he had drunk, but he knew he had started to feel a little light-headed. The warm breeze and the stunning views, along with the jubilant atmosphere and the never-ending supply of chilled champagne made for an intoxicating cocktail.

Graham was relaxing into his role as George Miller. He could understand why his brother was so at home in an environment like this.

He had spoken to both Doug and Bernie at some length about the game, his knee and his future. Bernie had asked him to come and see him the following week for a chat. There were a number of subjects he wanted to discuss with George, but now wasn't the time or the place. Graham assured him he would talk to Brenda and sort something out with her.

As his glass was once again replenished, Graham sat himself down on one of the large, comfy sofas and looked out over the Barcelona skyline. This really was a good way to live, he thought to himself.

He had just decided to finish his drink and head for bed when he felt the dull vibration of George's phone in his trouser pocket. He looked at the screen. There was a text message from an unrecognised number.

Hi, George. Surprise surprise! It's me Debbie Morris. Congratulations on your fantastic victory. I'm in reception downstairs and wondered if you could spare me a couple of minutes Dx.

Graham was astounded and horrified at the same time. Debbie Morris here, now! He had been amazed when Frankie De Costa had shown up completely out of the blue, left almost dumbstruck when Mr Morotoni had introduced himself and now Debbie Morris. This was beginning to resemble a bloody school reunion. Why was it whenever the road to success and safety seemed clear of obstacles, something or someone, completely unforeseen, would crash into view and muddy the waters again? He thought hard about what he should do. He considered calling George and asking him, but decided that would only confuse the issue even more and send his brother into a new bout of panic. If he ignored the message, or palmed her off, she might never show up again. He knew how much they had meant to each other all those years ago and how George still cherished those memories. He knew his brother was desperate to find out what she had been doing over the years and would give anything to meet up with her again. He would have to see her if only for George's sake, but it was taking yet another massive risk. So far Graham had managed to fool everyone including Doug and his teammates who saw George on a day-to-day basis. If they couldn't tell George from Graham, surely Debbie would not be able to after all this time. George had told him about their meeting in Newcastle, when they spent the night together, but they had seen nothing of each other since and that was seven years ago. All he had to do was meet her, find out what she was up to, make his excuses and arrange to meet up back in London if that's what she wanted. Then he could leave it all in George's hands. Graham, content with his plan, texted her back.

Come up to the sixteenth floor and I will meet you there.

As he stood to make his way towards the lifts, he stumbled slightly and had to steady himself on the back of the sofa. 'Easy does it, George,' came a voice from the increasingly blurry crowd.

'Mind that knee, George.'

Graham couldn't see who had said it and he didn't recognise the voice, but he waved a hand in that direction and continued to slowly and carefully make his way towards the door. He tried to convince himself that his fragility was a result of the physical and mental weariness he was feeling and not the fault of the champagne. On the way down he looked at himself in the mirrored walls of the elevator. He took a deep breath and arched his shoulders back trying to straighten himself up. He vigorously rubbed his face with his hands, leant forward and stared deeply into his reflected eyes, imploring himself to stay focused and concentrate.

The lift doors opened on the sixteenth floor and there she was. Debbie Morris. She hadn't changed a bit, thought Graham. As soon as she saw Graham, she flung herself at him engulfing him in her arms.

'George,' she squealed and planted a big kiss on his cheek. She squeezed him tightly and didn't seem to be in any rush to let go. She was obviously pleased to see him. Graham didn't know how to react. He had always been fond of Debbie, but not like George. She was more like a long-lost sister to him. He hugged her tightly.

'Debbie, how lovely to see you.'

They talked by the lift doors for a few minutes. There was an awkwardness between them. They had parted from their embrace and were indulging in small talk whilst dodging the stream of human traffic making its way in and out of the numerous lifts. Debbie's initial excitement at seeing George had ebbed slightly. She explained she was travelling to Australia at the end of the month and would be there indefinitely. She was disappointed when George seemed excited and enthusiastic at the prospect of her leaving. She had been hoping for a very different reaction. She told him that when she had discovered they would both be in Barcelona she thought it would be great to meet up one last time before she flew off to her new life. She noticed that George was slurring his words a little and seemed unsteady on his feet.

'Why don't we sit down for a bit? Or better still go downstairs to the bar,' she suggested. Charming as she was, the last thing Graham wanted was to be alone with Debbie. The intimacy between her and George was bound to come up in conversation and that was something he had definitely not been briefed on by his brother. It was a subject he was ill equipped and unprepared for.

'I've got a better idea,' Graham triumphantly announced. 'Why don't you come up and join the party? You can meet some of the boys.'

Debbie forced a reluctant smile. She didn't want to meet any of the boys. She wanted to be alone with George and try and understand how he felt towards her. Was the fire still burning as brightly in him as it was in her? She had rehearsed her speech over and over again in her mind for this occasion. Easing the subject back to their school days, recounting their passion and their love and trying to see if the twinkle was still in George's eye. It was so important to her to know how he felt. Her planned trip to Australia was destined to be a fresh start, a new beginning. She wanted to settle down and live in one place. Somewhere she could finally call home. She wanted to be with someone. She still hoped to have children, but there was nothing left for her in England. Nothing except George Miller. He was the one person who could and would change all her plans if his love for her was still as strong as hers was for him. She had to find out and that night was probably going to be her last chance. To be able to explain what was in her heart and try and see what was in his was going to be a difficult task, but to do it in a crowd of semi-inebriated footballers would be almost impossible. Disappointingly for Debbie, it appeared that was her only option. They crossed the hallway and entered the lift to the rooftop. As they ascended the few floors there was silence between them. Graham was struggling to know what to say, whilst Debbie was already wondering if it had been a good idea to meet up at all. Maybe George had changed over the years. He seemed different to the man she had been hoping to meet. The electrical charge she had always felt zap through her body whenever she saw him, or even thought about him was missing. Maybe it was the drink. He had obviously had a few, but then George had always been able to hold his booze better than anyone she had ever known, even at the age of eighteen.

The lift doors gently parted and they walked out onto the roof terrace. Debbie delicately slipped her hand into his. Their fingers used to fit together beautifully, entwining effortlessly. This time they felt alien to each other. Searching for gaps and clumsily filling them. Once the union was finally complete, Debbie squeezed his hand, but she felt nothing back in return. Her hopes of a fairy-tale reunion between the two of them began to fade. Maybe she had been unrealistic. She desperately hoped they would both be the same people they had been all those years ago. Maybe all her fears and reasons for not contacting him sooner were proving to be right after all.

Graham introduced her to some of his teammates. He took two glasses of champagne from the passing waitress and gave one to Debbie. She spoke with a number of George's friends. She even talked with Doug. He had vague memories of Debbie from his early dealings with George and his father. Her name had cropped up a number of times in those days. He was pleased to see her and made a fatherly fuss of her, but Doug was tired.

'Poor old boy like me needs his bed, I'm afraid, George. Don't stay up too late, son. Remember we are leaving at 9.a.m. tomorrow. And take good care of that knee.'

He patted Graham on the shoulder and said goodnight. The day had been a triumph for Doug and Bernie, but it had taken its toll. Bernie had thrown in the towel some time ago and now Doug trudged slowly off to his room. In his day Doug would have been there until the end, partying with the best of them, but now he was happy to leave the drinking and revelry to the youngsters. He left the party with a contented smile on his face. His team had fought and won an unlikely victory, in what was the biggest club game in Europe. Both he and Bernie would feel the warm glow of success and enjoy the plaudits from the footballing world again. But most of all, Doug's smile was about *his boy, George,* who had come good at exactly the right time. Not only proving his doubters wrong, but showing the world that he still had a future at the highest level.

35

The beast was asleep.

Graham was becoming more expressive and more expansive with each glass of champagne. His speech was now noticeably slurred and he was treating Debbie more like a support than a companion. His stories and recollections were becoming confused and muddled. On more than one occasion he referred to his brother as *George* whilst remembering tales of their school-day shenanigans. Fortunately, everyone listening to him was also pretty pissed and didn't pick up on the somewhat bizarre ramblings of their matchwinner. Debbie put it down to the drink.

She had enjoyed her time on the roof more than she had expected. She had felt comfortable in the company of George's friends. She made them laugh out loud when she recalled the time George and his twin brother Graham, had pulled "The Switch" on their school nemesis Frankie De Costa. She explained what had happened and how neither Frankie nor the headmaster were able to tell the difference. She slipped her hands back into Graham's again and looked lovingly into his half-shut eyes.

'And that was the beginning of our,' she paused, and thought for a moment, 'time together.'

Graham smiled back, but it was a vacant smile, with no warmth or sentiment about it. A smile from someone vaguely interested in the story, not someone excited by the memory.

He put his glass onto a passing waitress' tray. Finesse and delicacy had left his body long ago and the glass toppled over and fell to the floor, smashing into a hundred pieces.

'Oh, God, I'm so sorry,' Graham slurred.

'That's okay, sir, no problem,' said the young girl as she bent down to pick up the shattered shards. Graham bent down to try and help her. He was still apologising to her when he let out a loud yelp.

'Ah, shit!' A large sliver of glass had embedded itself into his finger. The cut was deep enough to produce a steady flow of blood.

'Bollocks!' he said as he examined the wound. Debbie helped him up and took a look at the gash.

'Come on. I think it's time you went to bed, Mr Miller. We will get a dressing for that finger on the way.'

Graham was happy to do as he was told. He had long since exceeded his capacity for drink and was now all but helpless. Debbie took his arm in hers and led him away. 'Good night, George. See you in the morning,' said the chorus of voices still left on the roof. The first aid kit behind the bar supplied the necessary antiseptic cream and plasters for his finger and Debbie supplied the necessary know how to clean and wrap the digit.

It was as much as she could do to keep him upright. He was a dead weight.

'What room number are you?' she asked as she struggled with all her strength to manhandle him into the lift. He was now nothing more than cargo. With what turned out to be Graham's last utterances of the night, he said '2204.'

The green light clicked on as the entry card did its job. Debbie pushed the door open. It was a very large room with two huge double beds. Igor's belongings had already been collected. Debbie managed to get Graham onto the nearest of the two beds. Once she had released her hold on him he fell back onto the mattress, bouncing up a couple of times before coming to rest. His eyes were shut and his breathing was deep and slow. Every so often he would let out a grunt or a snore. She looked at him sprawled out on the bed. She had learned nothing at all about him, or his feelings towards her. The only thing she had discovered was his tolerance for alcohol had diminished alarmingly. She had spent years dreaming of this moment. The two of them alone again in a hotel room, but this was certainly not how she had envisaged it. She started to undress him. His shirt, his shoes, his socks and then his trousers. Even though the body on the bed in front of her was no more use than a corpse, she started to feel aroused by the sight of him. She had waited so long for this and realised it would almost certainly be the last chance they would have to spend the night together. There was a sadness and a feeling of resignation about her. It would be a night only one of them would remember and neither of them would cherish. If she could rouse him or breathe some life into his carcass, they would enjoy each other one more time. For *old time's sake*, nothing more. It certainly wouldn't be the passionate or emotion-filled rebirth or finale to their glorious time together. She eased his boxer shorts down over his knees and there he was, the man of her dreams in all his glory. She looked at him and wished the man she had hoped to meet would suddenly burst into life and fulfil her expectations, but that was clearly not going to happen. If this was going to be her last hurrah with George, she was definitely going to say a loving and fond farewell to her oldest and dearest friend. She couldn't help herself. She ran her right hand up and down the inside of his thigh, stroking softly. She glanced up into his eyes desperately hoping to see some movement or recognition of pleasure. Just the suggestion of a smile would have been enough. She moved her fingers up and wrapped them around what had given her so much happiness. She caressed and squeezed him gently, but sadly it was as unresponsive as the rest of him. She wondered if her mouth would have more of an effect. That had always been guaranteed to get George's attention. She slid the flaccid flesh between her lips, using her tongue as she had done so many times with him before, taking him as deep as she could, but there was no twitching or pulsing to be felt. Even her best friend was incognizant to her efforts. The beast was asleep. She held onto him for a while longer massaging him with both hands, desperate to get a reaction, but to no avail.

She took the duvet off of the other bed, lay down next to him and covered them both. She cuddled up to him keeping one hand between his legs and her other hand between her own, just in case he woke up. Debbie fell asleep with a bitter sadness in her heart.

Graham blinked and slowly opened his eyes. He was a little confused. Where was he? Why did he feel so awful?

The phone by the side of his bed was buzzing in a loud and extremely annoying fashion. He grabbed the phone. It was reception giving him the early-morning call that had been ordered for him. He sat up in bed and tried to come to terms with his surroundings and his hangover. His eyes were well ahead of his brain. They were taking in images his mind was unable to explain. There was a loud bash at his door, followed by a voice shouting. 'Leaving in one-hour, George!'

It was the Australian tones of Steve Denton. Graham's head was pounding, his mouth was dry and he was still a little confused. As soon as he heard Steve call him *George*, it slowly started to come back to him.

'Okay. I'm up,' Graham shouted back. He looked around the room and hoped his brain would hurry up and fill in some of the numerous gaps in his memory. At the bottom of his bed he saw his clothes. They were beautifully folded in a neat and tidy pile. Graham frowned at them. How did they get there?

On top of his neatly arranged clothes was a piece of paper. He reached over and picked it up. It was addressed to Mr G. Miller.

I hope your head is okay this morning. It was great to see you last night and I thoroughly enjoyed your company. Be lovely to see you again before I leave for Australia. Please call me if you fancy meeting up. Well done last night. You were wonderful. Debbie x. Underneath was a mobile phone number and another kiss. The mist began to clear and the memories started to seep back bit by bit into his aching brain.

'Jesus! Debbie Morris. Shit!'

He remembered her texting him and then going up to the party. He remembered her dressing the wound he had inflicted on himself when picking up the broken glass. He looked at his finger. She had done a good job. He remembered her suggesting it was time for bed and carrying him into the lift, but after that it was all blank. He looked down at his neatly folded clothes. He lifted the duvet and stared down at his naked body. She must have put him to bed. He glanced over to his left and saw the indentations in the pillows next to him. They had obviously slept together. Had he…? Did she…? He looked down at himself again in disbelief and horror. He had been so drunk he couldn't even remember if he had had sex or not. He read the note again hoping it would tell him something new, but there were no hidden clues or reminders to be found. *You were wonderful.* What the hell did that mean? He covered his face with the palms of his hands and tried to search back into the murky past of a few hours ago, desperately hoping for some spark that would ignite a memory rush, but all he could see was the darkness and blackness of his amnesia.

There were so many questions rebounding around in his head. Had he let the cat out of the bag? Had he blown it so close to the winning line? He remembered talking about the Frankie De Costa incident with some of the boys, but couldn't remember if that had led to anything more damaging.

What the hell was he going to tell George?

'I met your old girlfriend, got drunk and can't remember if I fucked her. Also, I don't know if I gave the game away to her or anyone else.'

Hardly the triumphant epilogue they had hoped for.

He was now more confused than he had been at any other time since they had started this. He would have a shower and report down at reception and see what the atmosphere was like. Any comments or remarks from his teammates might give his memory the nudge it needed; but would he want to remember? Would his memory or his teammates reveal that in fact he had blown the entire deception? This was the beginning of the last lap. He should have been feeling euphoric, but instead was feeling utterly dysphoric. Maybe his head would clear in the shower and allow a few more details to emerge.

On the journey to the airport all he got from his teammates were schoolboy giggles and innuendos.

'She was a cracker, George. Where did you find her?'

'I saw her leaving about six this morning. She looked like she was in a hurry.'

They were still calling him George which was a huge relief, but the comments he heard raised more questions than they answered. If she had left at 6.a.m., they had obviously spent the night together. But did anything happen?

After all the glamour, excitement, luxury and hero worship he had experienced over the past few days he now wanted this to be over. He wanted to swap phones, jewellery, passports and most of all, identities. He would grow his hair and his beard, longer and bushier than ever and become Graham again. It couldn't come quickly enough. His head was still throbbing.

36

Graham was Graham once more.

The sound of Graham's key in George's front door should have heralded the end of the saga. Home safely and no one suspecting a thing. It should have been the final curtain coming down on a theatrical performance unequalled by any thespian or troupe. The end of a covert, undercover, top secret mission, unsurpassed by any CIA or MI5 agent. George sprang to his feet and rushed to welcome his brother back. By the time the door was fully open, George was there, face to face with the returning hero.

'Graham!' George shouted triumphantly with his arms spread wide and a smile on his face to match. He rested his hands on Graham's shoulders and looked him square in the eye.

'We did it! We did it!' There was as much relief in his voice as celebration.

'Well, you did it, Graham. You pulled it off. We are in the clear. I don't know how I can ever thank you. You've saved my life and my career.'

George stepped towards his brother and threw his arms around him, hugging him tightly and patting him vigorously on the back. But Graham's body was rigid. He showed no emotion whatsoever. There was no response to George's embrace. George pulled back, sensing there was something wrong and looked at his brother. Graham's eyes were cold, blank and vacant.

'Everything went okay, didn't it?' George said both smiling and frowning at the same time. Graham's expression remained frozen.

'Yes. I think so. But …'

Graham paused, trying to think of how best to relate to his brother the events of the past eighteen hours.

'What's the matter, Graham?' His smile had disappeared and his frown had deepened. George's face was now a picture of concern bordering on panic. Graham's eyes were focused beyond his brother. He walked past George towards the two large sofas.

'What is it, Graham? What's happened?' George's voice had now become more demanding and the anxiety in his eyes was matched by the fear in his tone.

'Come and sit down. There are a couple of things I need to tell you,' Graham said as calmly as he could. He gestured to the sofa. George's body language had changed drastically in the few seconds Graham had been in the apartment. From the wide-eyed, wide-armed exhilaration of a few moments earlier, he had become twitchy and agitated. He looked hunted and worried and could sense the imminent arrival of bad news. Bad news had never been an option. Even the slightest blemish to their scheme was liable to be fatal.

'What do you need to tell me? Please tell me everything is okay, and we are in the clear.'

He was now begging his brother for information. Graham paused and tried to gather his thoughts. The silence was deafening and the tension almost unbearable. Graham took a deep breath and looked at his brother on the opposite side of the coffee table. The colour drained from George's face. He looked white. He looked terrified.

'Everything went beautifully, until after the game. No one gave the slightest hint of suspicion. The only person who questioned my identity during this whole affair was Frankie De Costa, but he was only showing off to his mates. Everything went as smoothly as I could have hoped or dreamed. Even the frightening moment I was told to go on for the last ten minutes went reasonably well. After all the traumas and unknowns, all the possible pitfalls and minefields and then finally the most feared scenario of them all coming true, once I walked off that pitch and got back to the hotel, I was sure we were home and dry. When I spoke to you back at the hotel, I truly believed we were in the clear. It was just a case of keeping my head down and getting home. I went up to the roof club bar to join in the celebrations. I felt it was what you would have done. I thought it would be very suspicious if *George Miller* didn't turn up to celebrate with the rest of the team. I had planned to only stay for an hour then sneak away.' He paused and took another deep and thoughtful breath.

'But the atmosphere was incredible. The buzz amongst the players was extraordinary. It was wonderful to be part of it. To feel part of it. The camaraderie was something I have never experienced before, not in that extreme way. And the most magical part of it was, I, or should I say you, were the centre of attention. *George Miller* was the headliner. It was overwhelming and I lapped it up. I was George Miller and I loved every second.'

George shuffled closer to the edge of the sofa.

'Yes, yes, yes, that's great. So what's the problem?' George interrupted trying to hurry his brother along.

'Well,' he paused. 'You know what I'm like when I've had a few drinks.'

George's face collapsed in horror. His shoulders slumped, his head bowed and the air disappeared from his lungs.

'I just can't handle it like you can.' He looked at his brother apologetically. 'The champagne was flowing. I lost count of how many I had to drink.'

George's head was now in his hands. He could only imagine this ending one way. He had reluctantly started to prepare himself for very bad news. He needed to get to the end of this story and find out what sort of mess they were both in.

'So, did you give the game away and who knows?' George asked.

'I don't think so,' Graham said. 'From the reaction I got from everyone on the journey home, none of them were any the wiser. I was still George Miller, hero of Barcelona.'

George slumped back into the sofa. He was now totally confused.

'Something else happened. Something you should know about,' said Graham.

'For the love of God, Graham, spit it out. What the fuck happened?'

George now didn't know which way was up. He didn't know which one of his numerous emotions to let flow. Graham nodded, understanding his brother's frustration, but he had to get this right. He had to tell George exactly what happened, as well as he could remember.

'I received this text on your phone halfway through the evening. I was thinking of calling it a night and heading off to bed, but then I got this.'

Graham passed George his phone with Debbie's message showing. George almost snatched it from Graham's hand and read the message. As he read the text some of the sternness and fear left his face and a soft smile crept onto his lips. Graham left George to his thoughts for a few seconds, but even the thought of Debbie couldn't distract him for too long. He had to find out how it ended and what Graham was seemingly so concerned about.

'So, what happened? How is she? Did she ask about me?'

Graham almost burst into laughter.

'George, she saw you and spoke to you! She saw me, but I was you!'

A thoughtful frown washed away George's soft smile.

'Well, what happened, for God's sake?'

'I met her at the lift. She hasn't changed at all. I didn't want to get too close or involved with her for obvious reasons. Things that have happened between you two were not part of my briefing. It would have been very dangerous for me to have been alone with her. As well as all the intimate stories and secrets that might have come up she probably knows you better than anyone else, including me. I just didn't think it was worth taking the risk, so I invited her up to the party. It was either that, or not seeing her at all. She told me she was about to go to Australia and start a new life. She wanted to see me, sorry, you. I think it was to see if there was any spark or embers still burning in you for her. I thought it would probably be the last chance you would have to see her again. My plan, for what it was worth, was to spend some time with her on the roof surrounded by others, then arrange to meet back in London and let you take over from there.' Graham paused.

'And...' George verbally nudged him back into his tale.

'She fitted in beautifully at the party. All the guys really liked her. Even Doug remembered her from our school days. She was chatty, interesting and funny. George, she really is a wonderful girl. If I wasn't...'

'Okay, okay,' blurted George, 'yes I know all that. Get on with it.'

'Well, we had a few more drinks. I was beginning to feel a little light-headed. It all gets a little foggy from there on in. I remember we left the party and because I was struggling to walk straight, Debbie helped me to my room. She was talking to me, but I can't really remember what she said. I'm pretty sure she undressed me and put me to bed. Some of the boys said they saw her leaving the hotel at about 6.a.m., so she must have stayed with me in the room for a few hours. Apart from that, I don't have any other recollection until I got my wakeup call at eight o'clock. I found this note on top of my beautifully folded clothes, piled neatly at the bottom of my bed. They were not folded by me, that's for sure.' He passed the piece of paper to George who read it. George stroked his chin and looked very thoughtful.

'So, what happened after that?'

'Nothing,' Graham said in a truly anticlimatic way. 'That's it.'

Silence once again enveloped the room. Graham had told his story and George tried to digest it and make sense of it. Eventually George spoke.

'So, let me get this straight. You got drunk. Spent the night with Debbie, but can't remember what you did or said and when you woke up, she had gone and this note was left. No one said anything to you on the journey home and everyone behaved normally.'

'That's about it in a nutshell. I don't quite know what to say. I shouldn't have got so drunk. I know that, but I couldn't let Debbie slip through the net again. I know how much she means to you. I just didn't know what to do for the best. The champagne certainly didn't help but there we are. That's it.'

Once again George slumped back into the comfort of the sofa and tried to understand what he had just heard. From what Graham had told him it seemed they were still in the clear as far as Doug, Bernie and the boys were concerned. Debbie was the only unknown factor. What had been said between them? What had they done? Had she happily accepted Graham as George and just put everything down to the passing of time and too much drink? There were so many unanswered questions. Graham's voice interrupted George's thoughts.

'She said she was going to Australia at the end of the month to sort some stuff out concerning her move, but she was really keen to see me, sorry, you, before she left. Why don't you give her a call? If nothing else, it would put your mind at rest about what went on last night.'

George agreed. Not only was he keen to find out as much of what was said and done in that Barcelona hotel, he was also desperate to see her. He knew if she left for Australia the chances of them ever seeing each other again were remote.

'Good idea. I'll do it now.'

George's first two calls went through to her messaging service. The disappointment of not speaking to her was somewhat allayed by hearing her voice after all those years.

Hi, this is Debbie. Leave a message and I promise I will call you back as soon as I can. George didn't want to leave a message. He decided to send her a text. There was less emotion in a text and he didn't want to give anything away with the tone of his voice.

Hi, Debbie. Was great to see you in Barcelona. Really sorry I was so pissed. Would be lovely to see you again before you leave for Aus. Can we arrange a time in the next couple of days? I am pretty much free at all times. Fingers crossed. Gx.

The unanswered questions and mysteries about what had happened during Graham's last hours in Barcelona would have to wait.

The two brothers sat back and relaxed. They talked about everything that had happened since Graham first walked out of the flat on Thursday morning. George replayed the game on the TV and they both revelled in the winning penalty. Graham explained how the opposition goalkeeper had tried to intimidate him before he took the spot kick and how he had substituted Frankie's face onto the snarling giant. With every scenario Graham started to describe, George had even more questions. Graham even recalled the somewhat bizarre appearance of the mystical and mythical Mr Morotoni at the party on the roof. He was amazed when the old Italian gentleman managed to recall, not only the game he had seen them play and how awful it was, but also Graham's name and the details of the conversation he had had with their dad and Mr Ellis.

For the first time in a while, the flat was full of laughter and humour. Graham recounted every detail he could remember, even who sat next to who at dinner and what they had had to eat.

The military operation had come to a close and the debrief was complete. Graham got up and hugged his brother. This time the embrace was full of love, emotion and a huge sense of relief.

'Don't forget to call and make that appointment to see Bernie, will you? And good luck with Debbie. I hope it all goes well. Let me know, won't you?'

'Of course I will. Thanks, Graham.'

They embraced and Graham left. This time he was wearing his own clothes and shoes. He had his own phone, wallet, passport and jewellery. Graham was Graham once again and it felt bloody good.

An hour later George's phone pinged into life. A new text message.

Hi, George. Would love to see you again before I go. Am really busy tomorrow sorting stuff for Australia. What about Tuesday? Am free all day. Text me your address. I will come to you. Let me know what time. Dx.

George fired a message straight back with his address.

Am free all day too. Why not make it mid-morning?
Gx.

Sounds like a fine idea. See you about 10. Dx.

The fear that Debbie had somehow discovered their scheme or even had a night of passion with his brother quickly dissipated. He was going to see her again. All of the fear and tension he had been feeling over the past few days had now been replaced by excitement and anticipation, a buzz that he hadn't felt for many years. He would hopefully find out what had happened in Barcelona and they would undoubtedly talk about the past. But most importantly it was his chance to see what the future held in store for him. For both of them. He couldn't wait.

37

Little secrets.

It was nearly 10.a.m. on the Tuesday morning. George had been up since seven o'clock and had been pacing about his apartment. He had checked his watch several times and was convinced it had stopped on numerous occasions. Debbie Morris was due at any moment. He knew now, even more than before, just how much she meant to him. The thrill and expectancy he felt in his body was evidence of that.

The apartment was tidier than it had been for a long time. The cleaners had been in the day before and given it a thorough going over. Everything was in its place. He dared not touch, or sit on, anything. The cushions on the sofa were all plumped up and the flotsam and jetsam of apartment life had been stacked away in cupboards. He busied himself straightening up the perfectly piled magazines on the coffee table and brushed some non-existent dust from the arms of the sofa. It was bang on ten o'clock and right on time, the intercom buzzed into life and echoed around the room. Even though he was expecting it, the noise made him jump and he felt his heart miss a beat. George hurried over and looked at the screen. There she was. Graham was right, she hadn't changed at all.

'It's me. Debbie.' George pressed the entry button and watched her as she pushed the main entrance door open. Two minutes later she had reached the fifty-second floor and knocked on George's door. He opened it immediately. Before him stood the sexiest, most gorgeous girl he had ever laid eyes on. Her beautiful smiling face and azure blue eyes stared across the threshold at him. She was wearing a blue beret and a long blue woollen coat. She had the collar turned up to protect her from the chill of that late May morning. Her cheeks were rosy red. She glowed.

'Come in,' he said, struggling to keep his smile in check. As she passed George, she planted a kiss on his cheek. The kiss rather took George by surprise. He shut the door and watched her walk over to the sofas.

'It's lovely to see you, Debbie… Again,' he hastily added. 'As you can see, I'm a little more sober than when we last met. I'm really sorry I was so drunk in Barcelona. Tea or coffee?'

'Tea, please. Milk, no sugar.' He watched her take off her beret and coat and lay them over the arm of one of his sofas. George filled the kettle and clicked it on.

'It was one hell of a night,' he said trying to explain the inebriated state he had apparently been in. Debbie smiled at him. .

'Yes, it was. One full of surprises.' Under her coat she was wearing a very elegant dark blue dress with white polka dots. She looked fabulous. She was stylish as well as sexy. She always had been. Every inch of her wonderful body made him shiver with delight. He suddenly realised he was gawping. Eyeing her up and down and wallowing in the view. He caught her eye. She was looking straight at him.

'Sorry,' he said. 'I was just thinking what a lovely dress that is.' Debbie grinned back at him.

'No, you weren't. I know the workings of your mind, George Miller, and your eyes always give you away.' She glanced down at her frock. 'It is a nice dress, I agree, but that wasn't what you were thinking.' George felt himself start to blush. The kettle clicked off and demanded his attention, saving him from any further embarrassment. He turned to make the tea.

'Sit down. I'll bring them over.' Debbie sat down and straightened her dress. George sat next to her, placing the mugs on the table.

'Now, where was I?' George began again. 'Ah yes. Barcelona.' He was keen to learn as much about what had happened that night as quickly as possible. There were so many other things he wanted to talk to her about, but this had to come first.

'I can't apologise enough for my behaviour. If only I had known you were coming I would have shown a little more restraint.'

'Oh, I don't think you have anything to be sorry about. It was lovely to see you and nice of you to invite me up to the party. It was very swish. I thoroughly enjoyed myself. Meeting all of your mates and even talking to that lovely gentleman, Doug Fenner. He said he remembered me, but I think he was just being kind. You remember?' Debbie looked him in the eye.

'Err. Yes, of course I do,' George said with a little hesitation in his voice. 'It's later on I'm having difficulty with.'

'I hope you didn't get into any trouble because of me,' she said.

'No. Why is that?'

'Well, I know they can be a bit strict about you boys having someone in your room. Do you remember all of the shenanigans we had to go through that wonderful night we spent in Newcastle?'

A happy and contented smile washed over George's face.

'Oh yes. Yes, I do,' he said, this time with no hesitation or hint of a pause.

'Well, anyway, I thought it best if I left early so as not to embarrass you with your mates or get you into any hot water with the management. I got up and left at 6 a.m. You were still fast asleep, but then you had rather exerted yourself during the day.'

'I suppose I had,' said George.

'And of course, during the night.' She gave him a cheeky smile and a wink. 'I left you a note. I assumed you found it.'

'Oh, er, yes. Thank you.' His voice was beginning to stutter as he tried to process what she was saying into some clearer picture.

'Look, I hate to admit it,' George started, 'but I really don't remember anything about it at all. I know you came back to my room with me, but it all gets a bit hazy from then on.'

'Really?' said Debbie in a slightly hurt voice. 'Well, I remember every detail. We had so much fun. Do you not recall anything?' She looked and sounded astonished. George just sat there shaking his head apologetically.

'We practically did the Kama Sutra from cover to cover. I knew you had stamina, but that night was epic. I've never known anything like it in my life before. I've always treasured the memories of our love-making when we were at school. Then we had Newcastle, which was as magical a night as I have ever experienced … up until Barcelona that is. George, you excelled yourself. Three times in as many hours. Mind you, I thought I was pretty good too. We inspired each other like we have never done before. I'm surprised I could walk out of the room after you had finished with me!'

George's face was a picture. His eyes were wide open and his mouth was gaping. He looked dumbfounded and shocked. He looked rather "simple". Debbie continued.

'Oh, come on, George, don't you even remember asking one of the hotel maids to join us? She was very young and pretty. I think there was a moment when she seriously considered coming in, but she declined in the end. Even your charm and silver tongue couldn't persuade her. I hope she didn't go to the press. Think of all the scandal, for both of us. I've got a reputation too, you know.'

George's face was blank. He was staring flatly into space. Debbie chuckled to herself.

'Oh, George, you used to be able to hold your drink so much better.'

George's mind was a mess. He didn't know what to think. He had stopped listening to Debbie's words. He was just trying to make sense of what she had already said.

He was struggling to put the information together. He had seen Graham after he had drunk too much and he was lucky to have a pulse, let alone anything else. And if this was true surely even Graham, in a semi-conscious state, would have had some recollection of events. George looked up at Debbie's face. A cheeky smile flickered across her lips as she witnessed his bafflement, her eyebrows raised in a quizzical manner. She took hold of his hands in hers and started to stroke his fingers with her thumbs. She stared lovingly into his eyes, a look he had seen so many times before. But this time the only expression he could manage was one of confusion. Debbie had said all she was going to say. There was a hush in the room waiting to be broken by George. He looked into her lovely blue eyes. He felt she could see right through him. She had always been able to read him like a book. Maybe she still could. Her facial expression remained the same. A soft smile with her head tilted slightly to one side waiting for him to respond. He had managed to close his mouth. His eyes narrowed and a thoughtful frown appeared on his face. He searched her features for any clue or hint of what she was thinking; what she wasn't telling him; what she already knew. They stared at each other for a few moments, Debbie's smile slowly increasing with every second. After what seemed like an age of silence, George's searching look eased itself into the beginnings of a wry smile.

'You know, don't you?' he said in a guarded manner. Debbie's smile widened even more.

'Know? Know what?' she replied in an equally guarded and innocent tone, her head tilting another degree and her eyebrows edging ever more northwards.

George repeated himself.

'You know. You do, don't you?' He wasn't asking now. He was making a statement. Debbie lifted George's hands up to her mouth and kissed his fingers, still looking him in the eyes

'Yes. I know,' she said softly. George sucked in a huge breath, shuddering under the brutal impact from the intake of air into his lungs. But he felt no panic or sense of catastrophe. If it had been anyone else, his world would have just fallen apart. But strangely, because it was Debbie, he felt a warmth flow through his body. As if it made them even closer. He tried to regather his thoughts.

'How? What gave us away?'

Debbie lowered George's hands into her lap and smiled.

'When we met after all those years that night in Newcastle, you were the George Miller I had loved, still loved and would love for the rest of my life. From the moment you came over to my table in that hotel bar I was sixteen again. I know we haven't seen each other since then, but when I walked out of the lift in Barcelona, I was ready to feel the same. I didn't. I felt disappointed. Don't get me wrong, it was great to see you. Just like it would have been great to meet up with any old friend. But you are not just an old friend. The bolt of electricity I used to get every time I stood close to you didn't happen. When I kissed you on the cheek I felt nothing. I knew it had been a long time and wondered then if we had both changed too much in our feelings and expectations, but I hadn't prepared myself for such a noticeable change. By the time we got into the lift to go up to the party, I have to admit I was a little deflated. When we were at the party, you seemed at home and comfortable with your teammates and friends. You were great. The life and soul of the party. But the George I remembered would have made more of me. You always did. That was one of the things that set you apart from all of the others. You would have made me feel part of you. You would have put your arms around me and showed me off like some exhibit. You always did that, too. Even holding your hand felt awkward and strange. Our fingers used to fit together so easily'. She picked up his hand from her lap and threaded her digits into his. Effortlessly.

'See.' She squeezed and felt him instantly respond.

'You would have included me in the conversation and made me part of it, not left me to fend for myself with a bunch of semi-drunk strangers. It was okay, but I had to work myself into most of the chat and introduce myself each time. You were more content speaking to the boys. It felt like you didn't want to engage with me.'

George's face was now looking doleful and apologetic.

'I've seen you drink before and I know from experience that the amount of champagne you consumed at the party would not have made a mark on you years ago. It certainly wouldn't have left you in that state. As you became drunker, you started to slur your words badly. I've never heard you do that before either. Most of your stories concerned you and your brother and the pranks you used to pull. On at least two occasions you referred to your brother as George.'

A pained expression crossed his face.

'Shit,' he whispered to himself. Debbie continued.

'Most of the others who were listening were just as drunk as you were, so I don't think anybody noticed. I thought it was a bit odd, but put it down to the champagne. By then I thought it was time you went to bed. I had been hoping and praying for years that an opportunity like that would present itself to me again, but I was having serious doubts about it. When I got you to your room you sat motionless on the bed before collapsing like a felled tree, not to move again. I couldn't get any sense from you at all. I undressed you. All the way. When you were lying there on the bed naked in front of me, my heart was pounding and I felt extremely horny. Even then I still thought I would do with you what I had been dreaming about for so long. It was your fault you were in such a state, not mine. You might miss out on our last chance together, but I certainly wasn't going to. I looked down at my prize and I sat beside you. I stroked your thigh, firstly with the back of my hand and then gently with my nails. You didn't move a muscle. You didn't even make a noise. Then I stroked you where you love to be stroked. I held it in my hand. The one thing that had given me more pleasure over the years than anything else. Still, you didn't move and the limpness in my hand refused to stiffen. Even after all those years I thought my dear old friend would have responded.' She glanced down at George's groin.

'Whether you were asleep or drunk all I had to do was touch you and he would instantly stand to attention.'

Debbie decided not to mention the vigorous attempts at massage, or her efforts to stimulate him with her mouth. That would be her little secret.

'I covered you up with the other duvet and let you sleep. I did crawl into bed with you for what I assumed would be our last cuddle, but I was up and away at 6.a.m. I left you the note. Even at that point it hadn't occurred to me that you and Graham might have pulled the famous "Switch". I addressed the note to Mr G Miller only because you were no longer George Miller to me. Not the one I remembered, anyway. I looked back at you before I left the room. I was broken-hearted and I have to admit to shedding a tear as I closed the door on what I thought was George Miller, for the last time. I asked the receptionist to call you at eight o'clock to make sure you were awake. Then I left. I didn't really expect you to contact me after that. It was only later that day my mind started to ask questions about what had happened. I started to convince myself that for whatever reason and it must have been a bloody good one, you had decided to switch identities. I desperately wanted to believe that I had just walked away from Graham, not George. That would have given me a glimmer of hope. It would have explained so many things, but the more I tried to believe, the more I told myself you would never have done such a foolish thing. It would have been madness. Eventually I gave in to sensible reasoning. Of course you wouldn't have done anything as ridiculous as that. I just had to come to terms with the fact that what we had was special, but now it had gone. It was only when you texted me back to say you wanted to meet up, that the small ember of hope in me started to glow again.' Debbie took a deep breath and sighed. George had been listening intently.

'What makes you so certain now then?' he asked quizzically.

'On my way up today I kept telling myself not to be so stupid. Any thoughts I had about you and Graham switching were preposterous, but I had one more chance to see you and I could then gauge what the real, sober George Miller's feelings were. I told myself that if the magic between us had gone then so be it. Everybody changes and we were lucky to have had what we had. At worst I could walk away from you with all my doubts and questions answered for better or worse. But when you opened the door to me just now I knew for sure it wasn't you in Barcelona. As soon as my eyes met yours that charge of electricity shot through my entire body. My heart started to pound and my knees felt weak. Shivers shot up my spine. That bolt of electricity that was missing outside the lift in Spain hit me like a hammer as soon as I laid eyes on you. It only ever happens when I'm with you. I love Graham, I always have. He's a great guy but he isn't you. You set me on fire, George. I am and always will be that sixteen-year-old school girl who has got just what she always wanted, when I have you.'

A tear started to run down Debbie's cheek. She lifted his hands up to her mouth and kissed his fingers again.

'If I needed any other proof, it is here.' Debbie glanced down at George's hands. Again, George looked a little perplexed.

'You cut your finger on some broken glass at the party. It wasn't too bad, but it was deep enough to warrant a dressing. One of the last things I did before you passed out was to clean the wound and put a plaster on it.' She singled out his index finger on his right hand and inspected it closely.

'You are either a very quick healer, or this is the first time we have seen each other since Newcastle.'

The talking had finished. The explanation and evidence plain for them both to see. The room fell silent. They stared deeply into each other's watery eyes. Without saying a word they leant towards each other and kissed. Once their mouths had unlocked, they hugged each other tightly. The tension and angst had gone from his body. All he could feel was relief and an overwhelming passion soak through his entire being. He was sixteen again. George whispered in Debbie's ear,

'I think your old friend is rather pleased to see you again after all this time.'

Debbie smiled and put her hand on his trousers and gently squeezed.

'So it would seem,' she said, laughing through her tears.

'Shall we get you two reacquainted?' said George.

'Yes please,' replied Debbie. They took each other by the hand and walked into the bedroom.

At four o'clock that afternoon George emerged. He walked into the kitchen with a swagger. He picked out a cold bottle of Laurent Perrier Rosé champagne and two glasses and sauntered back to the bedroom. He was whistling. Debbie was sitting up in bed with the duvet pulled up under her arms. He was ready to go again, but first…, Champagne. He popped the cork and filled both glasses. As Debbie went to take one from him he pulled it away.

'What's the matter?' she said. George's face took on a serious look.

'I don't want to toast your new life in Australia,' he said solemnly. 'I don't think I could bear to lose you again.'

Debbie smiled at him. He looked like a sad little puppy. She reached out and stroked his cheek with the back of her hand then took one of the glasses. She looked lovingly at him and raised her glass.

'Here's to us. Forever,' she said.

George smiled and felt another tear start to form.

'What about Australia?'

'That was a new life. I don't want a new life anymore. I

want this one. With you. I think, George, that is all I have ever wanted.'

They clinked glasses and sipped their fizz.

A few hours and another bottle of champagne later, they were still cuddled up in bed.

'I will have to tell Graham that you know.' Debbie nodded in agreement.

'But absolutely no one else. Not Kerry, not Mum, Dad, not anyone,' said George.

Debbie wrinkled up her nose.

'It will be our little secret. Forever.'

38

Fortune favours the downright crazy.

George Miller had been here before. He was back in the lounge outside Bernie's office. It felt more welcoming and comfortable. Less claustrophobic and not as intimidating as it had before. It probably had something to do with his mood and state of mind. After the success in Barcelona, George was confident this would be one of the most positive chats he had had with the management for a very long time. The team had been back home now for nearly a week and the euphoria and celebrations were beginning to die down. They had paraded the trophy in an open-top bus around the local area as well as in their own stadium. Although George was happy to lap it all up and enjoy the adulation, he still felt a little distant from the others.

The season was over and most of the players and staff were now on holiday. There were a few people still there, keeping the club's heart beating. Bernie, Doug, David and the chairman still had plenty of work to do. There were deals to be done, including sponsorship, hospitality and players' contracts to be sorted. Who would stay? Who would be leaving? And who would be brought in to replace them? The eternal revolving door of every football club. Out with the old and in with the new. George was acutely aware that he would have been one of the names heading out of the club had it not been for their "almost" perfectly executed plan. If they hadn't pulled "The Switch", or if it had backfired on them, he knew he would have been one of the casualties of the end of season cull. His life and his career would have been in tatters and his prospects destroyed. He would have been unceremoniously dumped. Cast aside with no honour or respect left, walking out of the club and probably top-flight football forever. It had been a plan full of danger. A scheme so fantastic he still couldn't quite believe they had got away with it. George remembered their father, John, telling them once when they were boys that, "fortune favours the brave". Well, that was certainly true this time. Maybe it should have been "fortune favours the downright crazy". Crazy or not, they had taken the biggest gamble of their lives and won. The results of this meeting with Bernie would be the beginning of his rewards.

George looked out of the open window. It was the end of May. June was racing towards them and the sun was doing its best to trumpet in the belated start of summer. The biting chill of the wind over the last few weeks had been replaced by a warm breeze. There was no need for big overcoats today. The grey, miserable days that had reflected George's spirit were now a distant memory. Like George's mood, the world was bright, warm and colourful.

Brenda emerged from her office and walked over to

George. It was her final day at work before she left for a couple of weeks holiday. She sat down next to him.

'Hello, George. You're here to see Mr Roswell, aren't you? Have you been a naughty boy again?'

'No. I don't think so. I think this time it might be for a reward, not a slap on the wrist.' She laughed and clasped his hands.

'Oh good. Not even you can be naughty all of the time.' She stood up. 'Can I get you anything to drink?'

'A cup of tea would be nice, Brenda, if you don't mind.'

'Of course,' she replied. 'I watched the game last Saturday. It was very exciting. I do hope that Igor recovers quickly, he's such a nice chap. I thought you were fantastic.' He laughed.

'Thank you, Brenda, but I was only on the pitch for a few minutes.' She smiled and shrugged her shoulders.

'Well, I still thought you were great.' She turned and walked off to get the tea. She glided away from George with what he had come to know as her trademark wiggle. *Little minx*, he thought.

He sat back into the deep recesses of the sofa and looked around the room again. The room was pretty much as he remembered it from his last visit. There was, however, one change to the decor that caught his eye. At the end of the row of framed illuminated pictures on the wall, there were three new arrivals. The "Hall of Fame" had expanded. George walked over to take a look at them. He passed down the line, recognising some of his peers. Pictures he had seen many times. He stopped in front of the new editions. The first of the three was a photograph that had made it onto most of the back pages and even some of the front pages of the Sunday newspapers. A grinning, toothless Terry Bridges, holding the European Cup above his head. His long black curly hair stuck to the sweat on his face. He had no shirt on and his muscular torso just added to the image of a conquering warrior chief. The second photograph was a shot of the entire team along with Bernie, Doug, Steve and some of the backroom staff. They had posed behind the sponsor's advertising hoarding for the massed ranks of the world's press. The third and final snapshot of that memorable night was one that captured the drama of the final kick. A camera nestled into the top corner of the goal, with a wide-angle lens had caught the moment perfectly. It showed the penalty taker striking the ball. His right leg extended and his eyes fixed on the path of the sporting missile as it headed towards the goal. It showed the goalkeeper's body diving the wrong way and it showed his eyes, still fixed on the ball, knowing in that split-second he had been beaten. He would always have that look of pain and defeat on his face. It was a great photograph. The plaque below proudly announced "George Miller strikes the winning penalty to secure victory".

George looked at the picture, willing the frame to animate itself and for the ball to fly past the keeper, smash into the net and confirm it really had happened, but it stayed where it was, suspended in mid-air for all time. The picture itself was a piece of evidence from an unknown crime. As he stared at the motionless ball, his focus slowly changed. He felt himself being drawn deeper into the picture, past the two-dimensional image and beyond. A pair of eyes came into sharp focus. They were looking straight back at him and into his soul. George felt the intensity of the stare.

It was uncomfortable. The eyes were accusing and sinister. They knew about the secret hidden within the photograph. They were the secret. It was now George who was frozen, unable to break eye contact with the ghostly image. The still frame had animated after all, but not in the way he had wanted. From the dark recesses of the photograph the phantom that was his conscience, was reminding him of his fraud. While George looked into the eyes of the spectre he realised his reflection was the only true image of George Miller contained within the frame. He had achieved his ultimate goal. He had won a trophy, a medal and he had finally secured himself a place on the wall of fame. He was now part of the club's history. That's what everyone who passed by would think. Everyone except the three people who knew the truth and the haunting vision lying beneath the surface. Those eyes, those knowing and accusing eyes, would be there every time he looked at the photograph, reminding him of his deception.

Brenda slipped her hand into George's and squeezed gently.

'Here is your tea.' The suddenness of her presence made him jump and severed the connection between him and his accuser.

'It's a lovely picture, don't you think? You look so handsome in it.' They both looked at the photograph again. Brenda could see George taking, and scoring the penalty. The man she held so close to her heart. The man of her dreams. The man who in her mind was the truest, finest, and most honest man she had ever met. George could only see the reflection of his own face staring back at him, with black, menacing and piercing eyes. Those eyes burnt deeply into him, challenging his morality and his scruples, like a prosecution barrister waiting for a confession.

Brenda gave him his tea and wandered back to her office. George went back and sat on the sofa and sipped his drink. He looked at the illuminated frame at the far end of the row. The eyes were no longer watching him but he knew they would be there, next time and every time, waiting for him.

39

All about family.

Debbie rang the doorbell at number 75. George stood behind her and laughed.

'That thing hasn't worked for years,' he said. He reached around her and lifted the heavy lion-face doorknocker, rapping it onto the brass plate below.

George looked around the neighbourhood he had grown up in. Nothing much had changed. The plane trees and the silver birch lining the pavement were still there, their canopy of leaves creating a light-dappled tunnel effect along the length of the road. It was a time capsule for his many treasured memories. The door opened and there was the smiling, friendly face of George's dad.

'Come in, come in,' he said. Debbie went in first and took John's hand. John leant forward and kissed her on both cheeks then gave her a mighty hug.

'Dad, you remember Deb......' Before he had a chance to finish her name John cut in.

'Of course I remember. It's so good to see you again, Debbie. It's been a long time. You haven't changed a bit, after all these years.' Debbie smiled at him. He was still as lovely and as warm as she remembered.

'Thank you, John. It's good to see you too.'

George followed her in and gave his dad an equally big hug.

'Hi, Dad.'

'Hello, son. It's great to see you.' The three of them walked down the hallway and into the kitchen. Paula was chopping vegetables.

'Hi, Mum,' George said. Paula looked up, turned around and with a huge smile on her face, and arms spread wide, walked straight up to Debbie and wrapped herself around her.

'Hello, Debbie darling. How are you? It's so wonderful to see your lovely face again. You look fantastic. Still as beautiful as ever, I see.' Debbie started to feel a little overwhelmed. She had been confident John and Paula would welcome her back into their home, but she hadn't quite expected this much emotion. She cleared her throat.

'Thank you, Paula,' she managed with a little wobble.

'How are things, George?' John asked. 'I saw the game. Nice penalty. You must have felt a bit of pressure on your shoulders, what with being out of the team for so long.' George was dismissive of his father's concerns.

'Piece of cake, Dad. All that practice we had down the park with you, I just looked at their goalkeeper and imagined you standing between the sticks. The only difference was, he wasn't going to have to run fifty yards to retrieve the ball once he was beaten.' They both laughed.

'Glad I could be of some assistance to you,' John said. He handed George a cold beer and passed Debbie a glass of red wine. 'How did it go with Bernie the other day?'

'It was fine. He was very happy and relaxed. I think all my previous misdemeanours have been forgiven and forgotten. After the success in Barcelona, I think we can all start with a clean slate and that is fine by me. I think I've got a few more miles in these ageing legs if I look after myself. And that's what I'm planning to do. I want to keep my nose clean and stay out of trouble. Stay off the front pages and stick to the back ones.'

John nodded in agreement. He looked over at Debbie, who was speaking to Paula.

'There's another good reason for you to quieten down a bit, son.'

'I know, Dad. I know.'

Paula and Debbie were busy catching up with each other's news. She told Debbie both she and John had always hoped that one day George would find her again, or vice versa. She told her she always felt there was a piece of George missing after the two of them had gone their separate ways. Something maybe only a mother could see, but looking at her son now, that void had been filled. The piece that had been missing had returned and he was whole again. As Paula spoke, the emotion was clear to hear in her voice and not for the first time that day Debbie could feel the emotion rising in her as well.

Three loud claps from the heavy front-door knocker announced another arrival.

'I'll go,' said George.

He opened the door and there stood Graham and

Kerry. They were both weighed down with gifts. Graham was holding two bottles of champagne in each hand and had a large box of chocolates tucked under his arm. Behind him was Kerry who was carrying a huge bouquet of flowers.

'Hi, George,' Kerry said, popping his head out from behind the blooms.

'Wow,' said George, 'you two have rather outgunned me there.' He knew what the champagne was about, but Kerry didn't know that he knew. So, he played along.

As soon as Paula saw Graham, she shrieked. 'What have you done? Where is your hair and your beard?'

Graham had ten days growth on his head and his face and was already beginning to resemble the Graham of two weeks earlier, but it was a bit of a shock to his parents to see their two boys looking so similar after all the years of hirsute distinction. Graham glanced over at George.

'Ah, well, I woke up one morning when Kerry was away and I just fancied a change. So, I started to chop it all off. I hadn't meant to go quite so far, but once I'd started, well, I just got a little carried away. I knew I'd gone too far when I looked in the mirror. There I was, face to face with my not-quite-so-handsome brother. I can tell you it was an awful shock. So, I immediately decided to grow it all back. It shouldn't take too long.' They all laughed.

'You want to be careful, Debbie and you, Kerry, if he decides to do that again,' Paula said. 'You might both end up with the wrong brother.' That thought tickled everybody and the laughter carried on for a few seconds.

'I think we will be okay, Paula,' Debbie said holding on to George's arm and looking lovingly into his eyes, 'I'm pretty sure I can tell which one is my George. I've always been able to tell.'

Graham grabbed two of the four bottles of champagne he and Kerry had brought and passed them to George.

'Here you are, George. Would you do the honours, please?' He then relieved George of his beer.

'You won't be needing that for a while. It's champagne time.'

He stepped back and stood beside Kerry. They put their arms around each other and Graham turned to face his congregation.

'Mum, Dad, George, Debbie. Kerry and I are getting married. We are going to make it official.'

With perfect timing, the first cork shot out of the bottle and the celebrations and congratulations began. The first bottle was spent very quickly and the second cork careered out of its launcher soon after. It wasn't long before three empty bottles of Laurent Perrier Rosé sat on the kitchen sideboard.

'I'm surprised I can even look at champagne, let alone drink it after my last experience,' Graham joked. At that very moment, the room fell silent. George shot a glare at Graham who, realising what he had inadvertently said, glanced worryingly at Debbie. It was an awkward couple of seconds. Kerry broke the silence.

'Why, when did you last overindulge on the fizz?'

Graham stuttered and struggled to think what to say. He went a little red about the cheeks and looked suddenly uncomfortable. For a few seconds it felt like everyone was waiting for the answer.

'Oh, … I opened a bottle the other week while you were away. I was feeling a bit down and thought it might cheer me up. I only meant to have one glass but you know how it is. All of a sudden the bottle was empty. One leads to another leads to another and you know what I'm like the next day. I woke with a splitting headache and had to spend most of the day in bed feeling sorry for myself.'

There was another collective chuckle and the conversation started up again. Graham looked over at George with an apologetic face. Even though it was all behind them they knew they still had to be on their guard. It was a secret that had to be kept forever. A chapter in their lives that would always be lurking dangerously just beneath the surface like the accusing eyes in the photograph and it could rise up and destroy everything they had at any moment. It was a chilling thought but one that George, Graham and Debbie would have to be wary of for the rest of their lives.

The champagne and the wine flowed freely. Paula's roast beef was as good as it always was. John looked around the table. Opposite him was his beautiful wife, Paula. She was as gorgeous and beguiling as she had been when he first set eyes on her all those years ago. They had been married for thirty-two years and he couldn't remember a cross word between them in all that time. He was a very lucky man. To his left, Graham sat next to Kerry. John remembered the day they had sat around that same table and watched as Graham squirmed and suffered, with what he had imagined was a heavy burden. From that day to this Graham had never looked back. He had enjoyed and embraced life to the full. Now he was sitting next to the man he loved, excitingly discussing the arrangements for their special day to come. Graham was a happy man.

To John's right were George and Debbie. Holding each other's hands on the table just like they used to when they were school kids. They were smitten with each other, that was plain to see. They had both lead hectic lives since they parted company, but now they were back together, it seemed they were looking forward to a quieter, more intimate existence with each other. George was a happy man.

A shiver went down John's spine. This was surely the most content moment of his life so far. As the conversations continued, Paula caught John's eye. She smiled at her husband. She knew what he was thinking. She was having exactly the same thoughts.

The football match in Barcelona was mentioned a couple of times, but George didn't want to dwell on it. The day was not about football. It was all about family.